GAME, SET, MATCHMAKER

A Sweet Romance

EVIE STERLING

Chapter 1

Gemma

Mm. That smell.

Newly fallen maple and oak leaves. Grass that won't need to be cut again before the snow flies. I swear, I can smell a distant flock of Canadian Geese migrating south for the winter.

If this *exact* autumn smell could be packed into a candle, I'd buy a thousand of them.

It's the smell of fall in the New England suburbs.

Early October will forever remind me of golden-yellow school buses, metallic star stickers, and sparkly new pencil cases.

Ambition, awards, and straight A's.

This evening, as I grip the railing of the Manning's deck and look out across the string of fenced-in backyards, I feel the same excitement I used to feel as a kid.

Only tonight, my ambition is not aimed at anything related to being a student.

I'm here because of business.

When Carly joins me out on the deck, a glass of wine in one hand and her faded Boston University sweatshirt hanging loose over one shoulder, she frowns and gazes down on the string of yards splayed out before us. "I can't believe they took it down."

I know she's referring to the clothesline we had strung up between my bedroom, two houses down, and hers. We had a little bucket attached, and used to pass each other notes, books, and candy bars.

"And I can't believe it took them this long," I counter. "That thing was rotting, thanks to twenty years worth of sun, rain, snow, ice, and bird poop."

She utters a nostalgic sigh, like the fact that our old lifeline is now in a trash barrel somewhere is big news that we both should feel sad about.

I'm too giddy for nostalgia right now. "Okay, when do you think I should approach him?"

"Who? Dad?"

"*Yes*, your dad! Hello… The reason I'm here." I definitely didn't make the two hour drive out to Carly's parents house merely to enjoy her mother's famous pot roast, or reminisce about childhood, as pleasant as both those things are.

My work to-do list is a mile long, and I don't take time off on a whim these days. The only reason I took an entire week night off is because of what's at stake.

Funding.

Lots of it.

Carly twists, leans her back against the rail, and looks at the clapboard siding of her parent's house and then at me. "Remember that time in fourth grade when I needed help with my science report, and I flashed you an S.O.S signal? And then I filled the bucket with my terrible, chicken-scratch notes…"

"And I stayed up all night writing your report *The Fascinating Lives of Earthworms*. Yeah."

"I still don't know how you managed that. And you got me an A. I still owe you for that, by the way." She sips her wine. "You don't have to be nervous about this, you know."

"I really want to nail the pitch."

"And you will. You've been practicing for weeks."

"Months."

"If I know you, you have every word memorized by now."

"I've been playing the whole thing in my head like some song, except there's no catchy chorus. Only profit margins and interest rates."

She flashes a quick smile and tucks a strand of blond hair behind her ear. "You are such a dork. Getting butterflies in your stomach about profit margins."

"How'd you know I have butterflies?"

"Um, Gem…? I've known you since we were both in diapers. That's how I know. Go on and get in there. I just passed his office and he's off the phone now."

"You don't think I should wait until after dinner?"

"No. Because I actually want to enjoy the meal, and if you're all amped up about this pitch I'm going to pick up on your stress and I'll feel stressed. And then I won't enjoy Mom's pot roast and I swear, thinking about her pot roast is all that got me through the hellish week I just survived."

She points toward the patio doors. "Go."

I square my shoulders and level my gaze at the glass sliding doors.

Carly laughs. "You don't need to get all Amazonian Warrior Woman on this, Gem. He's going to give you money. That's, like, practically guaranteed at this point. You know he just handed out like twenty grand to some company making no-rinse shampoo? Shampoo in a spray can. How lame is that? You have a business that actually helps people. And, he loves you."

"I don't want him to invest because I'm a family friend. I want him to invest because he believes in Right Match."

She rolls her eyes. "You are such an overachiever. Just get in there and talk with him already, and then we can all scarf down a delicious meal. I'm starving, and Mom says it'll be ready in half an hour."

I set my jaw and march into the Manning household.

Carly's right. I have memorized every single word I'm going to say to her father. As I make my way through the living room, I run through all ten points for the millionth time. I can hear her mother humming in the kitchen. The smell of roasted potatoes, carrots, and beef along with baking biscuits hangs in a heavy cloud that I can nearly taste.

I really do have butterflies in my stomach. Tonight, my whole life might change.

I think Carly's right, and Mitch Manning will invest in my company, Right Match. And if he invests, I'll have the capital I need to finally get the brand online. We'll be set up to make millions.

Owning a multi-million dollar company by the time I hit thirty sounds pretty amazing to me. It'd be one huge life goal that I could put a big, happy check mark next to.

And I *love* check marks.

When I push open the office door and peer in, I spot Mitch and smile. "Mr. Manning? Do you have a minute?"

"Gemma, honey!" He waves me forward. "Come on in, come on in. Carly said you two had one heck of a drive getting out here. Rush hour traffic, construction on the Pike…?"

"It was no problem. Gave us time to catch up, which is always nice."

"You two never run out of things to talk about, do you? And it's been that way since you were tykes, barely big enough to scoot around on those big wheel tricycles you both loved so much. When you weren't over here, she wanted to be on the phone with you. And then that rope you had up between your windows, to pass letters after curfew… as if all us parents couldn't hear the crank turn squeaking. We had to take that down, by the way."

"I saw that."

"It sure was cute, that rope. Reminded me every day of how fun it was to have you kids running around. But Patty thought it was an eyesore. Well, you're all grown, now, there's no denying that." He sighs and leans back in his chair. "The end of an era, as they say. Did Patty get you a glass of wine? Some food?"

"I'm a little too nervous to eat, to be honest with you."

"Ah, pooh. This is nothing to be nervous about. How about a glass of whisky?"

"No, really. Thank you so much."

He picks up his own drink and gestures with it toward the couch. "Have a seat over there, then, and we'll get down to it. I've been looking forward to having a talk with you about this business of yours. Matchmaking. Is that it?"

"Yes, Sir. Right Match."

"Right Match. Great name, great name. It's all right there, spelled out, and that's a good thing. Makes advertising a heck of a lot easier, am I right? Anyway, I'm very interested in what you're up to. Always knew you'd do something impressive, and here we are. Carly says you're hoping for some help with funding?"

That's my cue.

I take a deep breath and then dive in.

Twenty minutes later, I rattle off my rehearsed conclusion. "We know the market's there. Everyone wants to find that right match—that's a universal experience. And with our track record, we feel confident that we can deliver. To date, 83% of the matches we make lead to marriage. That means we've facilitated over 300 marriages. Our process works. Moving to an online business model will really open the doors for us, so we can help more people."

He nods thoughtfully. "Hm. Interesting. A process for finding love… I like it, I like it. In business, the bottom line is you gotta sell something folks want. Who doesn't want love? Heck, all of us want love."

"Exactly."

"Now you've got me thinking. " He reaches for a framed photo on his desk and turns it to face me.

I cringe.

The Mannings have two children—Carly and her older brother, Parker.

I spent a lot of time in this house. Doing my own homework and helping Carly with hers. Letting her paint my nails and brush my hair. Sunbathing in the backyard by the in-ground pool, baking brownies and cookies in the kitchen, and poring over girly magazines in Carly's bedroom.

And almost every visit with Carly included some sort of run-in with her older brother, Parker.

By the time I reached eighth grade, I realized that Parker was not only a fearsome wielder of Supersoaker squirt guns, and a rival for the cherry flavored popsicles, which all three of us liked best. He was also hot.

Really hot.

Killer smile, washboard abs, shaggy-blond hair hot.

And that meant that when I raced Carly and Parker to the freezer for the last red popsicle, I ran extra hard because I *wanted* Parker to tackle me and drape me over his shoulder so he could reach into the popsicle box first. I wanted him to douse me with his Supersoaker, or flick little paper footballs at me while I made a show of trying to study, despite the distraction.

Eventually, neither of us could handle the flirting any more. We *had* to kiss. It was like we were two trains, locked into steel tracks and heading for one another without any way to change course.

I was eighteen and he was twenty-three when we both gave into the tension.

What a terrible idea.

It doesn't matter that his lips on mine made fireworks shoot through me. It was still a mistake. Because a few weeks after it happened, he decided it couldn't happen again. That night when I stayed up until sunrise it wasn't to outline and write a spectacular report about worms that eat dirt. It was because I was crying so hard, I thought my stomach was going to turn inside out.

Right now, seeing Parker's photo makes me remember how I actually crouched over the toilet bowl that night he broke things off, because I was crying so hard and my stomach hurt so much, I was sure I was about to throw up blood.

Mitch doesn't seem to notice my aversion to the photo. His voice sounds far off as he says, "My boy. He's in a rough spot these days. Have you heard?"

The sight of Parker's photo caught me off guard. Like I was sitting in a business meeting one minute, then suddenly getting creamed with a giant wrecking ball the next.

I blink as I stare at the image, and try to catch my breath and look like I'm not reeling.

It's a professionally taken shot, probably at one of the big tournaments Parker played in over the course of his tennis career. He's on a sun-soaked clay court, wielding a racket. His tattooed arms ripple, sweat glistens off his brow.

I cough into my fist. "Ah… hm?"

"I'm sure Carly's mentioned that he's living in Pines Peak these days?" He says this like he's bringing up the embarrassing fact that his son's chosen to spend his days hunkered under a rock. It's clear he thinks that Pines Peak, in Northern Vermont, is the sort of speck-on-the-map town acceptable for owning a second home in—which the Mannings do, a gorgeous log cabin—but that's about it.

"Oh. Yeah. She's mentioned it."

"He's had a rough go of it, since his injury forced him into early retirement. Off the rails, if you ask me. No direction, no sense of purpose. He's got a lot of energy, always has, and without an aim for that… Well, it's not good. He's getting in trouble. Fired from his job, living in a trailer. You ask me, what he needs is some stability."

"Stability. Right." I recross my legs and try to look professional. As though right now, I'm not thinking about that time Parker and I kissed for the first time.

It was right here in this house.

Parker was home for a brief respite from tour; I was gearing up to go off to college.

Mitch says something about his own company, Manning Light Fixtures. Maybe it's about his upcoming retirement? I'm not sure, because I'm too busy remembering that night a decade ago.

How the rec room couch felt scratchy behind my shoulder blades and thin tank top, when Parker crawled on top of me and finally, *finally* placed his lips on mine.

How he smelled like coconut tanning oil and chlorine, and he tasted like bubble gum.

How my world fell apart the instant our mouths fused. My reality shattered, and then came together in a brand new way that felt so good and right. Me and Parker. Together at last. I remember thinking: *This is it.*

Then, when he left town again, I learned that all life's incredible, breathtaking highs come with equally extreme lows. I also learned that if you're going to sob for hours and hours, you'd better have water handy because your throat is going to go so dry, you feel as though you'll never be able to speak another word in your life.

"... and he'd rise to the challenge, I think, if he feels the right motivation," Mitch says. "Besides, he can delegate all the tasks he doesn't want to do or doesn't know how to do. He doesn't have a head for business, as far as I can tell. But when it comes down to it he's good with people and that's what being a CEO *really* requires. People skills."

Welp. Now I'm lost.

Flashbacks: One. Gemma: Zero.

I stare blankly at Mitch, and then slowly his meaning catches up to me. He wants Parker to take over as CEO for Manning Light Fixtures.

But what does this have to do with me and Right Match?

Mitch tips the framed photo back his way and then picks up his whisky glass. "What'll get him back on track, you ask me, is a good woman. He'd stop messing around and finally want to take the reins from me, earn a steady income so he can provide for a family. What do you think?"

All I can think about is the taste of sweet bubble gum.

Mitch waits.

I do my best to collect myself and *not* think about Parker's body pressed against mine, down on that rec room couch. "I guess I'm wondering what this has to do with Right Match."

He smiles. "Now, now. Come on now, Gem! You're a

smart girl. I'm sure you get the picture. I want you to put your process to work for Parker. Like that company motto of yours you mentioned. Don't just find him a match, find him the *right* match."

Well, at least he was listening to my pitch.

My stomach twists. I'm sure my face has gone pale.

All the blood swirling so merrily in my veins at the prospect of getting oodles of funding for my brand has been drained away at this sudden detour into Parker-land.

Mitch goes on. "If you find him a girl he'll tie the knot with, then you got yourself a deal. How does five-hundred thousand sound to you?"

How does five-hundred grand sound? Great, obviously.

This other stuff, about finding Parker a wife? Not so great.

"Er. Um…"

"I know, I know. It'll be tough. I'm sure Parker will resist. He barely answers his phone these days, and you know how he is about technology. He'd rather spend the day out on that old mountain bike of his than on a computer answering emails from dear old dad, or anyone else for that matter. Sometimes I wonder if he even owns a computer. And you know for yourself how wild and stubborn he is."

Oh, I know.

You don't kiss a guy like Parker and then ignore the press about him. And his shenanigans kept plenty of journalists busy, over the course of his eight-year stint of pro tennis.

They loved snapping photos of him with his arm draped around various women, from professional beach volleyball players to underwear models. Or out on the town downing shots of tequila the night before a big match. The wild-child of men's pro tennis captured the hearts of millions, but most of those photos only made me feel resentful.

Turns out, resentment is fine fuel that can motivate a girl straight through college, graduate school, and into a fantastic line of work that she absolutely loves with all of her heart.

I really do love my work. I love helping people find their right match. I love getting Christmas cards from happy couples that met thanks to our services. I love that we have a mission and a purpose. I have a chance to make a difference in people's lives every time I step through my office door and sit behind my spotless glass-and-chrome desk, with the white orchid in the corner and my white Macbook front and center.

And if fixing renegade, wild, stubborn Parker up with a match is what it takes to take my company to the next level, that's what I'm going to have to do.

Half a million dollars.

If I had half a million to invest, I could absolutely, no-questions-asked turn Right Match into a multi-million dollar company by the time I reach thirty.

That'd be pretty freaking amazing.

And I know my process works. Technically, finding Parker's perfect match should be straightforward. Once he answers the questionnaires, I'll run the info through our system and the database will provide potential matches. A few dates later, he'll have *the one* right at his fingertips. And who can say no to walking down the aisle, once they meet *the one*?

"Okay. I'll do it."

"Excellent!" Mitch beams at me as he rummages in his desk drawer. "You've always been a brave girl, Gemma! I will say that about you. You'll have to travel out to Pines Peak to catch up with him, I'm sure. The boy's more apt to use his phone as a paper weight than an actual communication device, like I said. Here's the key to our ski house. Use the place for as long as you like. And, let me jot down the address for that trailer of his…"

He hands me a single brass key, and then I wait as he writes out an address and then hands me the paper.

Mitch and I shake hands over his desk. "Good luck," he says to me with a wink.

"Thanks." *I have a feeling I'm going to need it.*

Chapter 2

Gemma

The minute I get into the car with Carly, I start fretting aloud. "What have I done..." I groan, as I pull my seatbelt across my chest.

The dinner of perfectly slow-cooked, succulent pot roast and flakey, buttery biscuits did not ease my mind about the job I accepted from Mitch.

If anything, I'd spent the dinner doubting my decision to play matchmaker to a guy who pretty much stomped on my heart, when I was a little baby bird about to fly the nest.

"I have to do this, right?" I ask Carly "I mean, I can't turn down half a million dollars just because I don't want to deal with Parker. Sure, he was the first guy I fell for, stupidly, and he crushed me, but in the big picture, that's no big deal. *He's* no big deal. He's nobody, really. Sorry—he's your brother."

Carly, behind the wheel, looks grim as she fires up her Volvo. "He's my brother alright. Freaking Parker." She's not happy with the situation, either. "I can't believe my dad is asking this of you. He should've just signed over a check."

"No, no. I don't want a handout or a favor. He wants to know the process works before he invests. That's fair."

"I'm sure you presented the relevant facts. You are Queen of Statistics, Gem. At this point, Dad's meddling for his own entertainment."

She steers us down Woodberry Lane, past the house I grew up in. My parents still live there, but they're at my Uncle's place in Virginia this week, thank goodness. I have enough on my mind tonight without worrying about having to stop in and weather their questions about my personal life. According to my parents, I work too hard. They never made millions, so what do they know? If I want to reach my goals I have to apply myself full-on. Running a company like mine takes dedication. Commitment. Sacrifice.

Carly turns onto the main artery that will take us to the interstate. "And not only is he meddling in Parker's business, but he's putting you in a crazy position. I know how bad you had it for my brother."

"Really, it was no big deal. We never dated."

"You guys were practically inseparable for three straight weeks. If that's not dating, I don't know what is. Admit it, Gemma, even for a woman of steel like you, this is going to suck."

"All that happened ten years ago. It was nothing. Honestly. This is just one more hurdle to jump."

"You can lie to yourself, but you can't lie to me. I *know* how you were about Parker. I know how *every* girl is about Parker. I've been dealing with this my whole life. Last winter, I brought Hannah to the ski house for a weekend…? Remember that friend I had from Bikram Yoga?"

"Right." I've met plenty of Carly's friends over the years, and Hannah doesn't particularly stick out, besides a vague image of willowy yoga-physique and flower-printed leggings.

"Yeah, well, what a pain *that* was. We ended up running into him on the hill. For the rest of the trip I had to listen to Hannah go on and on… *'Where's your brother? Is Parker going out tonight? Can we meet up with Parker?'* It was ridiculous. And she *still* talks about him, every time I run into her at the studio."

"Carly, I was eighteen when I had a thing for him. That was forever ago and it doesn't matter now. This will be easy."

"Oh… ho ho. You are soooo wrong, dude. Easy has nothing to do with what you're about to attempt. First of all, he's not mature enough to even think about tying the knot. My brother will never grow up. It's like he thinks just because he moved to the town we used to go on family vacations to, his life can be one big holiday all the time. Like the rest of us have to grow up and become responsible, productive citizens, but he can goof off all day and it's fine. I swear, he drives me crazy."

"Maybe your dad's right, and he needs to meet the right person and settle down."

"Are you kidding me? *Settle down?* Are we even talking about the same person? No way. Every time I talk to him, he's dating someone new. My Dad's setting you up for failure. Parker's thirty-three going on seventeen, and that's how he's going to be for the rest of his life."

She takes a right onto the Mass Turnpike, and merges into the long parade of traffic that will carry us back into Boston. Rather than stick to the slower right lane, she presses the gas and her sleek Volvo catapults forward, launching us into the speedier, middle-lane traffic.

"His life's in the toilet these days," she adds, while scanning the radio for a suitable song. "The last time I went up to the log cabin, I went out to his place to see him... It's this cheap little double-wide mobile home way out on the edge of town. And did Dad tell you he got fired from the tennis center?"

"Yeah. I have some questions about that."

She groans as she glances over her shoulder to check traffic, then merge left again . "No kidding. I think we all do. Like how does a guy with two Olympic medals for tennis get fired from a job at a crappy little tennis center in the middle of nowhere? That place should've been kissing the ground he walked on. Instead, they canned him."

"Whatever happened must have been pretty bad."

"Totally. I'm thinking maybe he stopped showing up for work or something. *Ugh*, seriously, he is so irresponsible. I think he's working at some gross dive bar in town a few nights a week. The Tipsy Tavern. But still, he's probably totally broke. Hanging out with the same loser friends. When I visited, I tried to ask him if he even has any kind of savings account set up. Because even though I'm his younger sister, I feel about a billion years older than him, and I worry about him, and I want to help. So, I tried to tell him it's good to have three months' worth of emergency funds set aside and you want to know what he did?"

"What?"

"He threw a Fruit Loop at my nose and told me to chill out."

"Typical."

"*So* typical."

"But still, Carly, none of this changes the fact that I have to at least try. It's worth whatever pains and frustrations and suffering I have to endure. This is my business, and your dad's really giving me a shot at huge success. That's what I've always wanted."

"Oh, I know all about what you want. The Gemma Life Plan. Huge success, plus walking with Mortimer down the aisle, then a honeymoon to Switzerland."

"Precisely."

"You have it all mapped out. Wish I had something like that. The extent of my planning is that I seriously have to find a different job. My office is toxic. Did I tell you Serena actually went behind my back and complained to Lance about that software upgrade I pushed through last week?"

For the rest of the drive, we chat about Carly's work drama. By the time she drops me off at my brownstone apartment in West Cambridge, I've done my best to psychoanalyze a long list of behaviors, including her work-nemesis Serena's tendency toward passive aggressiveness, and her work-husband Lance's unresolved childhood issues.

Carly leans over the console to give me a hug. "As usual, I talked your ear off."

"I loved every minute of it."

"I think everyone should have a best friend who also happens to be a super talented licensed therapist."

I laugh as we part, and then hurry up the shadowy walkway to my first story unit. Inside, my cat, Queenie, brushes up against my calves as I hang my purse and coat on the rack.

I picked her up from the shelter the day that my then boyfriend, Mortimer Laughlin—a star player in the Gemma Life Plan—broke up with me.

It's sort of hard to walk down the aisle with a man you're not dating, so I'm going to have to fix that little blip in the schedule. I know Mortimer will want to get back together with me eventually... Once he takes some time for himself, and finishes whatever book he's working on.

He probably wanted space so he could focus on work, and I get that. I'm career minded, too.

But this "space" he asked for has turned into eight months of barely talking, and that's a little worrisome.

Also worrisome: the fact that I saw him at the Kendall Square Starbucks with his arm around a petite, ebony-haired woman in a red dress.

I will not dwell on that sight. *No problem.*

When is he going to come to his senses and try to get me back?

Any day now, I'm sure.

He'll call, tell me he misses me, and we'll be right back to where we started, treating each other with respect and civility. Two mature and responsible adults in a committed, loving, mutually-beneficial relationship. After all, he's my Right Match according to my own process.

It will work out, I tell myself, as I crouch to unzip my boots and then slip them off. I pet Queenie's back a few times while I'm down near the floor, and she rewards me by arching her petite frame up into my palm and gazing at me with her luminous green eyes.

I wish every relationship was as easy as the one I have with my beautiful cat. A pat here, a dish of water there, a can of Fancy Feast every night. Done.

In the kitchen, I pour myself a glass of chilled mineral water and then join Queenie on the couch, where she's curled into a ball. As I pet her, I continue an inner pep talk that I've given myself almost every day since Mortimer ended things.

The pep talk starts with how he'll finish writing his current book on economics soon, and it'll become another best-seller. It includes me steering my business toward international success, and then ends with us checking into a luxurious hotel in the mountains of Switzerland for a cozy, scenic, romantic, fourteen-day honeymoon.

Queenie's downy, feather-soft fur is warm beneath my fingertips. I give her a few more strokes and then reach for my laptop. Out of habit, I check my work email first, then click to social media. My usual rounds include a quick peek at the Mortimer Laughlin Author fan page, and I note that he'll be at a big economics forum in Vermont for most of next week. The speaker series starts on Wednesday evening and is scheduled through the weekend.

Next I toggle over to my calendar.

My priority has to be working out a "Right Match" for Parker. So, I have to head to Vermont ASAP.

Perfect, I think, as I scan my schedule. *I'll drive up to Vermont tomorrow after work, and spend the week there, tracking town Parker and dealing with his dating life.*

And while I'm in Vermont, I'll swing by the economics forum and see Mortimer at his conference. Since I'll be in the area and all.

I love having a plan.

Even better if it's an efficient plan, and this one does fit that description.

I snap my laptop closed and scratch Queenie under her dainty chin. "What do you think, Pretty Lady? You up for a trip to Vermont tomorrow with your Mamma?"

She closes her eyes and dissolves into purrs so loud, if I didn't know better I'd think there was a blender running under the couch cushions.

I'm going to take that as a yes.

Chapter 3

Parker

Duuude. What's this? A car, in the ski house driveway?

Lame.

My truck rumbles as I idle on the paved road out in front of my parent's vacation house and eye the light-blue Prius parked there.

It's Friday night, and I'm done with work. What I want so bad that my mouth is watering at the thought of it, is to eat the pizza I just picked up from Moe's, down at the center of town.

And I don't just want to *eat* the pizza. I want to *tear into* the pizza. Devour it. Demolish it. I'm freaking famished. My twelve-mile bike ride this morning up the steepest trail on the mountain must be catching up to me. I feel my stomach growling as I note the lights on inside the log cabin.

Skipping lunch to help Randy unload his pickup truck was not a good idea. Neither was picking up that shift at the bar without taking even fifteen minutes for a dinner break.

I want to crush a pizza, not deal with whatever friends my parents lent their house out to.

Probably some uptight and fussy couple from Wayland. I hate to be judgmental, but cars have personalities, and this one's sending out some serious uptight vibes. There are two university stickers in the rear window.

Not one. *Two.*

How pretentious is that?

The plate's red and white: Massachusetts. The tires are skimpy, too, like the rig's hardly seen a dirt road.

My hopes aren't high for the evening as I park and carry the piping hot pizza to the door. It's my own fault that I have to deal with this tonight. I didn't tell my parents I was here. So I'll put up with their friends, make small talk while I cram pizza into my mouth, and keep my fingers crossed that it's a one night stay.

Man, is this pizza hot. If I hurry and unload all the other crap from my car fast enough. I'll get to eat it while the cheese is still melted.

I prop the door open, drop the pizza box on a chair in the entryway, and then take a quick survey of the room to try to get a handle on what the situation for the evening is going to be.

I spot a pair of black ankle boots, neatly lined up against the wall. They're women's, with a little line of fur along the top and zippers up both sides.

The only other new item in the mudroom is a set of luggage: designer, paisley print, with little gold tags.

No other footwear. No other luggage.

Hm.

Either this lady has a hubby who's still wearing his own

set of sophisticated city boots as he unpacks shirts and khakis in the guest room, or the woman's here on her own.

Somewhere over near the guest room, a shower is running.

Interesting.

Not interesting enough to deter me from trying to get nutrients into my bloodstream as fast as possible. With my mind on hauling in the rest of the stuff from my truck back into the cabin quickly, I head for the door. I leave it propped open, hustle to my truck, and grab my bike out of the bed.

I never leave this puppy outside. The thing's worth three grand. I love this neighborhood and I'm a trusting guy, but I also know that it's best not to tempt fate. I wheel my baby into the garage, where my dad keeps his two "Vermont cars," a rusted Jeep and a refurbished classic Cadillac that he and my mom like to take out sightseeing, when they get around to it.

Which they haven't in years, as far as I can tell.

Mom likes the city more than the bugs and ice and mud of Vermont, and Dad's too busy working to stop and smell the roses—or the falling leaves, depending on the season.

Back at the truck, I load so many plastic grocery bags on one arm that I'm pretty sure I'm cutting off my own circulation. I slam the old truck's door closed and hike back to the door. Once inside, I notice that the shower's not running any more.

The next thing I see is a woman—petite, with wet, brown hair piled on top of her head in a bun.

She might be twenty or she might be sixty. It's hard to tell, given the fact that she has some sort of green paste smeared all over her face and she's wearing a plaid potato-sack nightgown instead of actual clothes.

"Parker?" the woman gasps.

That voice. I know that voice.

"Whoa, Gem, is that you?" I laugh before I can stop myself. "What's up with the alien mask? And the night-gown? I didn't even know chicks wore nightgowns anymore. Where'd you get that thing?"

Wow, it's good to see Gemma.

Unexpected, but that's how the best things always happen—unexpectedly, like little surprises that the Big Guy Upstairs lines up and then tucks down on earth like Easter Eggs for us humans to stumble on.

"What are you doing here?" I walk toward her, still laughing. Still amazed at the turn of events. No uptight Wayland couple after all. Tonight, I get to hang with Gem.

I want to hug her. Of course I want to hug her. I haven't seen Gemma Lafferty in ages.

Since, what… Carly's graduation from B.U.? That was… wow. Six years ago. Time flies.

Gemma, apparently, isn't interested in a reunion hug. She seems flustered as she ducks under my arm and strides barefoot to the door. "Yes, this is a nightgown. And I got it from your mother, by the way, for Christmas one year. And she got it here, in Vermont, at the Flannel Outlet store, and—Wait. What are *you* doing here? Your dad said I could use this place and he said nothing about you being here."

"Yeah, I'm sort of trying to fly under the radar. And if we could keep it that way…"

She reaches the door and her eyebrows pinch as she stares down at the ski boots I used to prop it open. Then she frowns and hugs herself as she steps outside into the darkness. "Parker, why'd you prop the door?" She looks left and right, then out toward the road. "Did you see a cat? Little, gray, pretty thing?"

When she whirls back to face me, I can tell that her face, beneath all that green goo, has turned pink as though she's upset.

Upset about what? The cat?

"Nah, no cat. But I was in the garage putting away my bike."

She huffs angrily, closes the door with a bang, and then cranes her head toward the guest room. "Queenie…? Queenie…?" she calls.

"Is Queenie your cat?"

"Yes, and I'm pretty sure you let her out. Oh my god, this is a disaster already."

"Already? What's that supposed to mean?"

What is Smarty Pants Gemma doing in Pines Peak, anyway? I wonder, as I watch her stride over to the guest room, her hands on her narrow hips.

Now that she's pinning the giant swath of fabric to her sides, I can tell she's still as fit as ever. Maybe a little slimmer and leaner than she used to be, even.

I remember how good she used to look in that little bikini she'd wear around the house, back when her and Carly were all about tanning out by the pool.

Back then, Gemma was Miss Perfect. Miss Valedictorian. Miss Goody Two Shoes.

I still don't know why she ever stooped down to my level and let me kiss her, for those few crazy weeks after she graduated high school.

She was probably bored with the Wayland guys. Once she hit that fancy college of hers she definitely moved on. These days, I've heard, she's dating some big-name author. What's his name again? I think Carly's mentioned it.

Morbid Phlegm-face.

No. Mort…. Mort-something. Cough-face. Coughlin. *Laughlin.* That's it. Laughlin.

I stare at the closed guest room door that Gemma disappeared behind. When she emerges, she's in matching purple sweat-suit and wool socks, and she's carrying a flashlight.

"Wow. From Granny Gown to this. Looking good, Lafferty."

She narrows her eyes at me as she shoves her feet into her boots. "I am going to look for my cat, whom you let out into the cold, dark night."

She's scrubbed the green stuff off her face, and now I can definitely tell that she's flustered. Her cheeks are flushed and her eyes keep darting over to me and then away as though I make her nervous.

Well, maybe it's not me making her nervous. Why should I make her nervous? It's probably her concern for this cat of hers that I'm picking up on,.

She crouches to zip her boots and then stands, stomps over to the door, and yanks it open. A drafty chill sweeps through the room. "She is a house cat and she doesn't know how to deal with wolves or… or… grizzly bears."

Laughter rakes through me. Man, is it nice to see this girl. Hear her voice say the silly things I used to get such a kick out of. "Gem, there are no wolves in Vermont. Or Grizzly Bears. Seriously, take a deep breath, have some food with me, and we'll figure out how to get Queenie back."

I'm about to explain how good a piping hot pizza from Moe's will taste when she steps outside and pulls the door closed behind her with a bang.

I give one last, longing look at the grease stained white box on the chair beside me. My stomach growls, but I ignore it and follow Gemma out the door.

Chapter 4

Gemma

Do not freak out. Do not freak out. Do not freak out.

Maybe if I tell myself that on repeat, I'll get my blood pressure down and manage to have a single clear, logical thought. As I traipse across the cracked pavement of the log cabin's driveway, my mind feels cloudy.

Parker's here.

At the log cabin.

And he just saw me in my old-lady nightgown.

I make my way past my own car, then a monstrous hunk of rusty metal that must be Parker's current vehicle. I'm too distracted to pay much attention to the truck's lift or knobby tires.

I *should* be distracted by the fact that my poor kitty is out in the wild. Even if Parker's right and there are no wolves or grizzly bears out here, it's still dark and cold and dangerous outside. There are owls out here. And… what? Moose eager to stampede over dainty cats, probably. I don't know. I've hardly ventured out of Boston for the past decade.

Queenie probably doesn't even know which house to return to, once she gets it in her kitty-brain that she should try to retrace her steps.

But it's not Queenie's predicament that's filling up my head with clouds of worry at the moment.

It's the dawning realization that after years of successfully avoiding Parker, I just ran into him while wearing a seaweed face mask and a plaid, flannel gown so big and bulky that I must have looked like a sailboat, waiting for the next gust of wind.

And what's worse than my mortifying display of sleep-apparel nerdiness is the fact that he's as built, tattooed, handsome, and relaxed as ever.

Mr. Cool in that white t-shirt and baseball hat pulled down low over his brow. Who wears a t-shirt when it's this cold outside? Parker, that's who. And I made a total idiot out of myself by screeching about Queenie and then storming out the door.

I hear the house's door close softly behind me, and then his deep, slightly croaky voice floats out from under the eves. "Hey, Gem? Wait up."

I turn and see him jogging toward me.

Oh, god. The embarrassing night continues. Now he's going to try to help me find my cat, and I'm sure I'm not going to give a good impression, given the fact that I'm shivering and flustered and slowly starting to actually worry about my fur baby.

I wanted to be on the top of my game when I knocked on his door, tomorrow. I wanted to catch him off guard, but now it's the other way around.

He caught me off guard by walking into the log cabin unannounced.

Why am I stressing about this?

It doesn't matter what he thinks of me, anyway.

I'm here for work, and that's it.

He catches up to me, and then uses a flashlight app on his phone to sweep light over a row of hedges on the side of the road. "Okay, hit me with the deets. We've got a gray cat… small and pretty. Anything else?"

"She's skittish. Really shy. It took me months to get her to warm up to me in the first place. When I picked her up from the shelter she was petrified."

"A sweet little fraidy cat. Got it." He aims his light up at a tree. "She climb?"

"Anything she can find. Yeah. The first few weeks I had her in my apartment, she kept making her way to the top of my refrigerator, into this cupboard that's up there. She'd burrow past the boxes of oatmeal and hide out for hours."

He laughs. "That's pretty normal."

What does he know?

"Do you have pets?" I ask, as I aim my flashlight across the pavement, toward a stand of pine trees. Poor Queenie. She could be anywhere.

"Nope."

"Okay, well, when we spot her can you let me try to catch her? She never even let Mortimer hold her. Every time he entered my apartment she ran and hid."

"*Mortimer.*" He snaps his fingers. "That's right. I couldn't remember his name. Hey, so, Carly told me you're doing great. Still in Boston, right?"

"I live and work in Cambridge, yeah."

"Sweet. Love that part of the city."

He matches my pace as we start walking along the paved road. The Manning's ski house is at the top of a loop. Every now and then, the wooded area that lines the road is interrupted by a huge vacation home of one variety or another. We pass a modern stucco-and-stone two story place, then a dark wood log cabin similar to the Mannings. Both look empty, and I don't feel bad about shining my flashlight beam over all the window ledges and into porticos and front porches.

Beside me, Parker does the same, only he aims his beam across the trees and houses on the other side of the road. Without even talking about it, we've split the search duties neatly down the middle.

It's weird, walking shoulder-to-shoulder with him out here in the dark. We've fallen into a silence that feels almost comfortable.

Impossible.

I haven't seen Parker in six years, since Carly's graduation from B.U. There's no way we can be sharing a comfortable silence.

It's him. He's doing that thing he does—pumping out the feel-good vibes. People gravitate toward Parker because he's one of the "easy to be around" types. Friendly and outgoing, When you're around him, it's always about *you*, never *him*.

I used to love that. So have all the other women he's ever been with, I'm sure. Including all of Carly's friends, Hannah and whoever else he's wooed over the years. I'm one more of her friends that fell for his charms.

I can just imagine how Yoga-body Hannah probably ogled Parker out on the mountain, practically drooling while lifting up her mirrored goggles to get a better look at his chiseled jaw and broad shoulders.

Yep, I used to be right there with ya, girl, I think, as I sweep my flashlight along a stone wall that borders a Swiss-style chalet.

This time around, I won't let him ensnare me in his spider web of charm.

If I have to be out here with him, walking down this peaceful country road without even one car in sight, I better use the time to my advantage.

Time to start working.

I cast a sideways look at him and ready my first matchmaking-related question, but then nearly get blinded when he flashes me a smile.

"Man, is it good to see you," he says. "Sorry again about the cat."

"Well I'd have warned you if I thought you were going to show up out of the blue. What do you mean you're staying there under the radar? Your dad said you were living in a trailer on the outskirts of town. What's the deal?"

"My place is sort of… not great right now. Noise level issue. Got so I wasn't sleeping, so I decided it was better to crash at the cabin for a while."

"What kind of noise level issue? I doubt there's some high-traffic jetway in a little town like this. Does a neighbor play the drums or something?"

"Just… an issue."

Okay, so he doesn't want to give me details. That means he's hiding something.

But, what?

My mind searches for possible answers as I swing my light out along a path that's cut into the woods. Maybe his mobile home is parked next to a rowdy bar or poker hall. Or some kind of machinery. Or truck stop.

Whatever it is, the noise is bad enough that he can't live there.

So, he's basically homeless. That does not bode well for his Right Match questionnaire.

I play my flashlight beam over the dirt path, hoping to spy a flash of gray fur. No such luck.

Parker heads that way. "We might as well walk this trail a little ways. She could've followed it."

He steps over a fallen log across the path's entrance, then turns and offers me a hand. His palm feels incredibly warm against mine. His grip is strong as he guides me over the thick trunk. Then we stand, facing one another.

The woods around us smells like pine needles and fresh, mountain air. Parker's features are shrouded in shadows, but I can make out his bright, brown eyes as they dance over me.

He looks me over, in that way that people do when they haven't seen you in a while.

And I guess now I'm looking him over, too. He's aged really well. I'm not sure how he managed it, but he seems to be in even better shape now than he was last time I saw him. That's quite a feat, given that the last time I saw him in person he was in the thick of a career as a professional athlete.

He's still wearing the t-shirt, like he ran out of the house without giving a second thought to the falling temperatures. It feels like the Arctic out here to me. Then again, it might be my anxiety that's given me such a chill. I hate when things happen outside of the bounds of my own schedule. I was supposed to see him tomorrow, not tonight.

On top of that I keep imagining a big owl with a ten-foot wingspan swooping down on my unsuspecting cat.

"Aren't you cold?" I ask, as I stuff my hands in the pockets of my sweatshirt.

"Nah." His mouth hitches up at the corner, in a quick grin. "My blood runs hot, I guess. I feel fine. You doin' okay?"

Then, with his eyes on mine, he reaches out and his hand threads around my neck. He gently tugs at the hood that's attached to my sweatshirt. His fingers brush against my neck as he fits the hood up over my head. Then he pulls both strings, and the gentle tug closes the fleece-lined material over my ears. "There. You'll be warmer."

He starts off down the path.

Don't read into it, I tell myself, as I stare at him. I can still feel a faint trail of warmth where he touched me. *He's a physical guy.* He touches people: hugs them, picks them up, knocks into them. I've seen him give handshakes that *start* as handshakes, but then within seconds turn into bear hugs.

"What about the tennis center?" I call out, as I hurry down the path to catch up with him. He's right. My ears are much warmer, tucked inside this layer of fleece.

"What about it?"

"I hear you were fired." *And that makes you both homeless and unemployed.*

Again, I think of the questionnaire I'll have to help him fill out. Being homeless and unemployed is not good, when it comes to dating. Not good at all.

His shoulders ripple as he laughs. "You ask a lot of questions, you know that?" Then his laughter dies down and he slows his pace. After a minute, he stops walking altogether.

Uh oh. He might be onto me.

I stop, too.

He turns to face me, slowly, as though he's thinking. This time when he looks at me, it's with a hint of wariness. "Wait a sec… I get what's going on here. My dad gave you my address… so he wanted you to visit me. You're a therapist these days. What, does he want you to try to fix me or something?"

What can I say to that?

It's not exactly the truth.

But the real truth—that I'm supposed to find Parker a wife—might be a harder pill to swallow.

So, I lift my chin a quarter of an inch. "Sort of."

"Oh… oh, man. There's more, isn't there?"

"Maybe."

"Ah. Okay. I get it…. You've got that matchmaker business." He fidgets with the brim of his hat, pulling it low and side to side, then he turns around and starts walking again. "No thanks."

"No thanks?"

"No thanks, I don't want to be a lab rat you experiment on."

"I don't need lab rats. My company's process is completely dialed in at this point. It really works, and your dad wants—"

"You don't have to tell me what my dad wants. I know."

We walk in silence for a few minutes, until a far-off yipping, howling sound pierces the air.

I catch up to him instinctively. Better to be walking right next to a broad-shouldered, six-foot-two guy when you're out in the woods like this—even if he is a guy who broke your heart, once upon a time—than lagging behind where the critters can catch you and make a meal out of you.

"I thought you said there were no wolves out here?" I hate that my voice is high-pitched and quavering, but it is.

"There aren't. Those were coyotes."

"And they're… harmless?"

"For the most part."

I don't like that answer.

And I don't like that Parker has tried to shut down the only reason I'm here in Vermont in the first place, with two words. *"No thanks."*

I'm not a girl to spot an obstacle in my path and simply turn around. I hurdle obstacles, no matter what it takes.

"Your dad thinks maybe if you find the right person to settle down with, you'll be happier," I say, as the path curves uphill. Tall pines loom over us. "I can help you do that. It's sort of my specialty these days."

I *will* convince Parker to let me help him.

I *will* find him a match.

I'll find Queenie, too, and then we're both going to leave Pines Peak in the dust.

And I'll do my best to never, *ever* walk side-by-side with Parker in the dark woods again. Because I don't think it's healthy for me to feel like this—like he's my safety. My protection. My friend, even.

Being out here in the woods with Parker Manning is bringing up way, *way* too many memories. The last thing I need right now is to relive one of the most painful experiences of my life.

"It's not even that hard," I hear myself say, as I ward off a fresh batch of kissing-Parker mind-movies. "One questionnaire, a couple interviews… we run the numbers, and *voila*. You're good to go."

Chapter 5

Parker

Maybe it wasn't a good idea to take this path.

Being out here in the woods with Gemma reminds me of the time when we were younger, and I drove us out to the Wayland Bird Reserve at the far edge of town. We parked and I carried a blanket out into the woods, and we laid on our backs and stared up at the starry sky and talked all night.

I remember how lucky I felt, when she rested her head on my chest and wove her fingers through mine, and spilled out all her dreams to me. She wanted so many things, and I admired that.

Every time she kissed me that night, I thought about how it couldn't last.

I knew I had to go back on tour.

I was only home that summer so I could rest my wrist. Not that it did much good. The thing still ached like a mother during that last set of the US Open, and my backhand was weaker than a limp noodle.

I also knew that night at the Bird Reserve that Gemma had her whole life ahead of her. That she'd follow her dreams, just like I was following mine.

And she did. She skyrocketed toward success like everyone knew she would.

Good for her.

This Mortimer guy, whoever he is, is really lucky.

I probably shouldn't have even helped her with that sweatshirt hood. She sort of stiffened up when I did that, like it was out of line.

Noted. Do not touch Gemma, even if the gesture's meant to be friendly.

She's taken, and I'm just a random guy at this point.

Not a guy who has the right to tuck her sweatshirt over the top of her head so she feels cozy and warm.

I want her to feel warm, though. Her hair's still wet from her shower and the temps are dropping out here. I want to find her cat, too. And more than that, I want her to stop talking about my dad's latest scheme.

But she won't.

While keeping perfect pace with me, she rattles off a few lines about some questionnaire and an interview process. As I listen, I slide my light across the green, lush bough of a nearby evergreen tree.

"Honestly, it's painless," she says. "If we sit down and I help you fill out the questionnaire it'll take you like one hour. Two, tops. And the interviews are sort of fun. You get to talk about yourself and learn interesting things about your own personality. Like, for example, how do you feel about social engagements? The introvert-extrovert divide is a huge deal, in couples therapy."

"Gem, I don't need therapy."

"No, I know, that's not what I'm saying. I'm saying that therapists who deal with marital problems day in and day out see common issues, and our process—the Right Match process—helps people avoid all those issues straight out of the gate. It's based on thousands—like *hundreds* of thousands—of data points that we collected from couples therapists all over the country. Super comprehensive."

Is it bad that I think it's cute when she gets jazzed about numbers?

Yes. It's bad. *She's taken*, I remind myself. "Hey, I appreciate that you're into your work, but it's really not for me."

"I'm offering you something that plenty of people pay big bucks for."

"Yeah, well, I'm not interested."

"Your dad thinks—"

"I already told you, Gem. I know what my dad thinks. He thinks I need to do exactly what he did… Find a wife, buy a house, raise two kids, and play Scrabble every Saturday night with the neighbors."

"What's wrong with Scrabble?"

"Nothing's wrong with Scrabble. I'm saying that what makes him happy isn't what makes me happy. *This* makes me happy, Gemma." I stop short on the path and we both stand in silence for a minute. A feeling of wellbeing flows through me, unstoppable. Sometimes this happens to me. They don't last long, but they're pretty cool.

"This?" she asks.

"This," I repeat. "Just being right here, outside, in the fresh air, without any clue what's going to happen next. I like it."

She wrinkles her nose and eyes me as though I just rattled off a monologue in Chinese.

"You can't be *happy*, Parker. You're homeless and unemployed. You're saying you don't need help with anything, but that's not true. All of us can use a little help.

So would you quit being stubborn and just let me try to help you? I went to school for this stuff."

Ah... Ah ha.

'Homeless and unemployed.' Clearly, she's been drinking the Manning Family Kool-Aid, lapping up whatever gossip my parents and sister dish out. I don't mind. They don't get me or my lifestyle, and they never have.

"Look... whatever my dad cooked up and roped you into—I'm sorry. I don't want any part of it."

"I'm not asking you to give up your happiness, Parker, or change your life, like, at all. You do you. Seriously. If this is your happy place, that's great." She waves her hand around at the trees dismissively. "But what's wrong with dating a nice girl who *adds* to your happiness? What's wrong with finding a person who you want to spend your life with?"

"There's nothing wrong with that. And when the time is right, it'll happen. On its own. Organically."

I can't believe I'm out here in the woods with Gemma Lafferty—the first girl I ever really fantasized about, and the first person I ever fell in love with—and she's trying to set me up with someone else.

Talk about bizarre.

But I meant what I said about how I like not knowing what'll come next. Life's full of surprises, and that's what makes it fun.

And the big surprise of today is the fact she's actually here in Vermont. It's so good to see her—even if she is trying to find me a wife that's not her. She's still *Gemma*, and I'm lucky to be hanging out with her right now.

So I try to forget about her twisted motive for visiting Pines Peak, and appreciate the fact that at least she's here.

Chapter 6

Gemma

My beeping alarm jolts me out of sleep so abruptly, I literally gasp for breath as though I've just surfaced from a deep dive into the ocean.

With one hand over my chest, I gulp in oxygen and take in my very unfamiliar surroundings.

Log cabin.

Pines Peak.

Parker.

That last thought makes me feel lightheaded.

I'm in a house alone with Parker Manning.

We were out until at least one last night, searching for Queenie. We didn't find her. But somewhere between fixing the hood of my sweatshirt (which was so sweet, I can't stop thinking about it) and refusing my professional help as a therapist (which was so *infuriating*, I can't stop thinking about it) he promised me that Queenie would be okay. And his voice was so deep, sincere, and certain that I actually believed him. And I still believe him.

Queenie will be okay.

But until I find her, I can't leave this cabin.

So even if every cell in my body—well, at least, um, the majority of the cells in my body—tell me to get out of this house, I have to stay.

It's going to be challenging, being under the same roof as him.

Because there are things about Parker I'd be much better off not knowing.

For example, I wish I didn't know that he sleeps in dark blue sweatpants these days. Nothing but dark blue sweatpants. No shirt. Bare chest.

Bare, *ripped* chest.

I found that out last night, when we almost bumped into each other on the way to the bathroom.

Oh, and not only that. I also discovered that he has a new tattoo across his right shoulder and pec. Or at least, new to me. The last time I saw a photo of him online, this ink wasn't there. It's of scales, perfectly balanced. Probably something astrological. Parker has that woo-woo side of him. The side that believes in fate and destiny and all sorts of stuff. Stuff that maybe I'd believe in, too, if I ever had time to think about it.

But I don't have time to think about things like that because I have work to do.

My company doesn't run itself. I am a hands-on boss, and my employees count on me to be there for them when they need me.

So, with my mind on work—and also sort of on that image of shirtless Parker— I stumble all the way to the kitchen.

When we met in the dark hallway outside of the bathroom, he placed his hands gently on my elbows to stop us from actually bumping into each other. *"Thought I heard a noise out here. I'm a light sleeper, I guess. You go first, Gem."*

My eyes were barely open at the time, but the minute he touched me awareness flooded my senses. I picked up on everything about him, including the way his dirty-blond hair stuck out in all directions because of bed-head. And the way his deep, sleepy voice resonated through me, all the way to the tips of my wool socks.

Would it really have been so bad to actually bump into him?

This has to stop. I can't walk around this house in the dark thinking about colliding with Parker.

That'll get me in trouble.

I fumble my way through the process of making a pot of coffee in an unfamiliar machine. Not easy, in my sleep-deprived state.

I'm used to being short on sleep, but even for me, getting nothing but three hours is extreme.

I wish I could turn over and fall back to sleep, but I can't.

The business world is competitive. If I slow down, I'll fall behind. I'm in the rat race these days. I hate how I haven't had a day off in forever, but what can I do? If I want to be successful, I have to keep running like everyone else.

It's 4:15 now, which means I'm already fifteen minutes behind schedule. I like to have the most pressing emails answered by five at the latest, so I better get cooking.

Perched on a barstool near the marble counter, I sip java and stare into the wormhole that is my MacBook screen.

This morning my emails are relatively tame. I fire off a few to my Head of Marketing, Claire. She's only been on the staff for four months, and so far I'm impressed by her work ethic. I recruited her after Right Match was featured in a documentary, *Love in the Modern Age*, at the Cannes Film Festival back in May. The documentary won a major award and in the weeks that followed, the office phones were ringing off the hook. Now that Claire is on board and handling inquiries from the press, I can focus back on big-picture stuff, which is where I excel.

Last night, it seems, Claire was burning some major midnight oil. *You go, girl,* I think, as I open her last email, which arrived in my box only a few hours prior. It's about a marketing opportunity: a YouTuber with a big audience wants to interview me.

I quickly read through the details and discover that he typically gets over a million views per video that he posts. Am I up for the interview? Um... hello! *'Yes, absolutely,'* I type. *'Set it up.'*

I polish off the last drops of coffee and hit send.

Up next, I have to tackle The Parker Issue, as I've mentally labeled it.

And for that, I'm going to need a second cup of coffee.

The caffeine's starting to work, and I feel a bit perkier as I settle back onto the stool, a second mug of brain-fuel cupped in my hands. I pull up the main questionnaire that I'll have to get Parker to fill in, and then stare at it.

It's long.

There are sixty-eight questions that he'll need to fill in, and most of them require serious thought.

But Parker said "No thanks."

That's not going to work for me. He can turn down my offer to help, if he wants. He's stubborn. He's Parker. But I'm here to get this done, and I'm not leaving Pines Peak without giving this Parker Wife Hunt one-hundred percent of my effort.

The thing is… how is my effort going to help, when *he's* the one who has to answer all these questions?

I could tie him down and force the answers out of him. Ha. I wish. He's about twice my height and twice my weight.

Okay, brute force won't work. Hypnosis?

No… that won't work either. Even if I learned how to hypnotize a person by watching the videos I am sure are out there on the internet in abundance, knowing Parker he'd probably fall into a stupor and give me confusing, nonsensical answers, like how the woods make him happy for no reason.

My mind drifts to last night.

How he stood there on that path and acted like he had his feet planted in paradise.

What's wrong with him, anyway? Can't he see he's on a dead-end road, and if he doesn't change his ways soon, he's going to be in big trouble?

Mitch is right. I feel sure of that. His son's up to no good, holed away in this little mountain town. Parker can't even live in the metal box he calls a house, for some mysterious reason that, now that I think about it, might have to do with rats. Yes, there are probably rats in his trailer, and that's why he can't sleep there.

I feel bad for him. I really do.

He's falling into bad habits and he'd be better off in Wayland, running Manning Light Fixtures.

I drum my fingers against the ceramic mug I'm clutching like my life depends on it. My life sort of does depend on this coffee, actually; if I stop drinking this stuff, I might drop to the floor and fall asleep for days.

And then it hits me: *I know how to get this job done.*

I'll fill in the questionnaire *for* Parker. When he was a big deal in men's tennis, he was constantly featured in the media. All I have to do is Google 'Parker Manning' and I'll find countless interviews to pick through. I can get into his head that way, and then use my research to fill out the Right Match form.

Where there's a will there's a way, I think, as my fingers fly across the keyboard.

My brilliant idea begins to feel less brilliant an hour and a half later, after watching two-dozen video clips that feature Parker sprawled on one interviewer's couch after another.

In every clip, he's the same: confident, content, chill, and super cool. It's like he has one mood, and one mood only: Relaxed.

He's never "on" or "off" and he never seems to have a bad day.

I don't think there's enough coffee in the world that would make watching video after video of your first heartbreaker enjoyable. Maybe I need a bowl of oatmeal or a grapefruit or something. I shouldn't do this to myself on an empty stomach.

Right. Like food is going to help.

Any way you slice it, this research is pretty much torture.

Parker dumped me, and now I have to delve into his psyche so I can try to find him a wife.

A feeling of sadness swoops down on me as if out of nowhere… like that owl I felt so fearful of, last night.

The feeling descends heavy on my shoulders and threatens to yank me into a serious pity-party, so I abort my Parker research. It's a relief to close the tab that featured a huge photo of him, shirtless again, holding his racket. *'Dreamy Parker Manning Would Rather be Playing Tennis'* the caption says.

Yep. I'm going to need a third cup of coffee, some breakfast, and some actual daylight before I read that one.

For the next couple hours, I focus on much more enjoyable work tasks, like going over our third quarter Profit and Loss statement and communicating with the company accountant.

By ten, I've showered, dressed, and ticked off half the day's to-do items. This remote work thing isn't so bad. It's dangerously easy to work from a vacation house.

I've gotten so much done, in fact, that I deserve a break.

I'll call Mortimer. See what he's up to.

I've barely contacted him since we split. But being out in the woods with Parker—standing so close to him, and feeling his warm fingertips brush my neck—all that made me want… no, *need* to remind myself that I have a man. A man who's right for me, not all wrong for me, like Parker.

According to the Right Match process, Mortimer Laughlin is a 93% match for me. That's really good. Our company policy is that anything over 85% is a green light for marriage. The numbers are all based on hardcore statistics, and I trust them completely.

Numbers don't lie.

People, on the other hand, lie all the time. They say things they don't mean. They act in contradictory, confusing ways.

But numbers are pure and direct.

I think about that number, 93, as I listen to Mortimer's phone ring. When he picks up, I can hear sounds of the city behind him. "Gemma? Can you hold for a moment?"

The corners of my mouth tug downward and I tap my pen against the marble countertop. It's not a great feeling, to be put on hold. Then again, he's a busy man.

When he speaks again, it's rushed, "Hey, sorry about

that, hon. I had my publicist on the other line. How are you?"

"I'm..." *I'm stuck in a log cabin with an irritatingly hot guy who I used to be in love with.* "I'm fine. Just wanted to hear your voice. Catch up a little, you know."

"Aw, that's sweet of you. It's always nice to hear from you, too. Business good?"

"Great. Hey, I'm actually in Vermont. I think I saw that you're going to be up this way...?"

He hesitates. "Er, yes. Yes, in fact, I am. Making the drive tomorrow morning, actually."

I wait for him to extend some more details, but he doesn't. Maybe he feels awkward about this because we're not officially an item any more. But he did call me "hon" just like he used to...

He should invite me to the conference. I want to go. I want to see him.

I have to take matters into my own hands, clearly. "Central Vermont, right?" I prompt. "The economics forum? I read that it's a really good lineup. Nice that you're getting there early. That should give you a little time to unwind, before you lecture. I'm sure you're speaking...?"

"That's right. They have me giving a keynote speech Wednesday night, plus presenting two talks on Saturday. *Volatility in Income* and *Labor Force Dynamics*. Rather drab stuff, but I'm saving the cutting-edge show-stoppers for the Cornell Lecture Series in January, after this next book launches."

"Wow, awesome. Good for you. Hey, would you be up for a visit, maybe Monday? I'd love to take a drive, and it'd be great to see you."

"Ah... er." He clears his throat.

I tap my pen against the counter top faster. What is going on here? It's almost like he doesn't want to see me.

I'm going crazy. That's what's happening. Being stuck in this log cabin with shirtless, bed-head Parker is making me lose my grip on reality. I can't let that happen.

Get your head straight Gemma, I tell myself. *Mortimer Laughlin is your Mr. Right. Star of your Life Plan. The man who will one day slip your great-grandmother's engagement ring onto your left index finger.*

I reach for the vintage ring I wear on a chain around my neck, every single day.

"It's been a while and it'd be really great to grab a cup of coffee, maybe, and chat," I say, as I run my fingertips over the smooth ridges of the ring. "Plus, I'd love to see your lectures if you think you can get me seats on Saturday. *Volatility in Income*… that sounds really interesting."

Chapter 7

Parker

I could sleep for another two hours, easy.

But I can hear Gemma out in the kitchen, and as I lie in bed I realize that I don't want to miss this time with her.

She'll be back to her life in the city in no time, knowing her.

Gemma was always busy, back when she was in high school. It was like she always wanted to be two places at once: presiding over a student council meeting *and* playing field hockey. Gossiping with the girls at the lunch table *and* running on the track.

Perfecting her backstroke in the backyard pool *and* flirting with me on a lounge chair in the sun.

I close my eyes and remember exactly what she used to look like, when she'd perch at the end of whatever chaise lounge I was sprawled across. She'd flick water over me or tease me for being lazy, and I'd eat it all up like a marathon runner at a spaghetti buffet.

I can almost feel the hot sun on my chest, and smell her

suntan lotion and that marshmallow lip gloss she used to wear.

Man, that lip gloss used to drive me wild. It sparkled on her lips and made me think about kissing her every single time she layered it on.

I think she knew it, too. She'd pull the tube out of her pocket whenever I entered a room, and then look me in the eye as she passed the wand over her bottom lip. Then she'd rub her lips together, all the while holding my gaze.

Now she's here, right out in the kitchen.

I wonder if she's wearing lip gloss today. Or, has she graduated to lipstick? Or is she a no-muss, no-fuss kind of woman these days, forgoing makeup for the natural look? Gemma doesn't need makeup, obviously. Her face is perfect, even with green goop smeared all over it.

I almost laugh, as I think about last night.

Then I sit up, swing my legs over the side of the bed, and run a hand through my hair.

Out in the hall, I smell coffee and oatmeal. I can hear the soft murmur of her voice, but I can't make out what she's saying.

She must be on the phone.

When I reach the kitchen, I see her. She's sitting on the edge of a barstool, her phone pinned to her ear. Her back's to me, and she's tapping a pen nervously against the counter. *Rat-a-tat-tat-tat.*

What's got her so keyed up?

Her tone sounds stressed, too. "Oh, is that right?" she says, her voice so tight it's like there are hands wrapped around her neck, rather than the cashmere scarf she's wearing. "That's great, Mortimer. I'm sure that's going to be a fascinating talk. Good for you for doing all that prep work. Maybe we could meet up after you log a few hours of research, then…? Late afternoon is fine for me. I mean, that is, if it's convenient for you and everything."

Ugh. Mortimer. The boyfriend.

She hesitates, maybe listening to something he's saying. Her shoulders look so tense, I want to walk right up to her and rub them.

That would definitely be out of bounds.

So instead I linger in the doorway. This conversation seems to be important, and maybe private, too. I don't want to interrupt.

"Okay, great. Where are you staying?" she asks. There goes the pen again, drumming even faster now.

The girl should have been a percussionist.

"Oh, really? Neat. I didn't realize there was a hotel right there. Okay, so I'll see you Monday around three then." When she hangs up, she pushes her laptop out of the way, and then rests her arms on the counter and plants her forehead down over her stacked palms.

I make my way to the side counter that has the coffee pot on it.

She must hear me, finally, because she picks her head up and fixes her scarf as she says, "Oh, hey. You're up."

"You doin' okay?" I ask, as I pour coffee into a mug. The pot's only a quarter full. Either she only brewed a half-pot, or she's been up for quite a while.

Based on what I know about Gemma, it's the latter. She never liked to sleep in.

"I'm fine," she says quickly. "Why?"

Because people who are fine don't usually do a face-plant after getting off the phone.

I wander toward the stove. "Just asking, that's all."

There's a pot on the stove, and I lift the lid. Nice. Oatmeal. And she added raisins and cinnamon, and maybe some maple syrup, too, based on the smell. "Hey, can I have some of this?"

"Knock yourself out," she says miserably.

That seals the deal. She's really not fine. "You don't have to keep stuff from me," I tell her, as I shovel a heap of cooked oats into a bowl. "If there's something wrong, you can tell me."

"Nothing's wrong."

She's lying. I know she's lying. "Good talk with Mortimer?"

"It was fine," she grumbles.

"You sure?"

"I'm sure. He's fantastic, I'm fantastic. I'm going to see him tomorrow, late afternoon. He's presenting a couple talks at a big conference center down in Broad Hollow this week and he's super busy with research and writing…."

"Yeah, I heard you figuring out where he's staying." *Which is weird, since he's your boyfriend.*

At the fridge, I pull out a gallon of milk. I pour a dollop on the oatmeal and carry my bowl to the counter. When I sit down across from her, I get treated to the whole dazzling Gemma-effect. Her straight-brown hair is pulled back in a high ponytail, like she used to wear it. She's in a fitted, heather gray sweater and designer jeans, and she's wearing a plaid scarf around her neck. Her skin glows, and—jackpot—she's wearing a coating of sparkly gloss on her lips. Why does it make me so happy that she still wears lip gloss?

"I think we're going to get married one day," she says quickly.

I yank my gaze away from her lips and poke at the warm oatmeal with my spoon. "That right?"

"Probably. If things go to plan."

"*Hrmph.*" I snort into my spoon and then manage to

swallow a bite. "Still with the plans, huh? You're something else."

"If you want to accomplish things in this life, you have to have a plan," she says. She pulls her laptop back to her and stirs it to life. While tapping the keys she says, "You don't seem to be all that worried about accomplishing things these days, though."

"What, two medals at the Olympics isn't enough?" I tease. Then I shovel in more oatmeal. "Wow. This is dank."

"Hey!" she retorts, feigning anger. "You know dank means damp and cold, or, like, moist and humid, right? Are you insulting my oatmeal?"

"Nah. I'm using the term in the best possible way. Excellent. Rad. Epic. As in, 'that pizza we had last night was dank.' Or 'Gemma's teeny-tiny Prius is dank.' "

She grins and shakes her head. "Okay, now you're making fun of my car."

Score. I got her to smile. "No way, dude. I like that little thing. I bet it's great to have a car you could pick up and cart around in your purse, if you needed to. Bet she gets you about a million miles to the gallon or something."

Still studying her laptop screen and typing, she says, "Parker, it's a *Prius*. It uses *electricity*. Not like that dinosaur gas guzzler you have parked out there. What is that thing, anyway? Did you buy it from Fred Flintstone?"

"Aw, no! You're ripping on my truck. That's a Chevy. You should see the thing tear around these back roads. If you want to, we could take a drive later."

She glances up at me over the top edge of her laptop, and concern flashes in her hazel eyes.

God, her eyes are pretty. I could get lost in them.

Her gaze holds mine for two seconds, then she looks back to her work.

Just like old times. Gemma, expert multi-tasker.

As she taps keys she says,"I'm not going to cruise back-roads with you. Unless you answer some questions while we drive."

"Back to this, huh?" I don't want to talk about the dating questionnaire again. She brought it up plenty of times last night, and I already told her I'm not into getting set up. "You're like a dog with a bone."

"You better mean a pretty, intelligent dog with a bone."

"Of course. A drop dead gorgeous, smarter-than-I'll-ever-be dog with a bone."

That makes her smile again. "Okay, that's more like it."

Why do I feel so lucky when she smiles like that? I want her to keep smiling. It's a simple desire, with a complicated foundation.

I'm not going to dwell on my reasons for wanting that smile to stay on her lips.

Maybe it has to do with our history, and the fact that I never stopped loving Gemma—not really.

Or, maybe it's just the fact that it's a beautiful fall day, and she's a friend from my past, and we're spending some time together and I want it to be fun for us.

Yeah, right.

It's more than that.

I know it, and she knows it, too. I can tell by the way we keep catching each others' eye, like we used to do when we were young. Back then we traded so many secret looks, when no one was looking. I grin back at her. "You'd like the back roads around here, Gem. There are some cool lookouts, up on the mountain. We could go for a hike or something. Or, do you mountain bike? I have an extra. I know this awesome lookout, that's really quiet. No one would be up there but us."

I can't help it that my voice has dipped low, like it used

to when we were a pair and I was saying something for only her to hear.

My gaze snags on hers. I feel heat simmering in my body, when I think of spending time with her alone, in a cozy wooded spot. I see a spark in her eye, too. Maybe she's having the same memories I am.

Memories of being young.

Memories of how it felt, when we snuck away from everyone and got to be alone.

Her brow scrunches, like she's having some sort of argument with herself.

"Don't overthink it," I tell her, even though I'm probably overthinking it, myself. "Just a ride."

"I'm not overthinking it."

I laugh. "Yeah, you are."

"You and Carly both act like you know me better than I know myself."

"Maybe we do." I polish off the last of the delicious oatmeal.

She types busily for a minute. When she finally looks up at me it's with pursed lips, a lifted chin, and a determined spark in her green eyes. "I'm serious about being here to work, Parker. And since you're being completely and totally uncooperative about this, I've taken matters into my own hands. I've been watching your interviews for hours. There's something I don't get."

"Fine. Hit me."

"Okay…" she glances down at a notepad at her side. "On your Podcast with Eddie Stuart, you said that you— and I quote— '*don't really care about winning*.' Then on your ESPN interview a couple months after that, you said you don't even know where your Olympic medals are. Now, come on. That can't be true."

"I don't lie, Gem."

"Everyone lies, whether they know it or not. You were making that stuff up, right?"

"Nope. I really never cared about winning. I only cared about *playing*. Everything's more fun that way. After I won those medals they were shipped somewhere. Probably the Wayland address, because I didn't have a house then. Mom and Dad probably put them in the basement or something." I shrug, carry my bowl to the sink, and rinse it out.

When I turn back to her, she's scrutinizing me through narrowed eyes. "But, that doesn't make sense. You have to be competitive. You excelled at a competitive sport."

"Tennis is competitive if you make it competitive. Just like anything. Chess, baking, skiing… whatever. Some guys wanted to win, and that's all they cared about. But those first few years I played in the big tournaments, I figured out that when I got narrowly focused on the outcome, I got too wrapped up in my head. Better to get out of my own way and just have fun and play my hardest."

"Hm." She thinks this over, then types something up on her computer.

I spot a stack of cat food cans on the counter near the fridge and grab one off the top. The lid makes a scraping sound as I peel it back, and that gets Gemma's attention.

"What are you doing?" she asks.

"Gonna put this in a dish, and then try to catch myself a cat. Your friend is probably hungry by now. Most animals rely on scent cues and this stuff stinks."

She narrows her eyes at me again. "How do you know so much about animals? I thought you didn't have pets."

A sucking sound comes from the can as I turn it upside down over a bowl. The wet food inside drops down onto ceramic. "You got yourself some trust issues, along with that fancy therapist career of yours?" I ask her. "I really don't have pets. I didn't lie about that."

"But you *are* keeping something from me. Something about your house. Or, trailer, or whatever it is. You haven't been... um... feeding, like, rats or anything, have you? Because that's the kind of dumb thing that would get you a big rodent problem."

"Chill out. I don't have a rodent problem," I assure her with a laugh, as I carry the bowl across the room. "I'm going to put this in the garage and freshen up that bowl of water we left out, too. You coming or what?"

She makes a big show of looking down at her wrist watch. "Thirteen hours, thirty-six minutes."

I arch a brow at her as I grab my baseball hat and fit it over my messy hair. "What's that—the amount of time you're going to spend bugging me about this dating thing?"

She laughs as she hops off her stool and joins me by the side counter. "No, that's exactly how long it took you to tell me to chill out."

"You're lucky. I thought it the minute I saw you."

"Oh yeah? Funny. Because when I saw you, I thought: he hasn't changed at all."

"Is that a good thing, or a bad thing?" I reach for the coffee pot and without asking, top off the mug in her hands. I return the pot to the burner and switch the thing off.

She looks down at the cup, smiles, and glances back up at me through her lashes. "I think it's a double-edged sword, if I'm being honest."

"I'm all about honesty."

"So you say." She brushes past me, and I catch a whiff of something sweet. Good lord, I think it's marshmallow.

Chapter 8

Gemma

What a day.

The sun is about to sink down behind the mountains. I've been sitting here in the log cabin's rustic-chic kitchen, with the polished marble countertops, the bird-motif wall clock, and cheesy moose-print wallpaper almost the entire time the sun traversed the sky. Besides that brief foray to the garage with Parker and a walk around the loop to look for Queenie, I didn't leave this barstool.

My work is paying off, at least.

I've endured the torturous task of watching Parker on Youtube videos and ESPN clips and reading about him in blog articles and newspaper articles. Thanks to all that, I filled out the entire section of the Right Match questionnaire that has to do with the nitty-gritty of how his mind works.

It's not perfect. But maybe, if I'm lucky, it'll be good enough to find him a decent or even above-average match.

I've done my best to get into his head and answer the questions the way I believe he'd answer them.

Now, however, I've reached a section of the digital form that puzzles me.

This part has to do with his resume, so to speak. Education, work experience, and all that. The first question is about his employment history.

I have a general idea. His first real job was playing pro tennis.

He did that for eight years, from the time he was twenty, to twenty-eight. Then, when his wrist acted up, he retired and moved here to Pines Peak.

I'm pretty sure he started teaching at the tennis center around then. Apparently, that's over now.

Why?

That's a mystery I'm going to have to solve, if I want to complete this section of the form—which I do. Badly.

But it's dangerous being around him.

This morning when he asked me if I wanted to go for a bike ride with him, I almost said yes.

As if being out in the woods with him last night wasn't bad enough.

I must have a masochistic streak or something. I want to cause myself as much pain and suffering as humanly possible.

Parker is a human wrecking ball. He attracts women, then breaks their hearts. I had it happen to me. And yet, when I'm around him, my mind wants to throw down a veil of forgetfulness. *Heartbreak? What heartbreak?*

"Sure, Parker, I'd love to toodle around the back roads with you, taking in the scenic glory of Vermont in fall while intermittently gazing into your gorgeous brown eyes or eating up the eye-candy that is your hunky body."

Ugh. Someone, slap some sense into me. If Carly was here, she'd do it.

I'm as bad as Hannah probably was.

Or, maybe I'm even worse.

I think I actually batted my eyelashes at him this morning. And I *know* I whipped my favorite lip gloss out of my purse a few minutes after he entered the kitchen, while his back was turned and he was helping himself to oatmeal.

I smeared that shiny goop all over my kisser and then ran my hands through my hair. These are old, old habits. There's a saying about a condition like mine: *Old habits die hard.*

Well, I wish they'd die already, even if it's a difficult end.

Because the last thing I need to do around Parker is primp my hair or coat my lips with gloss.

Once I actually fix Parker up with a match, I'll rein my eighteen-year old self in. She's running rampant now, but she'll behave if I can just set Parker up on at least one date.

Maybe two dates.

Hopefully, three. Historically, three's been the magic number for my clients. With three potential matches to choose from, clients have an excellent shot at finding Mr. or Ms. Right.

And that's what this is all about: Finding Parker his Ms. Right.

I lean forward and decisively close my laptop. *Time to get a move on.* I'm not going to uncover the reason Parker was fired by sitting on my butt in this kitchen. I have to go do some field work.

For a minute, I consider heading to the tennis center.

But I'm afraid of what I might discover there.

Things must have been really bad, if he was fired. Maybe I better start with something easier.

Parker headed out of the house a little while after we visited the garage together, with his bike hanging over the bed of his pickup, the front wheel resting on a black mat that he draped over the tailgate. He was probably going for that mountain bike ride he mentioned while scarfing down oatmeal. And, who knows what he got up to after that.

Since Carly mentioned that he picked up work at the Tipsy Tavern, I'll head there first. Either Parker will be there working, or I'll try to ferret out info from other staff members or locals. Either way, it seems like a good place to start.

I pile into my Prius and then wind my way down the steep, curvy road, heading for downtown.

Once I reach the heart of town, I pull up GPS on my phone and get my bearings. The Tipsy Tavern isn't far away, and soon I'm pulling into the crowded lot. Though I scan the vehicles, I don't see Parker's massive, black, rusted truck.

It's 6:30 by the time I walk in, and as far as I can tell Happy Hour was a success. The place is buzzing with rosy-cheeked, smiling people, talking over the loud music and occasionally bursting out into laughter.

The big tables scattered around one side of the room—across from an empty stage and dance floor—are chunky and thick, made out of split, polished logs. The walls are paneled in honey-gold wood, and there are photos up all over the place. Even though Christmas is a long way off, colorful strings of vintage bulbs dot the ceiling like stars, creating a holiday vibe.

An elk head mounted behind the bar has more colorful lights draped over his antlers. The animal's fur is tan, gray, and white. His eyes are black plastic, yet so real looking, I feel as though the beast is eying me as I settle onto one of the only vacant stools along the bar that lines one side wall.

Yep, that elk alone would earn the place the title of 'gross' in Carly's book. She's always been freaked out by taxidermy.

And maybe I am a little, too. I shudder as I glance up at the thing again then avert my gaze.

I peer down the bar and spot plenty of pints of beer, but little to no food except for baskets of something gray and lumpy looking. When I grab a menu I see why. The only option for food is something called Dirty Fries in small, medium, or large.

There's a slim, tattooed woman in her twenties behind the bar slinging drinks. She smiles at me but is too hung up with pouring beer from a tap to get to me just yet.

It's okay. I can wait to order my glass of soda water. I will not be dining on anything that starts with the word 'dirty', thank you very much.

The elderly man beside me gets up with a groan, says something about how he'd better "get home to the ball and chain" and then pats me on the shoulder like he knows me.

A few minutes later, his vacated stool, which is prime real estate, given how crowded it is in here, gets swooped up by a stout, gray-haired woman in overalls and giant, rubber boots. She turns, looks me over, then barks out. "You're not from here, are ya, hon?"

"No Ma'am."

"From the city?"

"Boston." I unzip my white North Face fleece and hang it on the back of the high stool. Then I hook my purse over it. "How did you know?"

"For starters, never seen you before. Then there's the way you eyed Big Ed, like he might come right down and bite ya."

Hm. I hoped for a chatty local to pump for info about

Parker, but I may be conversing with one leaning more toward insane, than chatty.

Fearing she's actually psychotic, I make a show of studying the menu. As if I'm actually going to treat myself to a 'dirty' dish, and now my dilemma is whether to stick to the small, or go big.

She bursts out laughing.

Batty. She's definitely batty.

After a long swig of her drink she says, "Here's a little local lore for ya. Ready?"

I don't want to insult her. "Sure," I mumble.

She points up to the elk head. "Big Ed, there? He met his end during a horrific snowstorm. Biggest blizzard we had up in these parts in the past century. Beautiful elk, he was. We all knew him, and it was a sad day when he passed on. I'm the town vet, you know. I actually tried to revive him. No luck. Poor fella had a ruptured spleen, and short of getting him a care flight to a big hospital somewhere for a transplant, there was nothing I could do."

"I'm sorry to hear that."

"Life and death… Nature taking its course. We all had to move on, but it's a good thing Susan Sullivan stuffed him so nicely because—here's the important thing, so listen close—he's still with us."

"Big Ed?"

"Sure. His spirit is right here, in this bar. Once in a while, you can hear him. Now, not really *hear* him, like a voice booming down from the wall there. That'd be nuts. But you'll get a *message*, is what I mean." She taps the side of her head. "So strong it's like he's speaking to your soul. Happens to me all the time, when I'm here. It's why I come in the first place, though the beer's not bad, either."

"Interesting…"

She chuckles. "You don't believe me, I can tell. But

you hang around this place long enough, you'll get a message. Mark my words. And when you do, you've got to do what Ed says. For your own good. If not—now, here's where the legend gets spooky—you'll be cursed. And if that happens, you're done. Kaput. Try driving? You might go off the road. Try shoveling your driveway? You can bet you'll slip and fall on a patch of ice you didn't even know was there. All sorts of terrible things can happen."

At that moment, the server walks over to us and slaps her hand down on the wooden bar. "What can I getch'ya?"

I'm so grateful for the interruption, I almost jump up to hug her. I ask for a seltzer, and a minute later she places it down before me, complete with ice and a straw. When I reach for my card she shakes her head. "Nah, on the house. When you're ready for a real drink or some food, you just holler."

She wanders off to deal with other customers and their "real drink" orders. I busy myself with sucking down some of the bubbly water.

The woman on the barstool next to me eyes my drink. "They got good beers on tap, you know."

"I can't wait to try one. But not tonight. I'm actually here for a work thing."

For the second time since sitting down, my companion dissolves in hearty laughter. This time she actually slaps her knee. "Ha! Good one. Work, on a Saturday night… here? Ain't no meetings going on, unless you count our precious dollars meeting that register over there. And if you pull a computer out of that big old purse of yours and start working remote, or whatever you kids do these days, I'll have seen it all." She shakes her head and smiles. "Work... heh heh."

Down the bar, the server turns to ring up a customer's

tab. She has a tattoo of a wolf on her left tricep and some sort of Celtic design on the right.

Maybe she'd be a good match for Parker. I could ask her to fill out a Right Match profile…

Then again, she's a little young. And just because she has ink like Parker doesn't mean she'd be compatible with him. Matchmaking isn't as simple as finding similar style traits. There's so much more to it than that.

Even though my process isn't perfect, given that there's a limited pool to work with, it's a lot better than trying to find a date with a blindfold on—which is like what most people do when they try to pick out partners on their own, without help from reliable data.

The woman beside me chats a bit about how "kids these days ought to have real jobs, not mess around on the internet all day." Then she finishes with, "So, you can't really be here for work. And you're not here to drink, clearly. What's really got you at the Tipsy Tavern, then?"

"My friend works here. He's not here tonight, though, as far as I can tell."

"Give me a name. I know everyone around here."

Great. "Parker Manning."

Her eyes light up.

"Actually," I say, "I've got a question about him, if you're up for it.'"

"Oh, goody. Sure thing, honey."

"Do you know anything about why he was fired from the tennis center?" I sip the cold fizzy seltzer, and wait as she draws in a long sip of her beer.

She sets the glass down and sighs happily. "Goodness, I love it here. Sometimes I get caught up on the latest town hullabaloo, and sometimes I get to dish the skinny out. You know Glenn at all?"

"Nope."

"He's the one that runs the tennis place. It used to be a bowling alley, you know. What's a town like this need a tennis center for? We have a field for baseball at the town park, plus basketball hoops, and that's plenty, you ask me. But then Parker moved to town and Glenn got it in his noggin that we needed a tennis center. So he started the place up and don't you know, got Parker to work there. Glenn charges a pretty penny for lessons with Parker, you can be sure. It's a real racket, pardon the pun."

I give the obligatory laugh.

She's settled into storytelling mode. "Those two didn't get along, is what I heard. Glenn didn't pay Parker enough, compared to what the tennis center was raking in for the lessons with a real, goodness-to-gracious famous player. I think Parker got fed up with it, finally. Just my humble opinion. He's your friend. You might want to ask him."

"I will. So, you think they argued?"

"Not just that. Parker broke into the place one night, real late. It's a good thing he's not in jail, you ask me."

I choke down my sip of soda water and try not to look as surprised as I feel. "Excuse me? He broke in?"

"What, he didn't tell you that?"

That's why I'm talking to you. "Nope."

"Well, shoot. Now I feel like I've spilled the beans behind his back…"

"Don't worry about that."

"Parker's a real good fella. Every one of us makes mistakes."

"So, he broke into the tennis center, and… what happened? What was he doing?"

"Now, don't get ahead of me. Let me try to tell it. It was about two weeks ago. Somewhere's around there. Jasper Mowrey was out walking his dog and saw lights on in the place, even though it was near midnight. I don't know, eleven or so. And everyone knows the place closes at eight pm. So Jasper called Glenn, and Glenn drove over to look into it, and don't you know it, Parker was there. He didn't even have a key. He let himself in through a window."

"What was he doing?"

"Probably skimming off the cash register. A couple hundred dollar bills… who knows? Whatever he needed. That's what some folks are saying. And then it came out that Katie Mowrey—that's Jasper's wife—she's been seein' lights on at that place at all hours for months, and she didn't tell anyone about it. Figured it was no big deal. So we all think Parker's been shimmying in through that window whenever he pleased. The truth is, I don't blame him for stealing cash. What Glenn was charging for one lesson was practically highway robbery. Three hundred dollars for a forty-five minute lesson! Can you believe that? And I'm sure he was only paying Parker thirty bucks a pop."

"So, Glenn fired him."

"Right on the spot, is what I heard. Can't have an employee squirming through windows and stealing from you, after all. Even if you are robbing folks blind yourself, day in and day out." She shakes her head ruefully, drains the rest of her beer, then flags down the server.

Once she has a second full pint glass in front of her, I try for more information. She seems to be a wellspring of it, after all. "Any idea what's up with his trailer, out on the edge of town?"

"No, what'd you hear? Something wrong with the place?"

"I heard he has a noise issue."

"Now, that don't make a lick of sense. There's nothing out by him except the mountain, foxes, squirrels, and a few birds. I suppose birds can cause a racket… and there I go with the racket talk again." She giggles into her pint glass.

The Tipsy Tavern is living up to its name, apparently. Her cheeks have a ruddy pink glow as she chugs down a healthy swallow.

"Any idea if he's going to be working here tonight?" I ask.

"Oh, he comes and goes whenever he pleases." She flaps a hand toward the door. "Hard to keep track of him. But since he's not here right now, I doubt he'll be coming in at all. Delilah's got us covered."

"Any guess on where he is?"

"Hm. Maybe he's off somewhere with that Veronica. I've seen them together an awful lot. Either she's coming in here, or his truck's parked in front of her place. I saw that three times last month, all late at night." She wiggles three fingers and then pokes her eyebrows up and down to emphasize the point.

She's got this 'dishing the skinny' thing down.

So… Parker's seeing this woman, Veronica, by the sounds of it. I shouldn't be surprised. Carly did say he's always dating someone new whenever she talks to him.

Then why did he invite me to go on a mountain bike ride with him? a little voice in my head asks.

Maybe it was Ed.

Then again. I don't think Ed would sound like a woman confused by Parker's mixed signals.

Sure, a mountain bike ride isn't exactly a romantic invitation. But it's an invitation to spend time together—just us. And given the past I have with Parker, that feels like a big deal to me. I'm sure I'm reading into the invitation too much, but I can't help myself.

The thing is, ever since Parker walked into the

Manning's log cabin and caught me in my nightgown, I've felt confused.

And every time he's looked at me for the past twenty-four hours, I've felt just like I used to when we were younger.

Special.

Really, really, amazingly special.

Like a perfectly formed snowflake; a little miracle that swirled down from the sky.

And I don't only feel special and unique.

I feel *wanted*. Desired.

It's a dangerously familiar feeling. Back when I was in high school I used to feel the same way.

We secretly wanted each other for so long. I remember how at night sometimes, after a day at the Mannings I'd look at the glow-in-the-dark stars glued to my bedroom ceiling and savor the long, meaning-laced looks me and Parker shared.

And then when he finally kissed me on that rec room couch, it was so validating. Like I really was the unique snowflake that he couldn't live without. He wanted *me*, and only me.

We let ourselves tumble headfirst into territory we had no business being in. We were just kids, basically. But I remember one night, sitting out by his pool, when he had his arms wrapped around me and he whispered in my ear, *'Gem, I think I love you.'*

And I was so stupid.

I turned and whispered it right back.

Then we kissed, and I thought I'd get to spend countless more nights just like that one. Whispering 'I love you' to Parker Manning while fitted perfectly in his strong arms. Laughing and looking at moonlight reflected on the pool's surface. Swimming through cool, silky dark water straight into his waiting arms, while everyone else in the neighborhood was fast asleep. It all felt so magical, and I assumed the magic would last.

And now it's like we're right back to it—trading secret signals that carry meaning.

But what if I'm the only one of us putting out and receiving signals?

What if it's all in my head?

What if he looks at me like I'm some kind of wonderful, unique, beautiful specimen because he's weird, wild *Parker*, and he's always happy and always amazed at life?

For all I know he gazes at parking meters and footballs in the exact same way. He always seems to be content with whatever life dishes up, so it's possible.

Beside me, Overalls chatters on about Veronica. How she's a single mom, working her "tush off" at a local inn, cleaning rooms.

I'm barely listening, though, because that little voice in my head is at it again. *He basically asked you out on a date this morning. Driving in his truck? Hiking…? Mountain biking… ?*

He even mentioned a private little lookout.

That's just like something he'd come up with when we were young. Parker was always finding secret places where we could spend a few hours, just us.

Also, his voice got so low and husky when he talked about that lookout. Like he remembering times in the past, how we used to kiss for hours…

Shoot. Parker told me not to overthink his invitation.

But I *did* overthink it.

I thought about being out on a mountain bike, with Parker helping me adjust the seat and then reaching around me to give me pointers on how to shift gears. I thought about how his arm would brush against mine when he gave the demonstration, and I wouldn't mind one bit.

I thought about how we'd get off the bikes and sit on some rocky overlook, and share an apple and laugh about something that happened long ago in the past.

I even pictured him putting his arm around me, or leaning in to kiss me…

But he *didn't* ask me on a date.

It was a freaking bike ride.

I scowl down at my seltzer and only half-heartedly listen to Overalls, next to me, who is still happily chatting about Veronica.

"... and sure, she's a good deal older. Forty-five, maybe? Forty-six? That has some people talking, believe you me. Good for her, I say, catching the eye of a young man like Parker. A young, *handsome* man like Parker."

She winks at me and grins. "I may be a grandmother of three, but I can still spot a looker when I see one! That Parker has the cutest caboose on him, that I just want to reach out and pinch!"

I can't even muster a polite laugh. My chest feels like lead.

It's happening. Again.

I'm jealous, just like I used to get when I'd see photos of Parker with his arms around some bronzed, bikini-clad Volleyball Goddess on a white-sand beach.

But I'm *smarter* than this. I'm *better* than this.

I don't need to sit here on this worn leather bar stool feeling sorry for myself about the fact that Parker Manning's currently out with some hot-ticket single mom from Pines Peak.

In fact, I could use this to my advantage. If Parker's actually into this Veronica woman, I could invite her to participate in the Right Match process, too. I could help speed along their romance.

I haven't even finished the glass of seltzer, but I can't sit here any more. I feel antsy, and eager to get a move on.

I'm also hungry, and not for Dirty Fries, whatever they are.

So I turn and snatch up my purse, and then wriggle into my fleece.

Overalls, beside me, uses her detective skills to take a stab at the meaning behind my actions. "Leavin' already?"

"Yeah, I better get back to where I'm staying."

She squeezes her eyes closed and then presses both index fingers to her temples. When her eyes pop open, she looks right at me. "Ed wants you to know something before you go. He says that if you've got a good heart in ya, you'll buy me a beer. Hm… lemme see. He says you should buy me a Long Trail Limbo IPA. Now, ain't that a funny message. What do you think?"

"Maybe another time," I tell her, before turning on my heel and heading for the door.

Behind me, she calls out her goodbye. "And be careful out there, ya hear? 'Cause, I'm sorry to say it, but now ya might just be cursed!"

I don't have to worry about getting cursed.

This trip to Vermont is a big enough mess as it is.

Chapter 9

Gemma

Back at the Mannings, I have to carefully squeeze my Prius into the patch of vacant driveway next to Parker's truck. Heaven knows I don't want to block the guy in, since he has such a vibrant social life these days. He's home now, but he might well be jetting off soon so he can spend the night with his current flavor of the month.

The garage bay doors are part way open, and music's blaring inside.

I duck under and then straighten up in time to see Parker, lying on his back on a weight training bench. As I watch he presses up an ungodly amount of weight on a barbell. He grunts as he straightens his bulging arms, and then, with control, lowers the weighted bar back to the rack above his head.

"Hey," I say, once he's no longer in danger of crushing his larynx. "What are you doing back here already? I heard you might be blowing off work, out on a hot date with Veronica."

He chuckles.

I'm tired of getting laughed at when I haven't said anything funny. Plus, I'm surviving on way too little sleep, and flustered, too. It's not easy to see an ex looking this good. "You know, since I'm in town to set you up on a couple dates, it'd be helpful if you mentioned your girlfriend."

Oops. That came out a little blunt. Parker didn't ask me to come here and meddle in his love life. But it's too late to take it back.

"Veronica? My girlfriend? Who told you that?"

"I had a talk with the town vet."

He heaves the barbell off the rack, presses it up toward the ceiling, then sets it down. Just watching him makes my arm muscles feel sore.

As I near his workout bench, I take in the fact that he's once again shirtless. He's also sweating.

The best thing to do, I think, when you're confronted with a situation that has to do with a sweaty, attractive man you used to be in love with, is to look away.

So, that's what I do.

I study the hand tools hanging from a corkboard on my right. I don't know what half of them are, and I don't really care to find out. All I need is something to look at — anything— besides the way that balanced-scale tattoo on Parker's shoulder and pec ripples as six different muscles pop out under it when he lifts the weight.

Not to mention the fact that his abs are as hard as always, with the same lower v-cut that disappears under the band of his sweatpants. These v-shaped muscles always used to make me swoon and apparently, they still do. My knees feel weak, I'm lightheaded, and my whole body feels limp and a few degrees too hot, given the actual brisk temperature of this unheated garage.

My eyes wander back over that way when I hear him huff out another burst of air—because I better make sure he's alive, at least, not getting strangled for stupidly trying to lift too much weight without a spotter in sight.

Bad idea! Bad idea!

He's still got the barbell up, and now his shoulders are bulging and his arm muscles are twitching, and I can see the tattoo of a mountain that winds around his obliques.

A flash of heat sparks through me and I stuff it way, way down and whip my head back toward the cork board.

Safer—much safer—to look at this silver hand tool here and wonder if it's a wrench or a ratchet.

The poppy electronic dance music he's playing fills the garage. At least I can be grateful for that. Besides getting in my catty comment about his love life, I have no reason to stay out here. It's not like we're going to have a conversation. I should head inside.

I hear the barbell clank as it settles back into the rack. Then, before I manage to take a step toward the door, Parker's next to me, scrubbing a towel over his face. He's pulled a t-shirt on, thank goodness.

He drapes the towel around his neck and gives me a smile. "The town vet, eh?"

Then he reaches for me.

Is this it?

Is he about to kiss me, because he simply can't resist? Is he going to sweep me up into his arms and kiss me, right here in this sweaty, loud garage?

Nope. He's reaching for the stereo that's sitting on the tool shelf. He twists the volume down and then grabs for his water bottle, also on the shelf.

He takes a swig of water and then chuckles again.

"Okay… what?" I ask. "If there's a joke here, I'm not getting it."

"That was Annie. She's not the town vet. Never was, never will be."

"Oh."

"She's a retired high school English teacher. Leads the local drama club these days. Loves to put on an act, especially for tourists. Let me guess… She fed you a story about how poor Big Ed died of a brain clot during a terrible rainstorm, and now he haunts the bar. And then she tried to get you to buy her a Long Trail Ale."

"Er… close. Ruptured Spleen. Blizzard. And she wanted the Limbo IPA."

He smiles, shakes his head, and helps himself to more water.

I TAKE a step toward the door that leads into the house. "I'm heading in. See you later." "Before you go, I have to show you something." He turns and grabs a sweatshirt. He pulls it over his head as he walks for the bay door and ducks under it. "Come on, Gem. You're gonna like this."

I feel hopeful as I duck under the garage door after Parker, and then follow him across the driveway. Did he spot Queenie outside or something?

He squats down and aims his phone, flashlight app on, at a patch of dirt between two shrubs. "Check it out."

I crouch down next to him. There, on the dirt, are four dainty paw prints. For the first time in hours, I smile. "Queenie!"

"She's here somewhere, I bet. I checked all around the driveway when I got home today and there were no prints. Then, about a half hour ago, I noticed these."

"Oh my god… so, she's close!" I bounce up to my feet and yank my own cell phone from my purse. I pull up a light and aim at the line of shrubbery that extends along the pavement.

"Queenie, baby?" I call out, gently and softly. The last thing I want to do is spook her.

"Maybe if we put her food out here…" Parker says. "I mean, she's around. That's really good. All we have to do is—"

"There she is!" I grip Parker's arm and point excitedly up toward the roof over the garage. "Oh my goodness, she's here!"

My ecstasy at seeing my furbaby takes over and I barely stiffen as Parker loops his arm around my shoulder and rubs my arm. "See? Told you she'd come back."

He's so warm, and his tall, hard body feels comforting next to mine. I find myself leaning into him. "You did! And there she is… But how are we going to get her down?"

"I got this, Gem." He gives my arm one last warming rub. "Keep an eye on her. I'll be right back."

As I stand in the empty driveway, listening to the mechanical whir of the garage bay door go up, it occurs to me: we just hugged.

I got happy, and I hugged Parker, and he hugged me back. And when I was tucked up against his side I breathed in his scent. He smelled exactly like he always did after working out. I hate myself for this, but I actually love the smell of his sweat.

My phone rings.

I keep an eye on Queenie, who is now parading along the rain gutter as if walking on log cabin roofs is a specialty of hers, and answer the incoming call. "Carly? Oh, thank god."

"What's wrong?"

"Er…" I bite my lip and watch Parker emerge from the

garage, a ladder hooked over one shoulder. *Your brother's pheromones. That's what's wrong.*

Plus, he still has abs of steel, and he says things to make me smile, and he's rescuing my cat as we speak.

"Everything," I mutter into the phone. Then I hold the device away so I can talk to Parker. "Should I go up the ladder, you think? And try to get her? She's really skittish."

"I got this. Trust me," he says.

On the phone, I hear Carly pipe up. "Was that Parker? What are you guys doing?"

"Queenie got away, and Parker's..." I fall silent as I watch Parker climb rung after rung. Annie was right. His caboose is still as cute as ever. He reaches the eves and hops up onto the slanted green-metal of the roof.

"Gem?" Carly asks. "You there?"

"Sorry.... Queenie got away and Parker's going to try to get her back."

"Got away where? At the ski house?"

"Yeah, last night." I hold my breath as Queenie, at the peak of the garage roof now, sits down on her bum and eyes Parker. He lowers himself down onto his haunches and mirrors her stillness.

Is this going to work?

"So, you've got Parker there with you, then?" Carly asks. "That is a bad, *bad* idea. You two there together, I mean. If he flirts with you, tell him to quit it, okay? Stick cotton balls in your ears and do not—I repeat—do *not* let him fool you. He's a pig. Seriously."

My pulse quickens as Queenie stands, her face tilted Parker's way. He has his back to me, and I can't believe how still he's sitting. If I didn't know better, I'd think there was a stone gargoyle sculpture up on the cabin's roof, not a warm-blooded, very-much-alive man.

Queenie takes a tentative step toward him.

Then another.

On the phone, Carly chatters on about how I've always been too "influenced" by her brother's charms.

But now I'm barely listening. My eyes widen as Queenie paces back and forth across the metal roof, each time drawing nearer to waiting Parker. I give a happy gasp when she then puts both paws up on his knee.

He reaches out and scoops her gently into his arms.

"What's happening?" Carly asks.

"He got her! He got Queenie!"

"Do I need to, like, drive up there and stage an intervention or something? I'm starting to worry about you."

"You don't have to worry." *I'm* not worried right now, for once. Parker has my cat safely in his arms and I feel a warm glow of happiness swirling in my chest. "We're good."

"There shouldn't be a 'we', Gemma. There's you, my best friend, and there's my irresponsible, off-the-rails, trouble-making brother. He's a walking disaster. Don't let yourself get caught up in his mess of a life, okay?"

I murmur my agreement and then hurriedly get off the line in time to accept the warm bundle of fur that Parker carefully hands over to me.

Queenie starts up with her loud purring the minute I hold her to my chest. I can feel the vibration travel through my body, as therapeutic as any medicine I've ever taken. "How did you do that? I swear, she's terrified of most people."

"Patience," he says. "I let her make the first move. Always."

"Now I feel like you're talking about how you get with women, too."

"You know it."

"Parker's secrets of seduction."

"Works every time. The girls aren't usually all about the fresh-water Salmon cat treats, though," he says with an easy laugh, as he tugs a bag out of his sweatshirt pocket. He takes a treat out and offers it to Queenie. Of course, my cat eats it right out of his palm. "Though, hey, maybe I should give it a try one day."

I grin. I can't help it. I'm holding Queenie nice and safe in my arms, and joking around with Parker feels right. Also—he has cat treats in his pocket, all because of my cat. Maybe he bought them today. How thoughtful is that?

Carly's warning feels a million miles away as Parker reaches out to pet Queenie's head. Her purrs get about ten-times louder with his touch.

"Maybe some dinner, to celebrate?" he says. "I picked up stuff for a Chinese stir fry. Broccoli, red peppers, carrots… Figure we could eat some veggies to make up for the pizza, last night."

"Mm. I love Asian food."

"I know." He runs his fingers gently under Queenie's chin.

Okay… he picked up cat treats *and* ingredients for my favorite cuisine? He's racking up some major points right now.

My quandary about mixed signals is at an all-time high right now, with Parker standing close, petting my kitty while she rests in my arms, and promising to fix us one of my favorite meals.

"You are being way too nice," I tell him.

"Nah. That's not possible. I'm happy you're here and I want you to have fun—even if you are intent on badgering me ruthlessly for the entire visit."

Right. I'm supposed to be badgering him about his dating life, not trying to insert myself into it.

I have a life in Cambridge, and a man that fits perfectly

into that life. Mortimer is successful, sophisticated, smart, and—most importantly of all—he's my 93% match.

Parker is crashing at his parent's second home, working haphazardly at a bar whenever he feels like it, and serial dating women in Pines Peak. He narrowly avoided getting sent to jail a couple weeks ago, if I can believe Annie's gossip.

Which, now that I think about it, perhaps I shouldn't.

"Hey, speaking of badgering. I do have a couple more questions for you."

"Oh, I know you do. You're not gonna quit. You're gonna have to do your poking and prodding inside, though, because I gotta start cooking."

He heads for the door, and I follow with Queenie in my arms. Though it's tough, I do my best not to take even one peek at Parker's cute caboose… but I'll admit that my best is not perfect.

Maybe Carly is right to worry about me.

Being here with him is trouble, and I'm old enough and wise enough to know better. Right about now, I should be putting my guard up.

Way, way up.

We're talking, Great Wall of China style.

When Parker holds the door for me, I grit my teeth and walk through.

Chapter 10

Parker

I don't have anything to hide.

Gemma can ask me all the questions she wants.

I'm going to tell her as much of the truth as I can, without veering into gossip territory. Other people's business isn't mine to share, so I have to keep certain things quiet.

I will do my best to give her straight answers.

Whether she believes me or not is up to her.

All I really care about is that it feels so good and right to be here in the kitchen with her, with the smells of garlic and ginger all around us, and a candle flickering on the counter top. Cooking her favorite food. Listening to her type. Hearing her laugh now and then, when I make a dumb joke.

It feels good—even though I know it won't last.

I slide a pile of ginger off the knife's edge and glance over my shoulder toward the counter, where she's perched primly with her white MacBook out in front of her.

Her fingers are poised over the keys. "So, that means you started at the tennis center four years and… let's see…" She pauses to do some mental calculations, "Eight months ago. For simplicity's sake, I'm just going to round eight months to a year and call that five years, total. Sound good to you?"

"You're the math wiz. Whatever you want."

The keyboard clicks as she types. "I know you're not into this, but thank you for at least humoring me."

"I know you. You won't give up." I drizzle a second round of oil over the chopped veggies, garlic, and ginger that I've piled into the wok and add a sprinkle of soy sauce.

"Not until I at least get you out on a couple dates," she says. "Is—um… is Veronica going to be upset if you go out with other people?"

"Nope. Definitely not."

"Wow. Keeping it casual," she mutters unhappily. "Good for you guys."

I grin down at the veggies. It's sort of fun, getting a rise out of her. "That's how we do it up here in the sticks," I tease.

"Gross. I don't need to know your weird country dating rules, Parker."

"You're the one asking about my love life."

"Yes, specific questions. Like—okay, here we go. I need a real answer for this. Why, exactly, did you get fired from the tennis center? Annie sort of filled me in about your break-in. How Glenn caught you. But I'd like to hear it from you."

"I entered the building after hours, through a window. Guess I wasn't supposed to be there. Funny how uppity business owners get about that kind of thing."

"I don't know if there's anything *funny* about getting

fired for breaking into a place and almost getting sent to jail. Okay, so what were you doing there?"

"I can't say."

"Come on. Stealing cash?"

"Gem, I really can't say."

"*Ugh*. I knew you'd be difficult about this whole thing but I didn't know you'd be *this* difficult. Moving on. Your boss caught you there, and you and he argued? Is that right?"

"He yelled. Said I was a crappy employee. He nearly had a hernia, I think." I grin, remembering how Glenn's face turned tomato-red that night he fired me. "I think he was bluffing, when he yelled that I was fired. I'm the reason he started that place in the beginning, and most clients come in to work with me. He figured I'd bow down and apologize. No way. I've been dealing with that guy for too long as it is. So, when he said I was fired, I said "thanks" and walked out of there. Didn't look back."

I add slivers of raw red pepper to the wok and stir them in. "Thankfully, he survived and I survived, and now we're both coexisting. Peacefully, actually, now that he no longer employs me. At least, it's peaceful on my end because I haven't seen him since. I don't know how it'll be when I actually run into him." I shrug. " I guess I'll cross that bridge when we get to it."

"All I can say is you're lucky he didn't call the cops," Gemma says. "That'd really mess up your eligibility, in the eyes of a potential mate. Okay, how am I supposed to word this whole thing succinctly?"

"It's your paperwork. You're going to have to figure that out."

There's a long pause and then I hear her read the answer aloud as she types. " *'My employment was terminated due to a conflict with my supervisor.'* There. It's true, but we're not going to dwell on the part where you broke an actual law. So, what's your job now?"

"I work at the Tipsy Tavern."

"Okay..." She narrates her typing again. " '*I am currently employed at a local eatery, where I work as a server.*' Is that right? Server?"

"Among other things."

"Like?"

"Bouncer. Bar back. Stage hand. Janitor. Whatever needs to be done."

"Great." She types some more. "And... that section's complete. Done. Finally. I actually think I can submit this whole form now. Thank you for at least being sort of truthful with me."

She actually sounds grateful.

Which means I have some leverage.

"Hey... since I gave you some answers, think you could do the same for me? Or are you gonna dance around my question with the fancy footwork you're so good at?"

"What are you talking about?"

"You and Mortimer. Everything good with you guys? 'Cause this morning you said it was fantastic, but I have a feeling that's not the full story."

She hesitates for so long that I have to stop stirring sizzling-hot veggies around the wok and check on her.

She didn't pass out or anything. She's just staring down at the counter top like maybe she's contemplating another face-plant.

"Look, if it's a sore subject, I won't pry. It's probably none of my business. But if you want to talk... I can listen. And you *are* asking me all sorts of stuff about my life."

"No, no. I get it. Fair's fair. Okay, just let me turn in this form so the software can start coding the answers." I hear her start tapping keys again.

She's stalling.

Which means I hit on a big, sensitive nerve.

I better tread carefully.

The last thing I want to do is cause Gemma any pain.

As she types, I check on the jasmine rice on the back burner. It's done, so I lift it off and set it on a waiting ceramic hot pad that I staged nearby. Then I give the veggies one last flip, and turn that heat off, too. I grab two bowls from the cupboard and fill both with scoops of rice and steaming stir fry.

Behind me, Gemma clears her throat.

I turn to her with a dish in each hand. She looks miserable, with a crease on her brow that definitely wasn't present a minute ago. I set one bowl before her, then take a seat at her side with my own. "Hey, if it sucks to talk about it, don't. I shouldn't have asked." I reach for the chopsticks I laid out earlier, and hand her a pair.

"I don't know why it makes me feel like this—to talk about it, I mean."

"Sad?"

She bites her lip and that crease digs deeper. "I guess, sad. Yeah. It's weird, though. I shouldn't feel sad. Every relationship goes through ups and downs, especially before the actual wedding, you know?"

"Nope. Enlighten me."

"'I mean, it's perfectly normal for two people to date, and then maybe take a break and spend some time apart, and then, when the timing makes logical, practical sense, get back together to walk down the aisle. There are certain, you know, life mile-markers that most people—" She flicks her eyes my way, "Okay, maybe not *you*, but *most people*—want to hit in a certain order. Mortimer wants to focus on his career, and I one-hundred percent accept that. Then, one day, we'll get married and start a family when the time is actually right."

Luckily, I'm fluent in Gemma-speak. I manage to sort through the optimistic projections into the future and find the nugget of truth hidden in her statements. "Okay, so you're saying you guys are taking a break? You separated?"

"Yeah. He needed some space. To write a book, probably. His books are brilliant."

A little whisper is stirring in my heart. *She's single.*

"Has it been a while? Since you broke up?" I lift a forkful of broccoli and red pepper. *Please don't say this happened last week.*

If Gemma's on a rebound from a recent breakup, I have to restrain myself.

If she and this Mortimer guy have been apart for at least a few months… it's game on.

She pokes her fork into her bowl. "He actually broke it off eight months ago."

"We can round eight months to a year. You said so yourself, right?"

She lifts the corner of her mouth in a half-smile. "Yeah, I guess I did say that." The smile fades and she bites her lip. Her brows pinch together again. "Wow, that's actually a long time. I haven't talked about this that much. Saying it out loud is sort of strange. Basically, I've been on my own for a year…"

"You had Queenie up in that cupboard, though."

"Yeah…"

"Hey, don't worry. You're still doing great."

"It's just—I kept thinking it was just going to be a temporary thing, but the months kept passing… Can I ask you something?"

"Anything."

"Okay, so… He travels a lot, and after we broke up I

barely saw him around Cambridge or Boston. But one day I was in this shopping square and I was passing a coffee shop and…" A frown flickers across her lips. Then she bites her bottom lip and studies the food left in her bowl.

"And, you saw him?"

"Yeah, and he was with a woman. He had his arm around her for a few seconds when they were in line. He gave her, like, this quick squeeze. Then they sat down across from each other at a table, but they had their heads sort of bowed together so their faces were close. Maybe they were both looking at a sheet of paper or something… Maybe it was a work thing."

"What's your gut say?"

She heaves a heavy sigh. "It says I shouldn't try to interpret something I know nothing about, really. I don't have all the facts, and—"

I wave my chopsticks at her to stop her from lying to herself any more. "Gem, you don't need all the facts. You don't need to use logic, or reasoning, or your brain at all. You don't need to write a term paper on this, just feel it. What do you feel?"

She places both chopsticks over her bowl and then uses her napkin to pat her lips. "I think I'm done eating. That was delicious. Thanks."

"You done talking, too, I take it?"

She nods. Worry clouds her pretty face and she pulls her laptop toward her. "Done talking about my relationship with Mortimer, at least. And if you could keep it to yourself that we're currently taking a break, that'd be great. I haven't exactly gone public about it. I'm supposed to be a relationship expert…. It's embarrassing that me and Mortimer are on the rocks."

"Relax. I won't tell a soul." Now that I know, that's all that matters.

Gemma Lafferty is single.

And she's staying in this cabin with me.

Even though she has her cat back, she hasn't said a thing about packing up and leaving. It'd be dumb to try to find a hotel room in this small town at such late notice. Gemma's lots of things, but definitely not dumb—so I know I have at least one more night with her.

I finish off my stir fry and then collect her bowl and mine. A few minutes later I've loaded them in the dishwasher, along with some other cooking utensils. The rest of the clean-up can wait.

Gemma's not the only one in this kitchen capable of coming up with a plan. I've hatched one of my own: a way to make the most of this night together.

"Grab your coat, plus shoes you can run in," I tell her, as I pull a couple water bottles from the fridge.

"Why?"

"You wanted to know why I broke into the tennis center. I gave a guy my word that I wouldn't be a loud mouth about it, but I don't think he'd object if I *showed* you what was up, and you put the pieces together on your own."

"Parker, what are you talking about?"

"The Gemma I know would be curious right about now."

"Okay, I will admit that I'm curious."

"Then come with me for a drive into town. I'll show you the reason I broke into the tennis center. And you'll figure out what's going on with me and Veronica, too."

"God, Parker, if you're dragging me out as the third wheel on some kind of small-town date, I'm going to kill you."

"I promise. It's not that."

"Good. Because I'm not up for 'gettin' mud on the

tires' or frolicking in the moonlit fields or whatever else you guys do up here for fun. Especially not while you and Veronica make puppy eyes at each other."

"Gemma… Relax."

She stuffs her laptop into its bag and then loops the thing over her shoulder. "Thank you. At least you're not telling me to 'Chill' anymore. Fine, I'll come, but I'm bringing work with me. By the end of tonight, I should have a couple potential matches for you."

I wish she was kidding, but I can tell that she's not.

Chapter 11

Gemma

Even if I tried for hours, I'd never come up with a logical reason for being here.

I'm in Parker's giant, toasty-warm truck, parked in the empty, dark Miller & Sons Groceries lot.

Yes, I'm curious to see what Parker has up his sleeve, but that niggling curiosity shouldn't have been enough to propel me out of the log cabin's front door, into his gas-guzzling truck, and down the long and twisty road into town to the tune of the love songs he cranked on the radio.

Logically, I should be at the log cabin right now. Not waiting in this idling truck on my own, staring at the dark grocery store's front doors and listening to more mesmerizing lyrics about slow dancing, red wine, and tangled-up bed sheets.

Parker disappeared inside a moment ago. Even though the front doors have a 'closed' sign on them, they opened right up and swallowed him whole. Either he's skimming off yet another cash register and I'm out here as an unknowing accomplice to his crime, or he's picking up his forty-five year old, single-mom lady friend for a rowdy night on the town.

Neither of the scenarios my brain conjured up sounds that good to me.

And neither includes a teenaged boy.

And yet, here he is now, walking toward Parker's truck with a big gym bag slung over one shoulder. The kid's tall and wiry, with a mop of black hair.

He has a big, crooked-teeth grin that I get to see close-up, when he loads in the back seat of the truck and sticks his head up between the two front seats. "Ms. Lafferty? I'm Ransom."

"Oh, no, no. I'm not your teacher or anything. Call me Gemma." *Who is this kid?*

Parker climbs into the driver's seat and fires up the truck. The engine rumbles as Parker steers slowly across the lot, then quiets down to a purr as he picks up speed out on a main road. "Ransom here closes up the grocery store on Friday and Saturday nights. Ain't that right, my man?" Parker lifts his eyes to the rear-view mirror.

From the back seat, Ransom agrees. "I clean the display cases out, mop the floors, count the cash. Wish I had my own wheels. Then I wouldn't need to bug Mr. Manning for a ride."

I don't get it.

Is Parker playing Dad, now? Giving this kid a ride home after work?

I want to rest my forehead on the truck's fogged windows, just to feel the patch of cool glass on my skin. It'd be a reminder that there's a whole world out there. A world that doesn't include me helping my childhood crush earn the title of Dad of the Year.

This single mom Veronica really must be a catch, if Parker's putting in all this effort.

We travel a few blocks in silence, and then Parker puts his right-hand blinker on… which doesn't make sense. The only thing over here is the highschool, as far as I can tell.

Parker steers us down a road behind the brick building. In the darkness, I can make out a couple wide swaths of grass: a soccer field and baseball field, I think. At least, there's an abundance of trimmed lawn, plus a few ragged, rusty looking chain-link fences and I think I see a single stand of bleachers, out there in the darkness.

Parker turns to me. "You'll get it soon. Don't worry."

"Okay… 'cause I'm not, yet."

He turns to Ransom. "You cool with it, if Gemma hangs out with us for our session? She's from out of town and she won't be a loud mouth about anything."

"It's cool," Ransom says, as he eagerly rummages in his duffel bag. He hauls out a pair of white sneakers and a racket, then pushes open his door and jumps down to the pavement.

Parker turns to me. "Think you could give me a hand and carry a light?"

"What for? What are we doing here?"

Without answering, Parker hops out of the truck, too.

What is going on? I have to push the heavy truck door hard to get the massive thing to close. At the back of the truck, I watch Parker, up in the truck's bed, wrestle with a stack of long, metal objects that are piled up in a stack. He frees one and hands it down to me. "Two should cut it, I think."

He untangles another and then jumps down off the bed with it in his right hand. He uses his left hand to grab his duffel bag. "Don't worry. You can play, too. I brought you a racket. You still use a size two grip?"

It takes me a minute to process what he's saying. "I'm not going to play tennis tonight." *Why would I?* "I haven't played in years."

"All the more reason to hit a ball or two."

"What are these things?" I nod down at the metal bars in my hand. I can make out a silver umbrella-like fixture on the far end.

"Floodlights," Parker says simply, as if the answer makes all the sense in the world. It's as if to him, carrying two floodlights and a bunch of tennis gear across a high-school parking lot at nine o'clock on a dark and cold October night makes perfect sense.

"Um, Parker? I don't even see any tennis courts."

"That's because the only ones in this town are at Glenn's center. So, we're gonna get creative. Hard to see 'em, but there are basketball courts over there. That way… see?"

I peer into the darkness and make out yet another rusted chain linked fence. Behind it is a sad-looking patch of pavement, a bench, and one lone, rusted basketball hoop. Ransom is back there, too, sitting on the ground hunched over. Trading his work shoes for the white sneakers, by the looks of it.

"I came by earlier today and put two pieces of plywood up against one of the fences," Parker says. "Painted a line across 'em, net height. We're going to use them as backboards to train against. This kid is good, Gem. *Really* good. He could be a pro one day, easy. I'm not about to let Glenn's greed stand in the way of that."

I have *so many* questions.

But I can't ask any of them, because seconds later, Ransom's shouting about how great the "backboards" are, and Parker's holding a gate open for me and telling me where to set the floodlight. Soon he's aimed at two big circles of white light on the pavement and plywood, and he's jogging across the court, waving for me to follow. "Get out here! There's space for all three of us, right my man?"

Ransom seems to be in some kind of tennis heaven. He has a big smile on his face, which puts all those crooked teeth on display in the floodlights. "Yeah, come on out, Ms. Lafferty!"

"No, you know what? I'm going to watch from right here."

"Are you sure?" Parker asks, as he hits a ball toward the wall. It ricochets off, straight to the waiting Ransom, who nimbly shifts his feet and whacks it right back.

"I'm sure."

I tuck my hands into my coat pocket and perch on a cold metal bench. It occurs to me that if I wanted to, I could take out my phone and check my work emails. I noticed, back in the truck when we first pulled up, that I'm picking up wifi. Better yet, I could go grab my laptop and dig into some work.

But laughter from out on the court pulls my attention back each time I think about getting onto the internet. So, for the next while, I let myself get caught up watching the scene in front of me.

Parker and Random both radiate joy as they crouch, jump, lunge, and run after balls. It's captivating, seeing how much lively energy and enthusiasm both have.

Neither seems to mind that the pavement under their sneakers is cracked and uneven with frost heaves, or the fact that it's so cold out, we can all see our breath. They're blissfully happy, in their element, playing a sport they love.

I still don't entirely understand why I agreed to come here.

Not completely.

But I *do* know that Parker is helping this kid with his

tennis skills, and that strikes me as incredibly gracious and generous.

He's a good coach, too.

Patient, like he was with Queenie.

Kind, like he is with me.

And so jubilant and ridiculously animated that I find myself laughing along a few times, when he jokes with his pupil.

"Ransom, dude, I'm giving you a bunch of aggressive returns, putting the hammer on you. You catching that? You have to keep me on my toes. Make me run ragged… Make me start here, end there." He makes a big show of launching himself across the makeshift court, racket extended. "As long as I'm getting tired 'cause of this runaround, I'm not gonna get there, see?"

The chain-link fence rattles softly, and I look over in time to see a slight woman in jeans and a big, puffy coat with patches of silver duct tape on the sleeves. She waves to the guys on the court.

"Okay if I keep him a couple more minutes,Veronica?" Parker asks.

"You're the coach. I'll sit right here." Veronica makes her way to the bench, and plops down beside me. She positions her leather handbag on her lap as she says, "Bless his soul. Are you his sister?"

"Me? No… old friend." *Or something like that.*

"You sure are lucky to have a guy like Parker as a friend. He's been a Godsend for Ransom. A real angel."

I might be wrong, but I'm not picking up on even the slightest hint of jealousy or possessiveness in her voice.

And the way he spoke to her wasn't at all in the gentle, croaky, deep intimate way he sometimes uses with me.

It was sort of… professional.

Maybe Parker's relationship with Veronica has nothing to do with hot dates or overnights, as I assumed.

Maybe it's… totally innocent.

Then again, I've been blindsided before, and I won't be surprised if Parker walks off this court and kisses her.

I hold my breath as Ransom hits one last ball and then does a victory dance. "I ran you ragged, Mr. Manning!"

Parker grips his knees, as if he's really worked. I know he's not—I can see it in his posture. But he makes a show of shaking his head as though exhausted. "Like I said, man, vary those shots. You killed it. Nice work." He straightens up to give the kid a high five, and then turns to Veronica, who's made her way toward the two.

I keep a close eye on them. *Please don't kiss.*

It shouldn't make me *this* happy when I see the two stop while still two feet apart, and settle into a friendly conversation. But it does. Giddiness sweeps through me, so strong I want to get up and do a victory dance just like the one Ransom did minutes ago. *Parker's single.*

"... I just want to thank you again," Veronica says, while digging in her purse. "This means the world to Ransom. Let me pay you at least something for your time." She holds out a few bills.

Parker waves the money off. "Nah. I can't take that. I love these sessions. We've got the best player in town right here, and I like getting time on the court with him."

Ransom's crouched at their feet, slipping off his white sneakers and tugging on the work shoes his mother brought out to him. "See that, Mom? If I'm the best player in town, I'm better than Mr. Manning and he won the Davis Cup."

Veronica shakes her head and eyes Parker. "What've you done? He gets it in his head he's that good, and he'll stop practicing."

"Nah," Ransom says, an exact mimic of his mentor's catch phrase. "I'll never stop playing."

"Well," Veronica says to Parker, "If you won't let me pay anything, at least think about letting me talk to Glenn and take some responsibility for that whole disaster."

"Don't worry about that. It was time for me to part ways with that place anyway. We'll keep up the schedule here at the high school. What do you think, bud? Tuesday night, say, six?"

Ransom nods and cheers, and then scrambles up to his feet. He gives Parker a bear hug and then accepts his sports bag from his mother and straps it over his shoulder.

I can hear him chatting excitedly as the two make their way back toward the parking lot. "*And then we worked on my backhand, the eastern grip that I told you about…*"

Before I overthink it, I get up off the metal bench and walk out to Parker. With my hands stuffed in the pockets of my fleece, I study his sneakers, which aren't that far from my leather boots.

When I finally raise my eyes, I watch the chilled cloud of our breath mingle in the small gap between us. "So, you're helping that kid. Ransom. Like charity. That's really sweet."

"Just don't let him hear you call it charity. Kid's too proud for his own good, and so is his mom. They want this kept on the down low. I can't blame them. No one wants to be pitied."

"And that's why you wouldn't talk about why you were fired. You were respecting their wishes about keeping it quiet. But I get it now. You were breaking into the tennis center to give him lessons for free."

"He's going places, Gem. Recruiters will watch him play at the New England Junior Championships next spring, and he's got a good shot at some full-ride college scholarships. Or, he might go my route, ditch the books, and just have fun."

I look out at the floodlights that bookend the makeshift backboard. "Yeah, if you can call becoming an Olympic athlete fun. I know that must have been hard work for you."

Out beyond this lit up area, night has really descended over the field and woods around us. But Parker and I stand in this pool of pale light as though it's heaven's spotlight, shining down on only us.

"It's not work if you love it." He bounces a ball a few times and then lobs it toward one of the boards. It hits the wall and changes directions. When it comes my way I tug my hands out of my pockets in time to catch it.

"What do you think, wanna play?" Parker asks me.

Play.

I haven't really played that much in recent years. Somehow I've managed to pack all my waking hours with work—despite being up before the sun and going to bed way later than my peers.

I love my work, and it feels fulfilling and important. But it's still *work*. Mosty administrative and managerial. Lots of it online.

Basically, I've been living on my computer for ages. I do ride a stationary bike for exactly 25 minutes every evening, before doing pilates, but that can hardly be called *playing*.

Now, with my laptop back in the truck and this neon-green, slightly scratchy tennis ball in my hands, I wonder if maybe my life's become a little *too* productive. On a scale with work on one side and fun on the other, I let the balance tip so far over that I almost forget what it even feels like to do something without a goal in mind.

That can't be healthy.

I lob the ball back at the board. To my satisfaction, it hits it and ricochets toward Parker. "Hey, the plywood works. It's almost like you knew what you were doing when you set this thing up," I tease.

"Give me a little credit. I have blueprints for all sorts of things up in my head."

"Do you, now?"

He chuckles and walks to his duffel bag. "Yeah. I can make a plan with the best of 'em. I had tonight mapped out, and you didn't even see it coming. But here we are, about to get our game on. You got your running shoes?" He pulls a racket from his bag and walks to me with it extended.

I take it from him, and for some reason, it feels like I'm accepting much more than a tennis racket.

Like his friendship.

"Thanks," I say. "I won't read into the fact that you had a woman's racket handy. That'll get me thinking about how you probably do this with girls all the time."

"The fact you just said that means you already thought it," he says with a grin. "But it's not true. I've seen a couple women, since I've been with you. But I never had to work this hard to get a girl to hang out with me. You've got me bending over backwards."

"Why *do* you want to hang out with me?"

"Because you're *Gemma*."

Whatever *that* means. Instead of trying to decode his statement, I head for the gate. "My sneakers are in the truck. I'll be right back."

"You need me to go with you? There might be grizzlies or wolves out there."

"Ha. I have it on good authority that's not true. I'll be fine."

I hurry to the car and trade out my leather boots for

my pink Saucony sneakers. *Am I going to be fine, though, really? In the long run?*

I'm going to Broad Hollow tomorrow to see Mortimer.

Mortimer is in my Plan.

Parker is not.

I hustle back to the court, and when I grab the racket again, I let thoughts about my Life Plan settle in the far back of my mind.

Out of the way. For once.

Parker goes easy on me at first, but when I start to warm up and give him some spicy returns, he laughs and puts more power to the shots he fires back.

Soon I'm running so much that I have to strip off my fleece. My cheeks feel flushed and my chest heaves with exertion as I jump up to make contact with a ball zooming over my head. The racket's strings bounce against the ball's weight. I land light on my feet, run up toward the "net" and lunge right in time to reach the ball again.

"Oh, ho! What do we have here? And I thought I'd have to remind you how to volley. You always used to hang out in no man's land." In the corner of my eye, I see Parker twist and use a double-backhand to return the ball my way.

"What, like you had a pro career and I've got nothing but a couple lessons at the Wayland town park plus some pointers from you under my belt?" I laugh as the ball flies past me, out of reach. I have to jog to get it, but I don't mind.

It feels good to move.

I line up my feet and angle my hips toward the wall. I might not remember everything from those lessons I took in fourth grade, or times in my past messing around on courts with Parker, but I do recall the basics of how to serve.

I give it my best shot, and Paker makes a big show of lunging, on his side of the pavement. "Dang! You put some power into that one, girl. Almost had me."

"Hey, I don't need you to patronize me." I can't help but laugh, because compared to his serves, mine was pathetic. "Then again, if it was a compliment I'll take it."

"It was a compliment. Gemma Lafferty—the power house."

We hit the ball back and forth for a while, and I have to move so much to keep up with him that I'm too out of breath to talk. The only sounds are the thud of the ball against the wall, our sneakers scuffing the pavement, and our mutually ragged breathing.

When he returns a ball just out of my reach, he raises his fist in the air and pumps it once.

I catch my breath as I jog after the ball. "What, suddenly after your years of being all Zen Master about athletic events, *now* you're competitive?"

"Yeah. Complete change of heart. I'm playing to win, and that's all."

"Not for the fun of it?" I tease.

"Who's calling this fun?"

I am. I am definitely calling this fun.

I pause with the ball in my hand. I should serve it, but I just want to savor this moment. I glance over at Parker and see he's watching me—with that you're-a-special-snowflake look.

Is it possible that I'm wrong about this look? Maybe I better get some nerve up and check. "What?" I ask.

"Nothin'."

"No really… *what*? You're looking at me like—"

"Like what?" he asks, his voice husky.

"Like… like you used to, I guess."

A beat of silence fills the space between us.

"Maybe… I don't know…" His voice is so deep and sincere that I can feel it resonate through my core. "I guess it's been sort of a trip down memory lane, you showing up in town."

My heart beat speeds up, even though I'm standing still.

He's been reliving old memories, too. Of course he has. There are memories we share. Memories that only the two of us have. "Yeah, it has, hasn't it?"

"A *good* trip. Really good. I missed you. I'm really glad you're here."

A pleasant, tingling shiver races down my spine, but I don't feel cold. I feel warm, like I'm standing near a ten-foot bonfire. I know that fire's Parker. And he's passing his happy glow to me, and I like the way it feels.

Here I was, thinking I was nothing to him. But he missed me.

"I'm glad I'm here, too," I say, in total honesty.

It feels good not to twist my words to mold some far-off ideal for once. I spend so much of my time trying to make things sound the way I think they should sound. Like saying I'm fine when I'm not really fine. Saying I have things under control when the truth is I'm as at the mercy of chaos as the rest of the world.

Right now, standing here under a ceiling of stars, I don't feel the need to lie to myself or anyone else.

I really am glad I'm here in Pines Peak. On this high school basketball court. Playing tennis with Parker.

Happiness bubbles up in me. When was the last time I felt this good? This free?

It's been ages.

I'm not stressed, I'm not rushing to get anywhere. I'm here, and *here* is exactly where I want to be. Where I need to be.

What an incredible feeling.

It won't last, but for now. I might as well enjoy it.

I savor the deliciousness of it for another moment, and then focus back on the ball in my hand. "Ready?" I ask, as I toss the bar into the air. "Here it comes."

Chapter 12

Parker

Adorable.

Gemma Lafferty is adorable.

Her serve is straight out of a beginner's tennis manual. Half the balls she hits arc up over the chain link fence we're playing against. A dog will probably come by in the morning and help himself to a few new toys, because I'm not going out there to collect those stray balls tonight.

No way.

I want to stay right here on this make-shift court at Gemma's side. Listening to her laugh and tease me, hearing her breathe hard after running for a ball. I love the way she swipes her bare forearm across her forehead, to get stray wisps of her brown hair from her eyes.

She sounded sincere, when she said she was glad to be here in Vermont. It's good to hear her say something and mean it, for once.

No fluff about what she should be doing or what her

future plans are. She let herself get into the moment, and I'm right there with her.

Having fun.

She's going to go back to the city, I remind myself, as we call it quits and head for the bench. *Don't get too used to this.*

Gemma's cheeks have a gorgeous pink glow. Her bare arms are toned beneath the black sweater she's wearing, rolled up to her elbows. The silver accents of her jewelry reflect the moonlight. She perches on the bench and tucks her knee up to her chest to untie her laces.

I watch her work.

Because she's beautiful.

She glances at me through her lashes. "You could take a photo."

"Hm?"

"It would last longer," she teases, shaking her head and going back to work. When she hops up to her feet, now back in her leather boots, she strides up to me.

I busy myself with packing up the duffel so I don't look like I'm gawking. As she nears I get to my feet, too, and loop the bag's strap over my shoulder.

"We'll leave the lights here," I say. "Might get smashed up or stolen if people come to play ball or whatever, but we'll deal with that if it happens."

"That's how you handle things, hm?" She stops before me and tilts her face up to mine. "Wait to see what comes up, then you deal. Maybe you should try thinking ahead more, instead of sitting back and watching things unfold. I think it'd help you. And I was joking, by the way, about the photo. I know you look at everything the exact same way you look at me. It'd be ridiculously self-centered of me to think it's just me. For all I know, you looked into that oatmeal pot this morning with the same awe-struck reverie."

"Well, it was good oatmeal."

"Par-keerr..." She reaches out and pushes my arm. And when the gesture ends, she's standing closer to me.

So close that I can smell a faint whiff of her perfume. Her shampoo. And that marshmallow gloss.

It's like every memory I have of her has come to life, here right in front of me.

If I closed my eyes right now, I'd be able to recall exactly the way she used to stand up on her tiptoes and wrap her arms around my neck before delivering one of her sweet, delicious kisses.

I used to live for those kisses.

For a long time, they only happened in my mind. I had fantasies about her for years. Then, for those few weeks, I actually got to experience them.

And for years after, I looked long and hard for another woman that would make me feel like she did.

Never found it again—that feeling.

Maybe it was because love was so new to us, that it felt so amazing. Or, is it something about her and me, and the way our cells and nerves and souls sparked up, every time we touched?

I don't know.

I don't have this stuff down to a science, like she apparently does.

All I know is it was different in a good way, what we had. And that even though I searched, I couldn't find anything quite like it again.

"Stop it!" she quips, as she gives me another swat. "You're doing it again!"

I chuckle. "What do you want me to say, Gem?"

"Tell me why you look at me like that."

"Can't. I don't want to come on too strong."

"Now you're speaking in code again. I don't know what to make of a statement like that, Parker."

"It's like… it's like I said in the driveway, about your cat. I'm going to be patient." *If you want me as much as I want you, you'll make the first move.*

I don't want to scare you away.

"I'm not Queenie," she says, as she bites her lip and looks up at me with big, hazel eyes. . "I'm not going to jump into your arms just because you offer me lots of treats."

"I know." *But I wish you would.* I'd give anything to feel Gemma in my arms right now. Her lips on mine.

She rubs her lips together. When she stops, the upper and lower part slightly. So plump, supple, and kissable I could die.

"I'm here to help you get your life back on track," she says, almost in a whisper. "Not re-ignite some old flame that's better off out."

"Might be too late for that." For my part, that old flame sparked up the minute I saw her. And now it's burning so hot inside me, I feel like it might as well be mid-July.

"It's never too late to get your life back on track."

"That's not what I was saying." I can't help it. I reach out for her cheek, and slide my fingertips from her temple to her jaw. Her skin feels so good under my fingertips. Warm and smooth. I rest my thumb under her chin and tilt her face toward mine as I step in closer to her.

She skims her hand along my arm, and for a minute I think she's going to reach up for my neck to pull me closer, like she used to do.

But worry flickers in her eyes, as she searches mine.

I can't lower my lips to her like I want so badly to do, while she's got that concern written on her face.

She runs her hand over my hard bicep again, and then pulls it away. "We shouldn't do this," she whispers, before stepping back.

I can hardly breathe.

It takes me a minute to suck air back into my lungs and stop my blood from rushing so hot through my veins, I feel like I might burst into flame.

When I clear the cobwebs from my brain I turn and see she's already halfway to the truck. I have to switch off the floodlights and unplug them from the electricity pedestal on the edge of the court, so it takes me a few minutes to join her.

When I make it into my Chevy, I find that she's pulled her computer out and balanced it on her lap.

"Hey, good news," she says, in a falsely-bright, chirpy voice. As though I'm nobody except a client of hers or something, and we didn't just almost kiss.

I should have let her make the first move.

I told myself I would.

I messed up.

If this unexpected visit with Gemma was a football game, I just fumbled the ball.

I draw in a deep inhale through my nose and run my hand through my hair. It takes every ounce of control I have not to bring up what just happened between us.

I want to talk about it. Get straight about what's going on. But she clearly doesn't want to, and I don't want to push this thing any harder than I am already.

"Yeah? Hit me with it." I crank the key in the ignition and the truck rumbles to life. I turn the heat up, and put the shifter into reverse.

When I loop my arm over the back of her seat, I'm achingly aware of how close I am to touching her again.

She studies her computer screen. "Okay, so I turned in

that questionnaire I filled out for you. We didn't do the interview portion—because you're being so stubborn—but I ran your numbers anyway, and the Right Match system located four potential matches for you. All within a 90 mile radius!"

I feel like I'm sitting in a dentist chair, and I've just been informed I have four cavities.

No, worse.

Four teeth so rotten, multiple painful extractions are right around the corner.

I just messed up bad with Gemma, and now she's talking about not one, not two, but *four* women that she wants to set me up with.

And not just 'set up' in a vague way, like someday in the future. I know Gemma's style. She's a take-action, check-the-boxes kind of girl. She's going to get me out on actual dates soon.

I want to kiss Gemma, not be forced into a date with someone else.

"And… that's supposed to be good news?" I shift to drive and press the gas. We barrel across the lot. The truck's headlights cut a swath of yellow light across ink-black stands of trees.

"Really good. I was afraid you'd only get one or two matches. Three's usually enough."

"Enough for what?"

"Enough to get you on the right track. You know… what we've been talking about. What your family wants for you. A wife."

"But I told you, that'll happen for me when the time's right."

"The time is right *now*. You're thirty-three. Statistically speaking, your wife will probably be within plus-or-minus four years of you. So, say twenty-nine to thirty-seven. If you start dating now and the relationship progresses at an average speed, you guys will still have time to have kids before she reaches forty. I don't have to sit here and give you a lecture about ovaries and eggs, do I?"

"Whoa, Gemma. This is sort of a lot to take in."

"You need to think about this stuff."

"Do I, though? Really? I'm doing fine."

"You *think* you're fine, but you're not. Not really. You're helping me unwind a little, so I might as well help you, too, right?"

"You think it's helpful to say this stuff about—" I cough and clear my throat, which is suddenly incredibly dry. *Where is that water bottle?* "Ah… um—ovaries?"

She reaches out, places a hand on my knee, and squeezes. "Don't drive off the road, there, Stud. Focus."

She's right. My steering did get a little off.

But her hand on my leg isn't helping matters. I mow over a stand of weeds and then manage to correct course before actually driving us into the ditch. Once I have the truck out between the painted lines where I'm supposed to be, I glance over at her. "Gemma, this isn't what I had in mind for tonight."

"I know… you had a plan. And we did your part. We had fun. But take it from me—an actual, experienced, bonafide planner—sometimes even when you map something out, it goes haywire at the last minute."

"Yeah, I'd call this haywire."

"Oh, come on. It's not that bad. I'm giving you the facts." Her face has a pale blueish glow to it, thanks to the light off the screen she's staring into. "Most women like to be engaged by age thirty, popping out babies a few years after that. That's the reality. You're not too far behind the ball, but if you keep dragging your heels like you are, you're going to be screwed."

She taps a few keys on her laptop. "Shoot. Wifi's getting weaker. Can you pull over here?"

"So you can harass me about this? No."

I can feel my blood rushing, still, every time I look over at her. I really wanted to kiss her back there.

I shouldn't have tried, though.

I scared her off.

"Fine, I pulled up one profile anyway, so it's okay." Her voice is hard-edged and a little too high-pitched.

You don't grow up around a person without learning their different moods. This is Gemma in fight-mode. You wouldn't catch it if you'd just met her, but I've seen her put this war paint on before.

If she's fighting, it means she must feel defensive.

She's afraid of what's happening between us.

Tonight, I watched her guard come down. I watched her shed her defenses, loosen up, and start to go with the flow. Then I tried to kiss her, and now *this*.

Was it that bad, me trying for that one kiss?

Maybe it was.

Maybe she's right and I'm trying to ignite an old flame. It sparked to life in me, and I thought it was heating up in her, too. The way she was standing so close to me… that had to mean something. *She wants me.*

Even if she does want me, though, she might be ignoring what she feels.

Overriding it.

Gemma's always been good at that.

Out of the corner of my eye, I see her lift her chin. She rattles off some stuff about the software her company uses, and then says, "Out of the four women your profile was compatible with, your best match was an 85 percent. That's great, by the way. Me and Mortimer are 93, but that's practically unheard of. Anyway, she lives in Northern

New Hampshire, an hour and ten minutes from here. Her name's Heidi."

"Heidi. Okay…" *Is this happening? Is this really happening?*

Gemma is the only woman I've ever tried to kiss who refused me and turned around to try to set me up with someone else.

She's really not going to drop this.

"Let's see…" she goes on. "She's 31, and she works at a micro flower farm. How cute is that! I mean, I don't understand if it's micro because the farm is small, or the flowers are tiny, or what, but it's still charming. She works with her hands… see?" She reaches out and hits my arm lightly. "That's perfect for you."

"Why is it perfect that she works with her hands?"

"Because, you're a physical guy. You're… you know, kinetic. Look, I don't know exactly how the Right Match process works, I just know that it does. The software says you two are compatible, so I think you should go out on at least one date with her and see for yourself."

There go the computer keys again. *What's she up to, now?* "Tell me you're not pulling up a second profile."

"No, no. We'll handle these one at a time. I'm making a note to myself to find a spot somewhere between here and her town in New Hampshire. A restaurant, midway between you guys. For your first date. How does tomorrow sound?"

"I'm not—"

"And *I'm* not taking no for an answer."

"When did you become so bossy?"

"I've always been bossy."

She's right. She has. I thought it was funny when we were kids, then, in my late teens and early twenties, I thought it was hot.

Right now, I find it irksome.

Because she's bossing me straight into a date with a woman I've never even met. Heidi, the flower farmer. When all I want to do is pull this truck over, lean over the console, and kiss Gemma.

"Please, Parker," she begs. "I came all the way up here to Vermont even though I am super, crazy busy back home. Your dad really wants this for you, and I think you should trust him. He's your father. This is important to him… and it's important to me, too."

"I don't get why you agreed to help him in the first place. Is he paying you or something?"

She sighs, closes her computer, and stuffs it in the bag at her feet. "Sort of."

"Truth, Gemma. Just say it how it is."

"Okay, he says he'll invest in my company if the process works on you. He's trying to be helpful. It could be a big deal, if he invests. We're at the brink of really big success, but we need a boost in funding to get there."

I hang a left onto Main Street. Most of the places are shut down, but the neon lights in the shape of a crooked mug of beer up on top of the Tipsy Tavern glow against the night sky. I note a bunch of cars in the lot as we pass.

"Please, Parker," Gemma pleads again.

When I look over, she has her hands pressed together as though she's praying. "For me," she adds, while searching my eyes.

I want to say no.

I really want to say no.

I have a thing for Gemma, and she's trying to set me up with someone else? If I had my head on straight, I'd probably be offended.

But my head isn't on straight.

It hasn't been, since I first laid eyes on her in that adorable, way-too-big nightgown.

How could I say "no" to the first girl I ever fell in love with? A girl I still have feelings for, to this day? She's looking at me with her big, green eyes.

"Fine," I mutter. "For you."

"Thanks. I really appreciate it." She tucks her hair behind her ear and turns her face to the window on her right, like she has something to say to the glass. "And… if I —if I… um… gave you mixed signals back there at the high school, you know, flirting or whatever—I'm sorry. I guess I got sort of swept up in the whole thing. Being out there, goofing around."

"You don't have to be sorry."

"I guess I have some old habits. Habits that just won't quit. I fall into my old ways around you, but I'm not eighteen any more. And you're older too, and it's—it's just better if we don't go down that road again… even if sometimes, against my better judgment, I want to, too."

I take a turn onto the road that will take us up to the log cabin. The Chevy downshifts for the slow climb.

I knew it.

She wants to kiss me, too.

She just admitted it.

But in true Gemma fashion, she's couched that statement in a tangle of other words that are mostly about *not* kissing me.

What am I supposed to make of that?

I don't know whether to be excited that she just admitted to wanting me as much as I want her, or bummed that her "better judgment" is getting in our way.

How does she know her judgment's that good, anyway?

Human judgment is a funny thing.

Usually, it's like tunnel vision. You can't see out past the walls around you. You get trapped into one way of thinking.

Pretty limited, in my opinion.

She keeps her nose pointed toward the window, watching the dark woods as it passes. "I'm going to head down to central Vermont Monday afternoon. Okay with you if I leave Queenie at the cabin, and come back in the evening sometime?"

"You bet. The house is yours for as long as you need it. I'll be careful opening and closing the door, now that we know we have an escape artist on our hands."

"Thanks," she mutters, as she studies more passing trees. "I'm going to be really busy with work tomorrow, but I'll text you the details about your date. You do use your phone, right?"

"Sure, when it's charged."

"Okay, well, charge it up and check it tomorrow, if I don't see you around. I'm thinking of finding a coffee shop or something to work out of."

"There's a good one down in town. The Steaming Mug."

I can see my family's cabin up ahead. The truck rattles as I pull into the driveway, as the rocks stuck in the wheel wells ping around a few last times.

"Great, thanks for the tip," she says, all business. She collects her computer bag onto her lap and reaches for the truck's door handle. At the last minute, before pressing the door open, she turns to look at me. "And, thanks for… um, for understanding. About back at the high school. I just forgot my priorities for a minute. No hard feelings about all this, right?"

"Right."

She lets herself out of the truck.

I lean back against the seat's headrest and groan.

Chapter 13

Gemma

I'm not in my office, but I wish I was.

Instead I'm padding toward the Manning's ski house kitchen, trying desperately not to wake the slumbering beast on the other side of an oak door.

He's in there, I know.

Freaking Parker.

Dangerous Parker.

In my bluetooth earbuds, my Head of Marketing, Claire, is in the middle of rattling off a long list of things she accomplished over the weekend.

While I was out there on Saturday night, losing my mind and pretending to be eighteen again, Claire Holt was hitting her work tasks out of the park.

Thank goodness I got my head straight yesterday, at least. I spent the day at a quaint little coffee shop on Main Street, sipping lattes, composing emails, and *not* drooling over Parker.

Which was good for me, I think.

Being around him messes with my head.

I start to forget what's important. Like Right Match.

"Thanks for the update," I whisper to Claire, as I lean down for Queenie's water bowl.

"Why are you whispering?"

"Because, I'm working twenty feet away from a sleeping beast and I don't want to wake him."

"Really?"

I'd answer, except now my ears are perked. I heard movement… coming from the direction of Parker's room.

Blankets rustling or something.

A soft, gentle groan.

Sounds I don't want to hear and wish I didn't hear. *I almost kissed Parker on Saturday night, and that would have been a huge mistake.*

What if something like that happens again?

I have to get out of here before he stumbles out here barefoot, with his hair poking out at all angles, and tempts me again.

"Really," I confirm, using the same hushed tone. "And I'm traveling today, so I might not be online consistently. I'll check in later this afternoon and again this evening. Hey, what's the latest on the YouTuber?"

"Right, let me pull that up…" I hear her clicking keys. "Got it here. *The Nikko Show.* I told him what you said, about how you're available for the interview Saturday, but only if he can travel to Vermont. He's psyched for the excuse to hit the road, and said he can meet you wherever works for you. He's going to bring a film crew, and says all they need is a location without too much background noise."

I pull a travel mug from a cupboard and pour some coffee in. As liquid hits the stainless steel, I furtively check over my shoulder toward Parker's bedroom door.

Still closed.

I'm still safe.

"Let me think a sec," I whisper, as I hustle to the counter and swipe my laptop up. I stuff it in my computer bag and then shrug on my fleece. "No background noise…"

That means the Steaming Mug is out. I look up and out toward the dark green couch and chairs positioned across from a picture window with stunning views. "I'm staying at my friend's vacation house for the week. Think Nikko could meet me here?"

"Send me the address. I'll check with him."

"Done." I lean over so my computer bag doesn't flop forward off my shoulder, and manage to scrawl a quick note on a spare sheet of paper. I'll add the item to my official, typed to-do list later. "Thanks, Claire," I tell her. "You're doing a great job. How's everything at the office?"

"Smooth sailing, but we miss you. Teagan's moving to that new apartment, so we're all going to her place after work to help her pack. Mark won't stop talking about some new video game he bought, and—Oops, hang on. He actually just walked in."

As a muffled conversation takes place on the other end of the line, I slip the note I wrote myself into my pocket. Then, careful to stay quiet, I make my way toward the cabin's front door.

I have coffee, my computer, and a relatively Parker-free headspace. That's everything I need for this trip to central Vermont to see Mortimer.

And seeing Mortimer should swipe the last remnants of Saturday out of my head altogether.

Once me and Mortimer talk, maybe I'll be able to face Parker without saying one single stupid, bumbling thing about how I'm so eager to make the same mistake he wants to make.

It really would be a mistake, touching him and kissing him.

I was *so* close to that trap, Saturday night. We're talking millimeters away.

He caressed my face and sparklers lit up in my core. I reached for him and almost, *almost*, let my fingertips move up into that warm space between his t-shirt sleeve and upper arm. I started to touch him like we were together. I wanted to fit my body against his, and let our lips fuse like they used to.

But we're not together, and letting myself give in to these feelings would just be asking for trouble.

I'm in Vermont because Mitch sent me to find Parker a life partner.

I have work to do.

Professional work as a therapist and business owner. And if I do my job right, I could secure a half million dollars in funding.

I can't let myself get distracted.

I can't let myself feel *all the feelings* for Parker again.

What good is that dazzling, can't-think, can't-breathe sensation?

The one where you feel dizzy and weak, and your heart feels like a warm ball of mush?

Feelings like that don't last.

My track record with Parker already proved that.

As I reach the entryway and go about slipping my feet into my boots, I hear Claire's voice in my ear again. "Gemma, you still there?"

"I'm here."

"That was Mark, actually. He says he checked on that profile for Parker Manning, like you asked him to. Hang on, I'm going to let Mark tell you himself."

A second later, my Software Development Specialist is

on the line, his voice so boyish I can picture his chubby cheeks and red-framed glasses. "Yo, Gem? I looked into the specifics of the Manning profile. His personality typing looks fairly solid. Not rock solid, but good enough, I think. You must have done okay with fudging the answers. Things are a little wonky with the Attachment Style coding, but I think it's good enough, too. That's what you said, right? Doesn't have to be perfect?"

"Right. I took educated guesses and that's all we have to work with."

"His profile would be a lot more accurate if he'd sit for the interview process."

Down the hall, I hear the soft thud of a door closing.

Shoot. He's up.

"He won't," I whisper.

Queenie, who's been following me around all morning, brushes up against my ankles. I rub her ears and mentally send her my loving goodbye. Then I open the door a couple inches and slip out without letting her follow me.

I don't think the hotel where Mortimer is staying would appreciate it if I showed up with a cat in my arms. Most places have health codes about that kind of thing.

"So, he's that stubborn?" Mark asks. "He won't even spend an hour or two on an interview? It sure would make me more confident about these matches."

"He's that stubborn," I say, as I stride toward my Prius.

It's already late morning. The day's bright and crisp. A blue sky forms a spotless background to the orange, red, and yellow treetops bristling up around the cabin. The car gives a soft beep when I press my key fob.

It's a relief to reverse out of the driveway and hit the road. I adjust the sun visor as I steer. "We just have to work with whatever numbers we have," I say, before slugging down a gulp of lukewarm coffee. "Thanks for looking into it."

"No prob, boss. Anything you need."

We get off the line. Now that I'm safely out of the ski house, I let my thoughts veer toward Parker.

How did his date go last night?

I holed up at the Steaming Mug all day and didn't see him, even once. But I managed to set everything up for him to have a cozy dinner with Heidi at a place called the Flower Cafe, which is sort of perfect, given that she works with flowers and all.

Did they hit it off?

Did he say sweet things to her? Maybe reach for her hand at the end of the night and pull her in?

Did he kiss her goodnight?

By the time I reach the highway, I've nauseated myself by playing through countless Parker-Heidi date scenarios on my mental screen. As I pick up speed on the interstate, heading south, I force myself to think about something else.

Like Mortimer. What I'll say to him. How he's going to see me, and tell me he wants me back. Of course he will.

When I reach the Broad Hollow hotel a couple hours later, I spend way too much time circling the thing and then finally nosing into a spot. I think I'm stalling, but I can't figure out why. I want to see Mortimer. I want to get us back on track.

My phone rings as I stride up a wide walkway to the hotel's impressively big entryway. A glass revolving door glints in the sun. I grab my phone and my heart squeezes in a little when I see it's Parker.

I turn away from the glass doors and squint out at a row of glittery, sun-washed cars. "Wow, look who's using a phone."

"These things are overrated. *Mrff mrff mrff.*"

"Are you chewing, in my ear? Gross."

"Sorry. Late breakfast."

I glance down at my watch. "It's one in the afternoon. When did you get in last night, anyway?"

"Two, I think. Two or three..."

"Hm." I feel my jaw clench. "Must have been a good date, to keep you out that late." *And I should be happy about that.*

"I'll tell you all about it. Later. Right now I'm wondering—where's the oatmeal?"

"I didn't make any this morning. I can't believe you're using your phone again. Your dad said you're more apt to use it as a paperweight than for making calls. Carly says you haven't called her in years."

"I went caveman. You're changing me."

"We'll see about that."

"I'll be at the bar later, working. You want to come by for some food?"

Dirty Fries. Small, medium, or large. They still don't sound at all appealing to me. Besides... "I'm traveling today. I told you. Central Vermont."

"Yeah, I remember. The guy. Morbid—"

"Mortimer—"

"Coughlin or whatever. You're visiting him."

"*Laughlin.* And yeah. We're getting coffee and catching up."

"Queenie misses you."

"I've only been gone for like two hours."

"She says she wishes you cooked some breakfast."

"She doesn't eat breakfast. You're projecting your own desires onto my cat."

"Sometimes I wish you weren't a therapist."

"And sometimes I wish you'd grow up. Are we done?"

"Almost. One more thing. It's Karaoke night at the bar. So you should really stop in, when you get back to town."

"I don't sing."

"I've heard you sing. You once belted out Mariah Carey's 'Fantasy' while wearing a pink tiara and using a fairy wand as your fake mic."

"That was when I was too young to realize that I'm totally tone deaf. Plus, I remember that afternoon. Me and Carly were alone in her bedroom and you were spying on us."

"I wasn't spying, I was trying to get a frisbee off the roof and I happened to look through the window."

"Yeah, well, that was a private moment."

"I like tone deaf Gemma."

"You might be the only one. I don't want to break anyone's ears."

"Eh, they've heard it all. Annie usually does a few Broadway numbers, and there's a guy named Frankie who likes to do his best with some country. You think *you're* tone deaf, try listening to that guy. Starts at seven, goes until closing time."

"I might not be—"

"See you there," he says, before hanging up.

I slip my phone back into my purse and surprise myself by laughing quietly.

When I turn on my heel and head for the revolving doors again, I can't even remember one word of the points I hope to get across to Mortimer.

Parker's voice is still ringing in my ears as I make my way to one of the sleek chairs set around a stone table in the hotel's massive lobby. I'm early, so I settle into one of the chairs.

To my right I can see through a wall of glass to a fancy looking restaurant. To my left there's a row of shiny countertops, backed by a line-up of hotel employees poised at computers, ready to help guests.

After setting up my computer, I send Mortimer a quick text to let him know I'm here ahead of schedule. Then, when I don't hear back, I call him.

No answer.

No big deal.

I know how busy he always is. He's probably neck-deep in research today, getting ready for his upcoming speech and lectures. Sometimes when he gets really immersed in research, he loses track of time. I do the same, when I'm in the zone.

This lobby is a wonderful place to work. A hushed quiet extends from the floor to the vaulted ceilings. Luckily, I have plenty to keep me busy, so I don't even stress about the fact that Mortimer isn't calling me back.

Before I know it, I've downed two lattes from the restaurant and spent the entire afternoon ticking off most of the tasks I'd set myself for the next day. I rarely get this far ahead, and it's exciting to think that maybe I have an actual day off on the horizon.

A whole day.

What would I even do with myself?

I straighten my back up and lift my arms to the sky for a stretch. Outside, evening is falling. I check my phone again while imagining what twenty-four hours off would feel like. Maybe I'd actually sleep in, for once.

That'd be a real luxury.

Or, maybe I could meet up with Mortimer again, and—

My thoughts of Mortimer abruptly halt as I catch sight of him, across the lobby. Designer suit. Receding hairline. Pointy, shined dress shoes. Gold watch. He turns back toward the elevator, and a petite woman steps out.

Her raven-black hair is cropped close to her head. Long earrings sweep across bare shoulders. She's in a sleeveless, blue wrap dress.

The same woman I saw him with, at the Kendall Square Starbucks.

What is going on here?

Mortimer says something, and she laughs.

The two head across the lobby. When Mortimer spots me, his laughter dies. "Gemma! What are you doing here?"

"It's Monday."

His face screws up with confusion, then pales as awareness dawns. "Oh, wow. I am really sorry. I *knew* I had something I had to do today. It kept nagging me, but I couldn't put my finger on it. "

"Don't be sorry," I choke out, as I scramble to collect my laptop, notebook, and empty latte cup.

I don't want a visit with me to be something that he 'has to' do. Something that 'nags' him.

I thought he would be looking forward to this reunion —like I was.

Or, was I?

I just sat here in the lobby for hours and hours, and I don't think I felt genuine excitement or giddy anticipation for even one minute.

My pen rolls to the floor. I stoop to grab it, and my notebook slides forward. I manage to gather it back into my arms before it falls, too.

Mortimer rushes to help. "Here, let me—"

"No. No! I can get it." I stuff the pen into the side compartment of my bag. In my periphery, I see the petite, dark-haired woman hovering nearby, looking confused.

That makes two of us.

"It's—It's no problem—" I stammer, while I grab my

coat off the back of the chair. "I was in the area anyway, like I said on the phone. Vermont's so pretty this time of year. I felt like taking a drive. Hey, we'll catch up another time or something."

"No, wait. I feel bad about this. Why didn't you call?"

"I did. I texted, too."

"Shoot. I think I put my phone on silent" He pulls the device out and makes a big deal out of scrutinizing the screen, like the answer to this mess might be spelled out on it.

My vision's blurring.

I think I have a fever, because my cheeks are flushed and burning. "I have to go." I get those words out without crying, but I think if I tried to say more, tears might start shooting out of my eyes.

I am an idiot.

A total fool.

I drove all this way to get blown off.

He *forgot* we were supposed to meet. And, why is he so dressed up? Why is *she* so dressed up?

I catch sight of the hotel's restaurant as I lurch toward the revolving doors. I don't know how I know, but I do—they're heading to dinner. *Together.*

I can see other couples in there, conversing over flickering candle light. The restaurant's tables are lined in white cloth. The lights are dim. I'm guessing something acoustic is trilling out over cleverly disguised surround-sound speakers, tucked up in the ceiling near fake potted plants.

Cold, night air washes over my cheeks. I swipe at my eyes, clearing a few tears that snuck out. When I start up my Prius, I draw in a deep, shaky breath. Then another. And as I let them out, I notice a feeling squirming into my body, and nestling in next to the oodles of shame filling me.

Relief.

Like some part of me knew Mortimer and that woman were having a thing, but I was ignoring it. Denying it.

My powers of denial are truly impressive, it seems. I really did a number on myself.

But seeing the two of them come out of the elevator like that… and seeing the way they looked at each other…

I can't ignore what I just saw with my own eyes. It was like the Starbucks situation, but amplified. They were practically shouting in my face that they're a couple.

How did I miss this, before?

I know how. I *wanted* to miss it.

I'm an idiot, I think again, as I roll past a lineup of sleek cars with plates from all over the tri-state area.

When I hit the main stretch of road, I roll the windows way down and stick my arm out. Wind tugs at my hair, pulling it free. I let it swirl around me. The brisk air dries a few more of my tears. When I turn on the radio, a love song is playing.

Typically, I hate love songs. They're full of stuff that's just not true about love—in my humble, if educated opinion.

Love—real love—is about commitment and dedication.

Enduring ups and downs.

Digging in and getting to know a person, with all their messy problems and quirks. Sticking with them and growing with them. Deep caring. Deep trust. Deep friendship. *That's* what love is.

I thought I was heading for all that with Mortimer. I thought with a few little tweaks, we could get right back on the path toward a committed, mature relationship that would last us a lifetime.

Sure, we weren't there yet. We never clicked, really. But I figured we'd get there… one day.

It looks like I was wrong about that.

As wind tugs at my hair and music swirls through the car, I reach up for the ring I wear around my neck.

It's the engagement ring that my great-grandfather gave to my great-grandmother. He made it by cutting and bending a spoon to fit perfectly around her finger. They didn't have money to spend on something extra like jewelry, but that didn't matter to either of them. She wore this ring for seventy years.

I knew her for a few of those. She lit up every time she talked about my great-grandpa, who passed away a couple years before I was born.

Then, when she passed away, she left the ring to me.

I'll wear it, one day.

I thought for sure Mortimer would be the man to give it to me.

When I hit the highway, I ease the windows up and set cruise-control.

By the time I make it to Pines Peak, my tears have dried. I drop my speed to 25 and crawl down Main Street. The sight of that tilted, neon, amber-hued beer mug jutting out from the roof of the Tipsy Tavern makes me tap the breaks.

Parker's working.

I could stop in and see him.

Is it a good idea?

I don't know. I *thought* it was a good idea to drive two hours to visit a guy who couldn't even be bothered to recall we'd made plans. I was wrong about that, so what else have I been wrong about?

I slow down more, and then take the right-hand turn into the packed lot.

Chapter 14

Gemma

The Tipsy Tavern is crowded.

Crowded, cozy, and colorful.

And it smells delicious in here. There's no way that's Dirty Fries I'm smelling… is it?

My stomach growls as I weave between two clusters of flannel-adorned locals. When I reach the bar I spot Parker, standing with his back to me. He's wearing a black half-apron around his waist and he has a rag tucked in it. His black t-shirt pulls taught over his back muscles as he reaches to a shelf for a bottle of liquor. The tattoos on his triceps disappear beneath the sleeves.

There are only two bar stools open. One of them's right beside Annie.

Just my luck. I actually know someone here besides Parker.

"Hey, Annie." I slide onto the seat beside her and nod up at the elk. "How's he handling this crowd?"

She grins. "Big Ed loves karaoke night. He's a musician

at heart. If he could, he'd treat us all to some loud, wailing bugling, the way he used to do when he was among the living, fightin' for a female this time of year. How you doin', hon? Nice to see you back here so soon."

"Thanks." I shed my outer layer and then reach for a menu. "Is there something else coming out of a kitchen somewhere that's not listed for the public? Because I smell something that's making my mouth water. Like, chicken and cream sauce or…"

"That'd be the fries. Take my word for it, you want the large. You have one, you want to eat a hundred more."

"Hm." I'm still having trouble believing it.

I hang my bag on the back of the stool and then turn to root through it for my wallet. When I swivel toward the bar again, Parker's in front of me, a bottle of Jack in one hand and a beer in the other.

His smile reaches his eyes, crinkling the corners. "Hey. You made it."

With his eyes still pinned on me, he places a shot glass on the counter and fills it with amber liquid. He slides it toward a man two seats down, barely even glancing that way.

"Yeah, and I'm starving," I admit. "And thirsty, too."

"Oh yeah?" His biceps flex as he wipes his hands on the towel at his waist. "What d'you want to drink?"

"A Cosmo would be great. Grey Goose vodka, or whatever you have. Light on the soda water, if you add that. I know some places don't."

"If I knew what you were talking about, I'd get right on it."

"You don't know how to make a Cosmo?"

"I think there's a book back here with recipes in it, but I haven't ever opened the thing."

I grin. "Maybe you should do some studying, Mr. Bartender."

"I have better things to do with my time."

"Okay, so do you know how to mix *any* cocktails?"

"Nope."

"Fine. What do you recommend, great server extraordinaire?"

"Two options: a pint of beer on tap, or a shot of whisky. Pick your poison."

"I haven't done a shot since college."

He pulls out a shot glass and places it on the counter. "Sound like the perfect night to—"

"No!" I wave my hand and then reach for the glass and push it aside before he can waste any liquor. "I will *not* be taking shots, college frat boy style." I have to lean forward and crane my neck to get a peek at the colorful labels of the beers on tap, not that far down. Because I'm now inches away from Parker, I can smell his cologne. Spicy, woodsy, and fresh.

I catch sight of a name I recognize, on the beer tap at the end of the lineup. "The Long Trail Limbo IPA sounds good. Two."

"So you *are* gettin' after it." He pulls out two pint glasses.

I laugh. "Nope. One's for Annie."

"I knew you had a good heart, hon." Annie places her wrinkled hand on mine and gives a squeeze. "I could see it in your eyes, minute you stepped in here. Prissy thing, but with a kind soul inside."

She leans in toward my ear as Parker steps aside to fill our pint glasses. "And seems to me like *he* sees right to that good heart you got, too. Lit up like a Christmas tree, when he saw you sittin' here."

A fluttering sensation stirs in my stomach.

Hunger?

Something else?

Parker returns with the brimming glasses. The minute he sets Annie's down she swipes it up. "Gotta leave you two kids to it. It's time for me to treat this crowd to a tune from *The Lion King. The Circle of Life*. This one's going out to Ed." She points up to the light-adorned creature looking down on us.

I laugh into my beer and then take a sip, and—oh my gosh , this is *so* much better than a Cosmo. It's smooth, juicy, and rich. The hops play over my tongue, and the faintest buzz starts up in my veins.

Maybe it's alcohol on an empty stomach.

Maybe it's the fact that Parker is now leaning on the bar with both elbows, looking at me with his incredibly gorgeous chestnut-brown eyes.

"So, you're up next," he says, in that deep, intimate tone he seems to use only with me. "Right after Annie. Got your tiara in that purse of yours?"

"No way. Not in a million years."

"The night's young," he says, his eyes dark as they lock on mine. "I'm gonna get you up on that stage."

I take another long sip of the flavorful beer. "I'll be on the floor, if I don't eat something,."

"One order of Dirty Fries, comin' up."

Before I can stop him, he leans back and shouts down the bar, so he can be heard over the crooning soprano voice now drifting toward the rafters—Annie, on the mic. "Yo, Delilah, a large, down here, when you got a sec."

I shake my head when he turns back to face me. "You might get in trouble, giving orders. Doesn't she mind getting bossed around by the temporary help?"

He shrugs. "Nah, it's cool. I help her out, she helps me."

I sink my lips down over the rim of my glass and draw in more liquid. Miraculously, I'm not fretting about *how much,* exactly, Parker and the tattooed, pretty young Delilah help one another.

How could I worry, when Parker hasn't even left the six inches of bar in front of me, despite the fact that this place is teeming with thirsty customers?

He's ignored everyone since he walked up to tend to me.

I might as well be wearing a tiara, because I feel like a princess.

"Good trip to Broad Hollow?" he asks.

"In a way, yeah."

He cocks a brow.

I don't have to lie to him. I'm learning that with Parker, I can just say it how it is, and I love that.

"I waited around for him most of the day, and then saw him come out of an elevator with this woman. And you know how you said I should just feel what's going on, instead of trying to intellectually analyze it?"

He widens his eyes playfully. "I said that? Wow."

"Not in those words exactly, but you know what I mean. You said *just feel it,* and I did. My gut knows he's with that other woman, and I think on some level, I knew the whole time."

This beer's making me chatty.

I lift it up and am surprised to see I've emptied a third of the big glass already. I take another sip. Okay, *gulp*. I've had a crazy day. All that embarrassment.

It's so good to be back in Pines Peak. Away from that fancy hotel and the stress I experienced there.

"It's kind of… weirdly refreshing," I admit to Parker, who's still listening attentively. "To stop being in denial about it. I think I've been in denial since I saw them together at that Starbucks. That time I told you about. And it takes a lot of mental energy to keep a wall up like that in your mind, holding back a truth you know, but won't let in."

"Good. It's good to try to see things like they are. Instead of how you want them to be."

"You're… wise. You know that? Not book smart like so many people are, but wise in an old man way."

He laughs. "I'm only thirty-three."

"I know, I know. You have a good perspective on things, is all I'm trying to say. You know how elderly people get, thanks to life experience? It's like you have *that.* And that's helpful. I went to lots of school, but sometimes all that learning doesn't do me much good."

"Give yourself some credit. You're doing fine. I looked up your company. Now that my phone's all charged up, figured I should use it. Pretty impressive, what you've accomplished. There were all sorts of articles…"

"I've been working hard." Too hard, maybe.

"And you were featured in a big deal documentary? Nice work."

"You should've seen me that week. I was a wreck, I was so nervous. But the filming went okay."

"Better than okay, I'd say. There were lots of articles about how good it was. How amazing *you* were."

"We did get buckets of new clients thanks to that."

I'm mid-sip when Delilah sweeps in and deposits a steaming plate in front of me. "Here are those fries." She pats Parker's arm as she squeezes behind him. "Hey, any word on that order of Labatts? We're low, out back."

"Danny's behind on deliveries," Parker says. "His wife just had the baby. He's got another guy covering, but they're way behind. Should be here tomorrow, though. If we run out tonight, let's put PBR on special instead. Tall boys, three bucks."

"Got it."

I listen to the two chat for another minute while I scrutinize the pile of food in front of me.

My scrutiny quickly changes to admiration. The cloud of scented steam coming off the thick mess of fries makes my mouth water.

"Okay, what's in this dish?" I ask Parker, once Delilah's gone.

I'd like to also ask him why he thinks he can call the shots about what beer's on special, but that particular question drifts to the back of my mind as I lift a drenched fry. It's dirty, alright. Dripping with a sauce of some kind. And down on the plate, there's a whole pile more of them, swimming in gravy, with chunks of unidentified white stuff nestled here and there.

"Try it," Parker instructs.

"I want to know what it is, first. What's this sauce? What are these chunks of white?"

He chuckles. "Would you take a risk for once? It'll be good for you."

More of that life-wisdom I just applauded him for having. Okay, he's right. I should try it without knowing every ingredient. It's not that much of a risk, and it might actually be enjoyable.

Or… heavenly.

The warm, rich flavors of chicken, savory spices, and hearty potato warm my tastebuds.

"We make 'em here," Parker says, as I reach for a second. "Local potatoes, hand-cut and deep fried. Locally-sourced chicken stock for the gravy. Even the cheese is from Pines Peak. It's a Canadian dish. The border's only fourteen miles away."

"Now you actually sound like a server extraordinaire. You could've told me all that before."

"Where's the fun in that? I wanted you to try food from a 'dive', and enjoy a pleasant surprise. Good to let life surprise you once in a while, Gem."

"Carly did describe this place as a dive, actually."

He laughs. "I bet she did. She's been in a few times. Not impressed. Probably because we don't have a coat check, and there's no valet parking."

I laugh, too. "Oh, come on. She's not stuck up."

"She's not used to simple stuff. Real gifts that aren't wrapped in fancy packages."

"Maybe you should write a self help book or something," I tease, as I swivel around to check my surroundings. It feels like Christmas Eve in here, it's so darn cozy. "She's wrong about this place though. It's really cute. Clean, vibrant, friendly, lots of character." *And crowded.* "Hey, if you need to see to other customers, go for it. I don't mean to monopolize you."

"Nah."

I laugh as I grab another fry. "You're not shooting for employee of the month, I take it."

"Delilah's got it. She'll clean up on tips, too, without me jumping in. I really just take up space back here. And these people are here all the time, they don't expect instant service. *You*, though. You're not here all the time. So I think I'm good, right here."

"Okay…"

He reaches for one of my fries and eats it before I can put up a fuss about how he shouldn't steal my food.

Not that I'm really mad. It'd just be an excuse to give him a hard time and keep his eyes on me.

Because I love that he's paying this much attention to me.

Is that wrong?

Probably.

But I'm half a beer in, now, and these fries are sending me into some kind of food high. I got badly embarrassed today but I don't feel embarrassed any more. I feel safe. And happy. And… excited.

It's the giddy feeling of anticipation that I never got, while waiting in that pristine, hushed hotel lobby for Mortimer.

I never felt one drop of anticipation there. No butterflies in my stomach, no flutter in my chest. No rushing feeling in my veins, or heat in my palms.

But now I have all of that, and it's an incredible feeling.

Parker reaches for another fry. "So…? What are you gonna sing?"

"Nope," I shake my head. "I'm sticking to my resolution of staying away from that mic." Even though it is a little, *tiny* bit tempting to take a turn.

Over by the stage, Annie's wrapped up, and a portly man in a cowboy hat is making preparations to sing.

"Howdy, folks," he says to the crowd as he untangles the wire on the mic Annie handed over to him. "Nice night we all go, here, ain't it? This one goes out to my wife, Sara-Jeanne. Honey, you're the love of my life. My light, my best friend, my rock."

Music starts up.

"That is so sweet…" I whisper to Parker.

The man starts to sing.

I do my best to mask a cringe with my beer glass. "Okay… *that* might not be so sweet."

Parker chuckles. "Told you. This is Frankie. We don't do something about it, he'll be on that mic for the rest of the night. You could save us all, Gemma."

"Why don't *you* save us?"

"I'm hard at work. See? I'm on this side of the counter."

"Ha. If this is you hard at work, I'm afraid to know what it would look like if you decided to slack off."

"Hey, if you sing one song, I'll take a half-hour off and come around this counter, sit right next to you."

"Be still my heart… I could actually sit next to you for thirty minutes?"

"You know you'd love it."

"Ha." I stuff a fry in my mouth. Because I'm hungry. And because I want to smile, but I don't want him to see me smile.

"You like the fries, don't you," he notes, before stealing another.

"I do, but unfortunately the bartender-slash-janitor is eating all of them."

"No one cooked me breakfast. And I haven't had dinner."

"No dinner?" That actually worries me. "Parker, you have to eat."

"I will. Later. We could grab a pizza from Moe's or something, on the way home. And salads. They make a mean Caesar. Dank, even, if you're hungry enough. That's what I grabbed last night. Chicken Caesar."

"Wait, last night? You were supposed to be out with Heidi last night, at the Flower Cafe."

"Sure, but that was early. Then I came here and helped out 'til close. Got home around two or three…"

"Oh." And I was so sure he'd been out so late with Heidi.

I sip my beer, hoping a little more of a buzz will soften the slight edge that's crept into my bones, at the thought of Heidi. It works. I feel a little loopy as I lean an elbow on the bar and prop my chin in it. "So…

how'd it go, anyway? Date number one, I mean. Big hit?"

"If by 'big hit' you mean total drag, then, yes."

"That's not at all what 'big hit' means."

"Ah. Well, then, no, it wasn't. It was a total drag."

Good.

The thought zips through my hazy mind.

Why? I set up that date. I wanted it to go well. I wanted it to be spectacular. Didn't I?

It's this beer. It's making my head cloudy, and I'm forgetting my priorities again, and—

Parker's holding a fork. With a ball of white stuff on it. He holds it out toward me. *He's going to feed me…?*

The sight makes all my worried thoughts evaporate. *Poof.*

"You haven't tried the cheese," he says. "It's really good. Mozzarella. Try one."

He holds the utensil over the plate. I have to lean in to wrap my lips around it.

The mozzarella cheese is incredibly fresh and flavorful—a caliber of cheese that any *Gourmet Magazine* foodie journalist could write a thousand words on.

I'm in Cheese Bliss.

It feels sort of like I'm floating on a cloud, and there could well be fairies and unicorns flitting through a purple sky around me. I moan.

Out loud.

In public.

Dear Lord, I must really be buzzed.

"Okay, that is seriously good," I admit, before taking a sip of beer. *And half of what made it so good was the fact that you fed it to me.*

I've stumbled into some sort of alternate universe where men feed women across honey-gold, wooden bars.

Where there are Christmas lights dancing around the room even though we haven't even hit Halloween yet. Where 'dirty' food tastes gourmet, and the man I've avoided for years and years and years is now the only person in the world I feel like hanging out with.

My mood is so good that even the off-key croning in the corner of the room actually sounds like good music for a moment.

Parker's glowing. Like there's a halo around him, or his skin's dusted in sparkles. Is it because he fed me cheese?

"Hey, I see what you're doing," I say, as I pat my lips daintily with a napkin. At least, I *think* it's dainty. But I'm definitely getting tipsy, and there is a chance my Tea with Queen Elizabeth manners are not quite as refined-looking as I'd like them to be. "It's the wild-caught salmon treats, but for me, it's mozzarella balls."

"Is it working?"

"Nope." *Yes. One hundred percent.*

"Yeah, it is," he says.

"Not on your life."

"You can't lie to me, Gemma."

"I can try."

"But, why? Admit it. You're attracted to me."

"I will never admit that, because it's not true. It was true, but not any more. But I'm sure there are plenty of other girls in here that'd gobble up your mozzarella balls if you wanted them to."

He chuckles. "You're cute when you lie to yourself. And I don't want other girls to eat off this fork. I want you to."

I am hungry. I didn't eat lunch. And I'm pretty sure there are actual festivals dedicated to cheese this good. I think I've seen them advertised, complete with catch phrases like 'farm fresh' and 'fun filled event for foodies'.

Plus, I can't pick up a cheese ball with my fingers. That would be very un-Tea-with-Queen-Elizabeth.

"Okay, one more. One." I hold up a finger to make my point.

He spears a chuck of cheese with the silver fork and holds it out to me.

I watch him as I take it off the fork with my lips. I blame the cheese *and* the beer I've consumed and Parker for the fact that I moan again. So good.

"I don't see how you can work on an empty stomach when you could order *this* for dinner," I say, as I grab a fry from the dwindling pile.

"I ate this every shift I worked, for like a year straight, when I first—"

"Wait, a year? I thought you just started helping out here a couple weeks back. When Glenn fired you."

"Ah. Yeah, well, I helped out before then, too."

"You should've told me that! I asked you all those questions, for your Right Match form."

Delilah approaches, counting bills while she walks. "We have some singles in the back office, do you know?" she asks Parker.

Parker eyes me. "Can you hang on for two minutes? Promise not to leave?"

"I'm not going anywhere." Not while there are still a few fries on my plate. Not while this bar is warm and cheerful, and the cabin is sure to be dark and lonely. Not while I'm this happy.

"Okay, great." He taps the bar in front of me and gives me a long look before turning and walking down the bar. He disappears through a set of swinging doors.

Delilah eyes my glass. "You up for another?"

"Maybe I should pay for this one so I'm ready to head

out in a little while. I saw there's one cab service in town. Mountain Shuttle, is that right?"

I reach for my wallet.

She holds her hands up. "I'm not taking your money. Parker would kill me."

"Why?"

She raises an eyebrow at me. "Girl…? He's not gonna let you pay. You're here with him."

"Oh, no. I'm not—he's my—I mean, we grew up together. And we used to be *together* together, like way back. Way, *way* back. Ten years ago. Now we're friends."

"I have two eyes, and believe me," she reaches over the bar to clap my shoulder, "you're a lot more than his friend."

I want to argue.

Then again, this chick looks tough, and do I really want to annoy her by protesting?

Because I know what it must look like. Me, sitting here, eating up the wisdom he imparts, laughing with him, and sliding food off of the fork he's holding.

We must look like two love-sick fools.

We're not, but no one else knows our history. We have this familiarity between us because we were in love when we were really young. A thing like that stays with you, even as you age. That's what they're seeing, Nothing else.

Right?

I munch the rest of the fries and Delilah clears my plate. A couple minutes later, Parker returns.

He hands her a stack of cash. While she fits it into the register, he makes his way back to me, ignoring a few empty glasses on the bar as he walks.

Those customers will have to wait.

He seems to only have eyes for me.

"You want another?" he asks, when he sees my drink's nearly gone.

"I'm not about to sit here drinking on my own."

"I told you I'd come around to your side, if you sing a song. I'll spend a half-hour right there." He points to the stool next to me, which is currently occupied by a guy in his early twenties.

"That seat's taken," I whisper to Parker.

He leans across the bar and puts his lips up to my ear. "I'm not afraid to fight that dude for it." I can feel his breath, warm on my ear and neck. "Also? I'm upping the anti. One whole hour."

"Sixty minutes with your company. Hm…"

"It's a one time offer. No big, bulky bar between us." He spreads his hands on the counter.

"I'm thinking…."

"Thinking about how great it'd be, to sit that close?"

"Thinking about what song I'm going to sing."

"Mariah. My vote's Mariah."

"You don't get a vote," I tell him, as I get up off my seat. I book it over toward the stage, because if I don't get there soon I might chicken out.

I reach the karaoke machine just as the portly guy holding the mic, Frankie, belts out the last few words of his song.

When he looks over at me, I wave. "Can I have a go at it?"

Assuming he'll say yes, I study the machine's screen. There are a couple different genres of music listed, and I tap the 'popular music' option. Better stick with something I know by heart, and that means pop.

But when Frankie doesn't turn up beside me to hand over the mic, I have to look back over my shoulder at him.

He frowns at me. "I still got a bunch of songs left before my turn's up."

"Says who?"

"That's how it works. Amateurs go first. Then Annie. Then me. We're the seasoned musicians. We know how to keep the crowd happy."

"I'd really like to do just one song, and then you can get back to it. Please?"

"No. Maybe later, but not right now."

No? I put my hands on my hips. "Come on, please? I just drank sixteen ounces of liquid courage, and I'm not going to be up for embarrassing myself later. It's now or never, I think. Just one song?"

"I'll arm wrestle you for it."

"For… the mic?"

He nods.

I survey his arms… which are beefy and thick. I'm not one to set myself up for failure.

"I don't think so. You'd crush me. How about a thumb war, instead?" I spent enough years in grade-school lunch rooms to know that while arm wrestling takes actual strength, thumb wrestling is more about strategy and speed.

He cocks a bushy, gray eyebrow at me as he considers my proposition. "You been practicin' or somethin'?"

I giggle. "No, I haven't been practicing thumb wrestling, on the off chance that I have to challenge a stranger at a bar. Believe me, this is not a part of my daily routine."

"You on vacation or something?"

I did mow through my to-do list today. I'm taking tomorrow off. "Yeah, I guess I am. And vacations are for doing things you don't usually do, right? And right now, for some crazy reason, I feel like singing. Maybe dancing, too."

He grins. "You got spunk, you know that? Okay, how about a duet. Classic country, I'll find us a good, old one. We'll share the mic."

Victory. I've always loved a good victory.

`I remind myself that I fought for this as he joins me by the machine to select a song, and gushes about how he's always wanted to sing with a cowgirl.

"Oh, I'm not a cowgirl," I tell him. "Nowhere close. I'm from the suburbs of Boston. "

"Ah, well." He's disappointed, for a moment. Then his face lights up. "Got an idea. Wear this." He tugs off his suede cowboy hat and hands it to me.

If I'm really doing this vacation thing, I might as well go all in.

I yank my pony-tail holder free and then jam the hat on my head, low over my brow just in time to take the mic from him.

I'm up first, so there's no time to feel self-conscious.

I hold the mic to my lips and start to sing.

Chapter 15

Parker

Delilah looks up from her work, stocking the fridge with PBR tall boys. "Is that your girl singing?" she asks, as Gemma's voice fills the bar.

I laugh. "Yeah."

"Thought Frankie was on the mic. He never lets it go, once he's on."

"That's 'cause he's never met Gemma before."

"Wow. She must be something else…"

"She is."

Delilah stands and joins me at the counter. We both watch the show going on over on the stage for a minute.

Gemma's holding the mic up at an angle, singing her heart out like she's a rockstar. Frankie's looking as though he's suddenly forgotten that good old Sarah-Jean's his wife of umpteen years.

He's clearly enamored. Gemma struts across the stage as she sings, with so much confidence, I have to chuckle again. Her hair's down over her shoulders, and she's wearing his big cowboy hat tilted sideways… and it actually looks good on her.

The crowd quieted down to listen. Plenty of heads are turned her way.

I think every single guy in this bar just realized there's a gorgeous firecracker here among us.

But those dudes are out of luck, because tonight, Gemma's all mine.

She's not tone deaf. A little off key, but her enthusiasm makes up for that. She dances over to Frankie and hands him the mic so he can sing his part, and a smattering of applause goes up for her.

Gemma's full of surprises.

One day, she's wound up so tight, I have to work to get her to smile.

The next, she's here, letting loose and having fun.

Good. I really want her to have fun while she's here in Vermont.

And I want more than that, too.

I want this thing that's sparked up between us to lead to something incredible. Something so surprising, it sweeps us both off our feet.

When she and Frankie belt out the last refrain, the mic between them and Frankie's arm around her shoulders, an honest-to-goodness applause rises up toward the rafters.

Sara-Jeanne pops up out of her seat to snap a photo of the two, which Gemma gamely poses for.

When Gemma makes her way back to the bar, she's flushed. "I can't believe I did that! That was—I don't know... Liberating."

"You made a couple fans, I think." I untie my apron and drop it on top of the cooler.

"No way. But they endured it and I'm grateful for that. There's something about singing… It's the craziest thing. It takes *actual* vulnerability. Like you're baring your soul or something. I mean, I've given plenty of scripted talks to audiences in the hundreds. That's not the same rush, at all. That was—whew."

"Catch your breath, cowgirl," I tell her.

She scrunches her brow. "What, you, with the cowgirl talk, too? Why am I suddenly putting out western vibes? Like I told Frankie, I'm east coast to the core."

I laugh as I walk over to the bar flap, lift it up, and step through. When I reach the barstool next to her, I tap the guy sitting there on the shoulder. "You mind?"

He gets up without protesting.

Good decision, dude.

I would have no problem booting him in a more direct way, if it came to that.

I settle on the puffy, worn leather, feeling lucky.

Really lucky.

I turn to face Gemma, who's angled toward me. "It might have something to do with that country duet you just fired off like you were up for a Grammy," I say as our knees touch, denim on denim. I can feel the heat of her body, and a shockwave passes through me.

There is no one else I'd rather sit next to tonight.

This girl showed up mere days ago, but she fits into this place like it's her second home. And she looks really, truly happy right now. That happy glow makes her even more attractive than usual, if that's even possible.

Her cheeks have little blossoms of pink on them, and her eyes are shining. She's still wearing Frankie's hat. It's too big, cocked over her brow, pinning her brown hair down.

I reach out and gently push the brim up an inch.

Now I can see her bright, vibrant green eyes. I can't help myself. I reach out and use my fingertips to slide her hair back behind her ear. Tingling heat passes over my fingertips, up my arm, straight into my heart. "Might be the hat, too."

"What?" She reaches up, and laughs as she pats her head. "Oh my gosh, I totally forgot I was wearing it."

"You look good with your hair down. And with it up. There isn't really a time when you don't look good."

She swivels on her seat to face the counter, then leans her elbow on it and glances over at me. "Parker's secrets of seduction, secret number three: tell her she's beautiful."

"I think I just got a peek in your playbook, too. You cast a spell over men by singing oldies but goodies."

"Slightly off key," she adds with a nod. "Gets 'em every time."

I chuckle. "Well, Superstar, what do you want to drink? If you save this seat for me—because I know another guy's gonna come up here and try to snag it—I can go grab you a refreshment."

"No way. Are you kidding me? I can't have another beer. I'm a total lightweight. One was enough, but thanks."

"Okay, no beer. I'll grab something else. You'll like it."

"You're on the clock, you know," she teases, as she taps her watch. "I get sixty minutes with you and if you leave, we start the clock back up when you return."

"Got it. Save my seat. Seriously." I make my way back through the flap, and pull two pint glasses off the shelf. Then I rummage through the side fridge and grab two bottles from the back. I pour one into each glass and add dashes of maple syrup, scoops of ice, and straws.

When I return to Gemma, she's hat free, and Frankie's ambling back toward the stage, his head-wear back in place.

Gemma gathers her glossy hair and pulls it over one

shoulder as she eyes the drinks I'm carrying. "I guess I'm not a cowgirl anymore…"

"You're whatever your heart tells you you are."

"Ha. Guru Manning. Hey, what are these? Or are you going to make me try first, analyze later?"

"I'll go easy on you this time. Don't want to push my luck." I slide a soda toward her. "Birch soda, made with—"

"Let me guess. Local bark." Without waiting, she pulls liquid up through the straw.

Those lips…

I have to really work hard to speak, not just gawk. "Yeah. Bark."

Her eyes widen. "No way! Really? I was kidding."

"Really." I nod. "Boiled, so it gets soft and releases the flavors. I added maple syrup. We call it the Tree Hugger's Special."

She giggles, lips still around the straw. "If I'm not careful, you're gonna brainwash me into tree worshiping, like you."

"I can think of worse things to worship."

"Yeah… like profit margins," she sighs.

"Hey—Superstar." I wag my leg so the side of my knee bumps hers. "Don't get down. You're doing your best like everyone is."

"Yeah… but I'm in the *rat race.* When did I get in the rat race? Do you know I haven't taken a full day off in over a year?"

"You're doing work you love."

"Yeah, I love it. But somewhere along the way, I forgot how to relax and have fun. I guess… I guess you're reminding me. I should thank you."

"Hey, I suggested you sing a little. That's all."

"It's more than that. It's… It's being here. It's the view from the log cabin, and all these leaves, and this quirky little bar with that big, furry head with the Christmas lights on the antlers. And—maybe I can't explain it. That's okay. Just—thanks, for putting up with me. I know I can be a lot, sometimes."

She twists on her stool again, and our legs collide. She leans in and squeezes my knee.

I can feel the warmth of her hand through the fabric of my pants. I rest mine over the back of her hand, letting my fingers fill the valley's between hers. And I know, in that moment, with her hand on my leg and my fingers settled over hers, that I won't let Gemma leave Pines Peak without talking to her about what's going on between us.

I think it's worth investigating.

Getting clear about a few things.

Like why, after all these years, I can still sit with her and talk like we're old friends. Why I feel *this good* around her. Why, now that we're touching like this, I don't want her to pull her hand away.

It'd be good to get clear on all that.

If we don't, she might leave, and I won't see her again—or experience *this* again—for another decade. I don't think I could handle that.

Chapter 16

Gemma

It is one o'clock in the morning.

When did it get to be one o'clock?

I've been sitting here laughing and flirting with Parker for hours, yet it feels like only minutes have passed by.

Frankie's still on the mic. My brain's adjusted to the sound of his voice. It's background noise now, like a fan on high when you're trying to sleep.

Not that I feel like sleeping.

I feel wide awake, and alive, and happy.

My beer buzz is long gone, but I'm still buzzing. The taste of sweet soda's still on my tongue.

Delilah headed out a while ago, so Parker's been splitting his time between work and chatting with me. Whenever he hops up to serve a customer, I get a minute to stop and think about what's happening.

But even when I think about it, I can't really figure it out.

I know Parker's trouble.

I know he's a serial dater, serial heartbreaker. I know he charms women, and then moves on and leaves them balling their eyes out.

Been there, done that.

But even when I take a pause to remind myself of those things, it doesn't stop me from falling right back into flirting with him when he rounds the counter again and sits down next to me.

It's late, though.

Really late.

I have an oversized, extremely warm flannel nighty waiting for me back at the cabin. Plus, Queenie. And I'm fine to drive, now that the alcohol's left my system. More importantly, if I stay here for any longer, I might do something I regret.

I know Parker won't let me pay, but manners dictate that I try anyway. So, when he returns to the stool beside me, I place my credit card down in front of him. "Hey, bartender. Think I could settle up my tab?"

"You leavin'?"

I have my purse already in my lap. I pull my fleece off the back of the stool. "Yeah, I should get to bed. Queenie's a cuddler."

"It's dark out. I'll drive us." He pushes the credit card back to me, then hops off his stool and puts his hand to his mouth. "Hey—guys!" he calls out. "We're closing early tonight. You got five minutes."

Frankie, between songs now, shouts a loud "Boo!" and his wife seconds it.

The thinned crowd stirs, sipping down the last of their drinks, wriggling into jackets.

I slip my card back into my wallet, which I tuck into my purse. "I *can* drive in the dark, you know," I say to Parker, once he's behind the bar again, but within earshot.

He collects a few empty glasses along the countertop and sets them in a sink. "I know you can, but I want to drive you home."

"You can't just close early because you feel like it. Won't you get in trouble?"

He grins as he accepts a couple dollars from a customer. "Do I look like I'm worried?" He fits the cash into the register.

"No, but *I'm* worried. This is your job now and I'd hate for you to lose it because of me."

"I won't lose it."

"You don't know that."

Around us, customers call out goodnights and goodbyes. Parker drifts toward the register again, and I watch him pull out the drawer and then disappear into the back.

By the time he comes out again, we're alone in the bar.

Parker switches off the lights by the door. Outside, I watch the tail lights of the Mountain Shuttle get smaller as it carries Pines Peaks locals toward their beds. I can make out the shuttle's cow-print paint and smell exhaust.

I stick close to Parker's side.

As we walk into the parking lot off to the side of the tavern the last of the cars pulls out.

Now the only vehicles are my Prius, across the way, and Parker's hulking truck. There are no street lights here in the lot. The sky above is dark and dusted with twinkling stars. The moon isn't up yet. I can barely make out a whisper of white, my breath, hanging in front of me as we walk. To the side, the string lights lining the bar's roofline sparkle.

When we reach his truck, he walks up to the passenger door. He opens it.

"You need a hand up?" he asks.

"That bar thing helps."

In the darkness, I see the corner of his mouth inch up. "You mean the grab bar. Yeah."

I take a step forward.

The truck's grab bar.

That's what I need to reach for.

But instead of doing what I *should* do, I hook my fingertips into the front pocket of his jeans and give a little pull.

He lets me pull him in.

My hand wanders from his pocket to his chest. The plane of his pecs is so warm and hard. The cotton of his black t-shirt is soft, thin and worn. I can feel his heart beating.

When I tilt my face up, his warm breath washes over me.

"It took you long enough," he whispers.

"It did, didn't it?"

"Man, Gem. I've wanted this." His warm, strong hand curls around my hip, and guides me closer.

"It might not be the best idea," I whisper, as my stomach flips and my heart flutters. "Because of our history, and—" I let my hand skim up toward his neck. His bare skin under my fingertips makes me want to melt into a puddle. I feel the wavy ends of his blond hair, down at the base of his neck.

I can't breathe.

His lips are inches from mine.

"Can you—can you kiss me?" he murmurs, "because if you don't, I might—"

"Might what?"

"I don't know. Go insane, I think."

"Then I better kiss you."

"Yeah," he whispers into my mouth, just before our lips touch.

I thought I found heaven earlier. In the bar, when he fed me that crazy-good cheese.

But no, that wasn't heaven.

This is it.

Right now, with his soft, warm lips pressed to mine.

Here, in this dark parking lot with twinkling lights of the bar off to the side and a sleepy country town's Main Street ten feet away.

Here, with our shoes touching and his hands on my hips, mine wrapped around his neck. Our bodies are fused together, and our mouths collide and search and taste.

As we kiss, we step backwards together.

I feel the cold, hard metal of the truck against my back. Parker's lips move against mine, and my brain, for once, isn't talking to me.

I'm feeling, Not thinking.

And the feelings coursing through me like a tsunami are delicious and delightful.

When we part, we're both breathless.

"So—the grab bar?" I stammer, as I peel myself away from the cold metal of the truck and hitch my purse on my shoulder.

He chuckles. "Yeah."

He returns to his earlier position at the passenger door and waits as I hoist myself up into my seat. Then he leans in and pulls at the seatbelt and fits it into place. He braces an arm against the console, and his thick, hard biceps flex. "You good?"

I don't know what I am.

I just kissed Parker Manning.

Tennis star. Wild child. The first guy I ever loved.

I never, ever imagined that we'd do this *again*. And it was good. So good, I still feel a buzz radiating through my body, straight down into my toes.

"Yeah, I think I am," I murmur. I'm still sort of breathless. My lips are wet, and I feel light headed.

"Good." He leans in and kisses me again.

Like this is our new normal.

And I want it to be our new normal. I reach up and fit my fingertips over the neckline of his t-shirt. Kissing him like this, I'm way more than good.

No words can describe the tingling, warm feeling that races through me, each time his lips part against mine.

With his mouth on mine, like it is right now, my world is right.

He tastes good. Like birch soda and a breath mint. A little sweet, like maple syrup. And his kiss is hungry, like he's nowhere near done kissing me.

When we part again, he tugs the zipper of fleece until it's zipped to my chin. "You cold?" he asks, still so close to me that my pulse is racing and my core has turned to fire.

I'm so far from cold, it's not funny. "Really, I'm good."

"You sure? I'll get some heat going in a sec. Tired?"

"Not really."

"Hungry?"

I reach out and place my index finger on his bottom lip. That soft, tender spot where his lip gives way to his perfect chin. "You're not my babysitter, you know."

He takes my finger from his lip and kisses the tip. "I know, baby. Just making sure you're okay."

"I can take care of myself."

"Yeah, but do you?" His brown eyes search mine, and he brushes his thumb across my cheek bone. "You're thin, Gem. You gotta eat. And you get up too early. You need sleep, too."

"I know..."

"I learned when I was training with some really good coaches, those first years I played the big tournaments. You gotta take rest days. They're as important, or more, than the days you go all out and push really hard. I know it's tempting to go hard all the time, but, believe me. It doesn't pay off."

When you get advice from a guy with two Olympic medals, you take it.

Even if he doesn't know where those medals are.

Even if he has messy, wild hair, and so many tattoos, they're hard to count. Even when he broke your heart, ten years ago.

"Thanks. I guess—I guess some food would be good." It's been hours since I consumed that plate of french fries.

"Great. I have buddies over at Moe's who will hook us up. I know we already had pizza, that night you got in. You up for a second go at it, or is that counter to some Gemma Rule I don't know of?"

"Usually, yes. Pizza twice in one week is a no-no. But I'm on vacation. Pizza sounds great. And one of those Ceasars you talked about."

He squeezes my knee. "I'll text to let 'em know we're on our way. Home, food, and bed for you. I know you must be tired." He kisses me gently and then closes the truck door.

I watch his dark silhouette walk around the hood of the massive truck, and realize that I'm glad he's driving us home. I feel safe.

Safe and cared for.

Parker settles into the driver's seat, fires up the engine, and adjusts the heating vents so they're all pointing at me. "Hey, what do you think Carly's going to say about this?"

"I'm not sure." I have an idea, and it's not all that pleasant to think about it. She warned me not to do exactly what I just did: fall into old ways.

But right now, I don't even care that she's probably going to scold me for my foolishness.

All I care about is when I'll feel his lips on mine again.

His hands on me.

When he'll whisper something to me in his deep voice that sweeps through me and makes me shiver in the best way.

Here in his warm truck, with him driving and music playing softly and dark buildings sliding past, I just don't care about my life back home. My responsibilities and reputation and future. I'm truly content and happy *in this moment*, in a way I don't often feel.

It might not last.

It *probably* won't last.

But for now, I'm going to enjoy the ride.

Chapter 17

Gemma

The last time I slept in this late, I was in the tenth grade and I had pneumonia.

It's nearing lunchtime. The puffy, moose-adorned quilt I'm nestled under feels too warm, now that sunlight's streaming through the guest room windows. I push the covers down and then reach for Queenie, who's curled up near my pillow. While I stroke her under her chin, I work on clearing cobwebs of sleep.

No, I'm not a cruise ship. That was a dream.

Catching giant squid in a net—also part of my dream.

Actual memories start to surface, and I squeeze my eyes shut. *Oh, no. Did that happen?*

Did I really make out with Parker in the Tipsy Tavern lot, and then again at home, here on the couch?

I pry my eyes open and look over at the bedroom door. It's closed. I remember leaning against it the night before, feeling ecstatic. My world felt like some kind of tilting, amusement park ride, spinning and whirling me around.

I remember climbing into bed feeling happy and giddy, almost like I was flying.

But now that it's morning—late, late morning, almost noon—I know that I wasn't close to flying last night. I was right here in this ski house in Pines Peak the whole time. The Manning's vacation house. Mitch Manning gave me the key…

I groan as I reach for my phone and dial Carly.

"So… I had a weird night," I grumble, as soon as she picks up.

If I slouch down far enough on this pillow, maybe I can escape some of the consequences that I'm sure are crowding in on me, as we speak.

Like the fact that Parker is probably somewhere in this house, right now. What happened last night is confusing enough… Now I'm freaking housemates with him, expected to drink coffee from the same pot.

Carly's laugh sounds distant. She's got me on speaker phone, I think. "That is an amazing way to start a conversation, Gemma. This is going to be good, I can tell. And I could use a good story. I just had the *worst* meeting with the District Supervisors. I swear, I almost quit on the spot. So, cheer me up, please. What happened?"

She might not laugh when I tell her.

She warned me not to fall for her brother again.

But, here we are.

"Are you alone?" I ask her.

"Yes. And now I'm thinking this is going to be *really* good—if you have to go to the trouble of verifying no one's going to overhear. What'd you do?"

"I *may* have challenged a guy to a thumb wrestling match last night. And I sang a duet—also with the same random guy. It was classic country, and I did my top-volume, pop-princess routine. The way we used to do when we performed in front of your bedroom mirror. Oh, and I ate cheese off a fork that I wasn't holding."

"Eek." She laughs. "So, you were drunk?"

Fair question.

"Only slightly buzzed, but then I sobered up." *Which makes the next part of my story even weirder.* I pause and reach for Queenie for support. She purrs as I run my palm along her back. "I also—I kissed him. Or, he kissed me. Both, I guess."

"Oh, wow, Gem, that's great! You kept saying how you'd get back together eventually. I was starting to worry that—"

"No, not Mortimer." I run my hand over my face, cover my eyes with my palm, then scrunch down farther into the too-hot quilt. *Here it comes.*

"But… you went to see him yesterday afternoon, right?" Carly asks.

"That was a total disaster. All the stuff I'm telling you about happened *after*. In Pines Peak. I decided I was on vacation, and I just wanted to have fun for a change."

"Wait… let me get this straight. The visit with Mortimer was a disaster, but thumb wrestling a random dude in a bar was fun?"

"I'm not bragging about the stuff I did. I'm confessing."

"Okay, so who did you kiss? The guy you thumb wrestled?"

"We never actually wrestled. And, no."

"Okay, then the guy you did the duet with?"

"Nope. That was the same guy, like I said." I bite my lip and consider burrowing so far under the bulky quilt that I won't be able to hear Carly scream when she puts two-and-two together.

But I called her, and I won't be a coward about this.

I need her advice, and the only way I'll get it is if I come clean.

I fidget with the edge of the quilt as I wait. A second later I have to hold the phone away as she squeals. "*You and my brother?*"

"Er… yeah. It's not that big of a deal. It was just—I—like I said, I wanted to have fun."

"Nooo! I told you not to do that! What were you thinking?"

"It's not as bad as it sounds. I have—I think I have reasons. Better reasons than that thing about being on vacation. That's sort of the truth, but not the whole truth."

"Do *not* tell me he's hot. I don't want to hear it. I'm going to plug my ears, which is dangerous because I'm going forty-five on Charles Ave."

Parker *is* hot.

Tall, built, gorgeous face.

But last night was about a lot more than physical attraction.

Which is… confusing.

If it was just physical, that'd be one thing. Maybe the kisses we finally shared would've burst the bubble of tension hanging over this cabin like a geodome. But it wasn't only about chemistry.

I looped my fingertips into the pockets of his jeans and pulled him toward me because he's thoughtful. He makes me laugh.

He's intelligent, in a way I never saw in all the grad school lecture halls I've sat in.

He's generous and a good coach and a good person, I think.

On the other end of the line, Carly starts a rant about

how all of her friends turn into fan-girls around her brother. "... and I thought it was bad enough when he was all over the press… But now it's like it's even worse. Like, now that he's not technically *as* famous, he's more approachable or something. I thought you were smarter. I thought you'd learned. The hard way."

"I haven't turned into a fan-girl," I promise. "This is more than that. I think we're—" I want to try to put it into words—how we've rekindled something real that never died, for either of us.

But Carly won't let me. "He's a *flirt*, Gemma. Not just with you. He does this with women because he's full of himself and thinks that just 'cause he went pro, he's God's gift to the female population. But he *never* gets serious and *you*—you're serious. By nature, like it's hardwired into you or something. You've been that way since we were little. Life's one big joke to Parker, but that's not the way you are… And I care about you, and I don't want to see you get hurt. *Again.*"

Oof.

Her statements penetrate the fuzzy, love-struck feeling that was starting to settle around me. "That hurts."

"Yeah, but it'll hurt more if you let this get out of control. Do I need to come up there and drag you back to the city? Because I will."

"No, no. Don't do that." Queenie rolls to her side, and I stroke her belly. "I'm fine. Maybe I just need to get some space today, to try to process what happened."

"Um, yeah… you think? Dude, you should definitely get some space."

That might be sort of hard, since I can now hear him out in the kitchen.

I want to ask my best friend how I should handle the

living situation, which is complicated, to say the least. But I'm not sure if I should tell her that Parker's here.

I cast my eyes toward the door and wonder how I'm going to make it through breakfast without walking straight up to him for more of what we did last night. As I listen to him clang pots and pans around, I close my eyes.

A vision of just-woke-up Parker sparkles behind my eyelids. Tousled hair. Relaxed, sleepy smile.

"Okay, you're hiding something big," Carly quips.

"Er—me? No…" I pick at a hem in the quilt. "Fine. Maybe. What if I told you… he's here…?"

"What, at the log cabin, with you? Wait… did you guys—"

"No! We didn't spend the night together, in the same bed. He's in a different bedroom. He's—" My nail scrapes the frayed thread. Maybe I shouldn't tell her this.

But she's my best friend and I need her help. "He's sort of… staying here. Under the radar. Your parents don't know, and he said he's hoping it'll stay that way."

"He's staying at the log cabin? Like, living there?"

"I think so. Temporarily. That's what I understand of the situation, anyway."

"First of all, what are you thinking? You're the therapist, Gem. I shouldn't have to tell you how much it can mess with a woman's head to spend time alone with her ex. Anyone in your shoes would slip into old ways. Get out of there. Book yourself a hotel. Better yet, kick him out. He has a house. Or, trailer, or whatever. He should sleep there."

"He can't. It's uninhabitable."

"Hm?"

"He can't sleep there. That's what he said. Something to do with noise."

"Yeah, I doubt that. It's more likely that he uses the cabin whenever he wants, even though Dad would be *so* mad. Which brings me to my second point: Dad's always said he doesn't want us to be spoiled. He wants us to make our own way, not mooch off him and mom, and the hard work they put into making what they have now. I can't believe Parker's using that place as his crash pad. I'm telling Dad."

"No—wait. Not yet. Let me look into the trailer situation, first. I've been wanting to do that anyway."

She heaves a sigh. "Fiiine. It's not fair, though. I grew up, and he never did. I can't believe he's living at the cabin… probably eating cereal and watching cartoons all day. He's a Man Child, is what he is."

My stomach drops. The amusement park ride I was on last night is now plummeting toward earth. *Did I kiss a Man Child last night?*

A guy who's technically nearing middle age, but still crashing at his parent's vacation house?

I want to argue that Parker doesn't eat cereal and watch cartoons all day, but… what do I know?

I've been in Pines Peak for a few days.

That's it.

I don't know what's really going on in Parker's life, besides the fact that he can't live in the structure he calls home, and he's a bartender who doesn't even know how to mix a cocktail.

I'm here to try to help him. Instead I drank with him and then made out with him near his truck in a dark, empty parking lot like we were two teenagers.

Time to put your big-girl pants back on, Gemma, I tell myself, as I get off the line with Carly.

I am going to take the day off from normal work stuff. It's good for me, this mini-vacation. I need it. I understand that now that I have a solid eight hours of sleep under my belt. Also, Parker's words of wisdom last night landed. He was a pro athlete, and he knows what he's talking about.

I was pushing my limits, and it wasn't healthy.

At best I was heading for chronically high blood pressure and an incurable caffeine addiction. At worst, I was heading straight for burn out. The kind of burn out that includes a weird collapse in a public place, an ambulance ride to the ER, and IV infusions plus bedrest.

Slowing my pace a little definitely feels right.

But just because I'm veering away from the routine of emails, meetings, and managing my team, that doesn't mean I have to actually laze around all day. Self-care can also mean getting fresh air, exercise, and maybe even a little snooping.

It's the snooping part that sounds the most fun, actually.

I'm going to do some honest-to goodness research today, with regards to Parker's life situation.

What is actually going on at his mobile home? I wonder, as I brush my teeth.

Back in the guest room. I tug leggings on and then lace up my running shoes.

Did he make up the noise issue thing, like Carly thinks, or is it legit?

And if it's legit… what is making the noise?

I ease the guest bedroom door open, peek left and right, then tiptoe down the hall.

I wince as the rubber sole of my sneaker squeaks against the floor. The door's latch clicks under my thumb, and I step out into the brisk, sun-streaked fresh air.

Once the front door is securely closed behind me, I bend my knee so I'm gripping the toe of my right foot. The stretch makes my quad burn.

I put my left leg through the same torture, then start down the road at a slow jog. I know from the maps on my phone that the Tipsy Tavern—and therefore my car—is four miles away. Most of it is down hill. I haven't jogged in ages, and this will be good for me.

Chapter 18

Gemma

It's cool out this morning, with a few clouds up in the sky that make the sun land in patches on the pavement. A few golden leaves twirl down onto my path, but I don't bother trying to catch them like I used to do when I was a kid.

Back then, I'd say a wish whenever I caught a leaf. I still do that on rare occasions, now that I'm grown. But this morning, I don't trust myself enough to even try to form a wish.

I'd probably wish for something stupid.

Like another night on that big, overstuffed couch, with the fire crackling and Parker's arms wrapped around me.

Each time we kissed last night, more of my reservations fell away.

All those inner protests—they twirled away from me like these leaves falling around me. And that left me bare and raw and vulnerable. More vulnerable than when I was standing on that stage, singing Karaoke.

What if Carly's right, though, and this is just fun and games to Parker?

I know Carly's hard on her brother. It's natural for siblings to be like that with each other. Competitive, even unfairly harsh.

I don't want to make judgements about Parker's life unfairly, like Carly seems to do. I'd rather collect more facts.

By the time I reach Main Street, my legs are burning and my throat is parched. I unzip the hip pocket on my leggings, pull out my key, and unlock my Prius. After tucking myself into my car, I reach for the water bottle I left on the front seat.

I sip down cool water as I drive slowly through town.

Near the library, I pull over to punch the address Mitch gave me into my phone while I still have Wifi. I have a feeling that by the time I reach Parker's trailer I won't be able to get online, so I take a screenshot of the map and save it. Then—because the icon is right there, so easy to tap—I pull up my work email.

There are a few messages I feel totally fine about ignoring until tomorrow. But one demands a swift response. It's from Mark. I dial his number.

"How's the skiing?" he asks.

"It's too early for that. No snow."

"Oh. In my head, it's always snowing in Vermont."

"Yeah, well, it's still leaf peeping season." I peer up at the treetops across the road, which are ablaze with color. The pavement is sprinkled with golden leaves, and there are piles on the lawns of the houses that line the streets. On this quiet, narrow, leaf-strewn road, the hubbub of Cambridge feels very far away.

"What's up?" I ask. "I saw your message that said urgent."

"Yeah, so, I had a strange call. Figured I should run it by you, sooner rather than later. Remember Jocelyn?"

"Of course." Jocelyn Radner was an employee of mine for a couple years. She used the Right Match process to find her own Mr. Right. These days, as far as I know, they're happily married, living on the South Shore and expecting baby number one.

Besides Carly, Jocelyn's the only one of my acquaintances who knows that me and Mortimer are on a break. The day he broke up with me over croissant sandwiches at Au Bon Pain, I returned to the office and holed up in the restroom and cried. Only for ten minutes. Enough time for Jocelyn to come in, use the loo, and then ask me if I was okay.

And I was just upset enough to come clean about what had occurred. I asked her to keep it under wraps, of course. Even at that early point I knew I didn't want the public to know that me and Mortimer were on the fritz.

As far as the public's concerned, my romance with Mortimer is proof that my Right Match system works.

I feel my palms start to sweat. "She's expecting that baby of hers any day now, I think," I say, before sipping down water to cool my tight throat.

His unexpected mention of Jocelyn makes me nervous. I suppose I always wondered if she might come out of the woodworks and blab to the press about how me and Mortimer split.

"She's called a couple times yesterday," Mark says. "She says she has something important to talk to you about. Teagan told her you were out of town for the week, and I said the same. But she insists she needs a word with you. She asked for your private cell number. What do you think—want us to give it to her?"

"I appreciate you checking with me, first." I watch a

car pass by my window without really seeing it. *What does Jocelyn want?* "Um…yeah, I guess you can give her my cell number. I better see what this is about. She didn't tell you?"

"Not a word. Said she wanted to talk to you directly."

"Okay… thanks, Mark."

"You betcha. Enjoy those leaves."

One swirls down and lands on the windshield. I lick my lips. "Yeah… I will. Thanks again."

It's weird, being a public figure.

I run a company that's gaining in popularity. I have social media accounts, followers, and email subscribers. I get interviewed in print and on video. I have to keep up a certain act. And that act—for me, at this point in my life—includes being totally tightlipped about my split with Mortimer.

As far as all those people know, we're in happy-couple la-la land, me reading over his manuscript to give him pointers, him cooking me Sunday Brunch.

I shouldn't have been so loud about how I used the Right Match process in my own life. I should've kept my private life private.

It's a little late for that, I think, as I cruise down a narrow paved road. When it turns to dirt, a little cloud of dust kicks out behind the car.

How did my love life get so confusing?

The thing that makes me feel like an idiot is that I basically studied love in graduate school. I completed a master's thesis titled '*Emotional Attachment, Romantic Love, and Marital Longevity*.' I felt so special when the Graduate Council applauded my opinions. They even encouraged me to publish the paper.

So, it is published now.

Anyone can find it and read pages and pages of my

fancy, intellectual-sounding ideas about what it takes to create a strong marriage in our modern society.

I brake for a doe who takes her sweet time crossing the road. While stopped, I bend over the wheel and rest my head on the cool leather.

I'm such an idiot.

I wrote about emotional bonding.

As if I knew—really knew—what I was talking about.

The doe bounds into a field of rust-colored shrubbery and long, wispy tan grass. *I didn't know anything*, I realize as I press my foot to the gas again.

Now I'm driving down a country road with fire-orange leaves blazing around me, realizing that all those words that I so carefully researched were really just letters, strung together. No meaning behind them.

It was all fluff.

Nonsense.

Gibberish.

I didn't know *anything*, because I was so busy stuffing down the only experience of love I'd ever known. That was with Parker.

If I really wanted to write about 'emotional bonding' I'd have written about the Wayland Bird Sanctuary. The way I felt with my head resting on Parker's chest that night, pouring out all my dreams to him and listening to him talk about his own. That night, it was like our souls were mixing, red food coloring and blue in one glass of water, turning the whole thing purple.

I remember listening to his heartbeat that night.

The dirt road I'm traveling down takes an abrupt hairpin turn. Then another, the other way. The zig-zagging continues for two miles, and with each passing minute I'm driving higher up into the mountain at the edge of town. At a bend in the road I catch sight of the small downtown area, far below.

The trees are a bit shorter up here. The rocks are bigger. The sky's more expansive.

I spot a mailbox with the white numbers painted on the side: 17. This must be Parker's place.

I haven't seen another house for a long time. The last one was a mile back, and had two beautiful horses out front.

I nose my way up the driveway, until a small mobile home comes into view.

It's framed by the most beautiful view I've ever seen in my life. Pines Peak Mountain rises up, towering and majestic. Beyond the mountain's rocky slope, there's a sea of green, blue, and lavender rolling hills that cascade out toward the distant horizon line.

Birds swoop through the air above me. Two spotted fawns nibble grass over by a few wispy saplings.

There's a gated area out front of the structure, and the fence line winds around the side yard, too. A lone motorcycle is parked in the dirt driveway.

Is it Parker's?

He hasn't said anything about owning a Harley, but then again, he also never told me that he owns a property with a view so picturesque, I want to take out my phone right now and snap a million photos.

The metal hinges along the gate creak as I open it. A bunny hops away from me as I walk up a stone path that leads to the front door. I knock, with no response. The door handle jiggles a little side to side, but won't turn all the way. Locked.

This place is so *Parker*. Simple. Unpretentious. No fancy trappings. So peaceful, I'm already thinking about suggesting to him that he run meditation retreats out of his backyard for a little extra cash.

I watch the sweet fawns as I make my way into the side yard. They seem to be under the place's spell as much as I am. One nuzzles the other's neck.

Good vibes. This place is doused in them.

I feel lulled by the beauty around me. Which is probably why it takes me a minute to catch onto the fact that a dog's booming bark is now emanating from within the trailer.

A dog?

My brain glitches, momentarily.

Parker doesn't have a dog.

Does he?

I'm too busy trying to smooth that brain-wrinkle to register the movement of a curtain in one of the trailer's back windows. But my survival instincts kick in when a flappy strip of rubber on the back door pushes out, and a big, boxy dog head barrels through.

The head seems to fill the doggy door, it's so big.

The body that follows is even bigger.

I've never seen a dog this big. He has black, pointy ears and a black nose, and the rest of him is tan. He's muscular, too. Something about my survival instincts puts his bounding forward movement into slow motion. I can see every ripple of his fur as he barrels toward me, like I'm watching a nature show.

Everyone knows that nature shows are violent when you least expect it.The videographer pans over a herd of antelope, and you think: *isn't that sweet, all those antelope, so peacefully grazing.* Then, *bam*! Lion attack.

Right now, I'm the antelope.

A lion's flying through the air, drool glistening in long

strings on either side of his face. His barks fill the air around us. I do what any good antelope would do. I run.

My legs are sore from my jog earlier, and the fact that I'm petrified doesn't help my coordination either.

I curse at myself as I fumble with the gate's latch in the front yard. My hands are numb and feel clunky and it takes me three tries to get the gate to open. I'd try to close the thing behind me, if it wasn't for the fact that I somehow managed to get my long-sleeve shirt snagged on the hook-mechanism.

I frantically tug the fabric of my shirt. It stretches and rips, but not enough to be free of the hook.

In my periphery, I can see the dog closing in on me, no longer slo-mo. He's in real-time now, which means that even as I tug my outer layer up over my head and then leave it hanging on the gate, I know it's too late.

I'm screwed.

Even more screwed when my sneaker makes contact with a rock I definitely didn't see, and I fly through the air.

The heels of my palms dig into the dirt as I land, and start burning instantly. Same is true of my knees, which probably made actual dents in this hard-packed ground.

I manage to roll to my back in time to see the dog bound through the gate, a big grin on his slobbery face. He's probably thrilled to be free of the gated yard, about to attack an actual intruder.

Which I am, I suppose.

I trespassed. This is my punishment. The impending attack is fair, and also brutal.

I register the fact that he's a Great Dane as he nears. From somewhere behind him, I hear a man's voice. "Mopsey? Mopsey, girl!"

The dog—Mopsey?—ignores the call.

She continues flying through space, until she reaches me and sticks her nose down toward my face.

This is it.

I'm about to find out what it feels like to have my face chomped by a slobbery Great Dane.

I throw my arms up over my face to try to protect myself. A warm, wet tongue slurps up the salty layer on my skin, thanks to my run.

This dog is licking me like I'm a popsicle.

"Mopsey, girl! Would you quit it already? You're embarrassing me and yourself. When I call you, you should come!"

I pry one eye open and peer through the space between my forearms. A man's face appears, wreathed by the partly-cloudy sky.

"Hey there," he says. A hand appears as he extends it out to me. "Sorry if this girl scared ya. She's a big goof. Need a hand?"

He pulls me up.

I didn't die.

My hands sting and my heart's thumping way too fast, but at least I'm breathing.

"Randy," the guy says with a smile. "You are…?"

"Gemma Lafferty."

I suppose that doesn't mean anything to him. He cocks his head. "Lost or something? You're sort of far from town."

"No, I'm—um—investigating. I mean, I'm a friend of Parker's."

He rubs his chin. "A lady friend of Parker's. Investigating, you said?"

"He mentioned a noise complaint. It's a long story, but basically I have a duty to figure out what's going on."

"A duty…!" His stubble covered chin lifts to the sky as

he tilts his head back to laugh. "Love it. Love it. That guy, man, he gets into the craziest jams. Leave it to him to get a girl up here, scoping out his digs. Checking on his story. What, you didn't believe him?"

I'm not laughing along with him.

I'm too busy leaning over to brush off my knees, one of which is exposed due to a hole in my leggings. Is that blood?

Mopsey gets up off her haunches and sniffs the spot. I have to give her a gentle nudge away so she doesn't treat my exposed, bloody flesh to more consuming-a-popsicle-style licks.

"I don't know what to believe," I admit to the still-chuckling Randy. "I'm here to see for myself."

He pats his chest. "You're looking at his noise complaint, babe. Here I am—a five foot nine noise-maker. It's the snoring that got to him. Guy gives up his couch for me, and I thank him by making a sound like a chainsaw every night. I felt real bad when he said he wasn't getting sleep. Made me wonder if maybe that's why my wife kicked me out, too. Food fer thought, you know?"

I narrow my eyes at him. "So, are you his room mate or something?"

"For now. 'Til Lydia lets me back in the house. *If* she lets me back in the house. We're trying to work it out."

"Hunh." I swipe the heels of my palms on my tank top in an attempt to ease the burning. It doesn't work. "This *is* food for thought. Thanks for filling me in, Randy."

"Any time, Jamie."

"Gemma."

"Right. Hey, you gonna see your man today? Tell him I won't need his help unloading the truck at the worksite later, like I thought. He's been a real trooper, helpin' me out so much. It's a good guy you got on your hands,

Gemma. Good guy. One of the best. Treats his friends like gold."

"Will do," I promise.

"Oh, and, maybe I better ask you this, even though those bright pink sneakers you got on make me think you're not from around here. Think you can keep that bit about me and Lydia quiet? Folks around here get hold of gossip like that, neither of us will hear the last of it."

"You got it."

I know a thing or two about wanting to keep a split-up hush-hush. I shake Randy's hand—*ow, ow*—and then pet Mopsey on the head before making my way to the car. Even pouring water over my palms doesn't ease the tingling pain.

By the time I get back to the heart of Pines Peak, I'm regretting a couple things.

For starters, I really wish I didn't give Parker a hard time about his housing situation. He's helping a friend through a crisis, for heaven's sake. That's honorable.

Secondly, I really wish I didn't trip on that rock and superman onto a dirt driveway.

Third, I fervently regret not starting my day with at least one cup of coffee.

I might have a vague plan forming about breaking my addiction to jitter juice, but it's never a good idea to go cold turkey. Better to ease off gradually, right?

I consider stopping at the Steaming Mug for a cup, but the sight of Parker's black truck in the Tipsy Tavern lot makes me turn in. It's hard to believe it, but more than coffee, I actually want to see Parker.

Maybe he's becoming an addiction, too.

Thoughts of him fill my mind as I head for the bar's front doors.

Chapter 19

Gemma

A 'closed' sign hangs on the front of the Tipsy Tavern, but I suspect Parker's inside so I push the door open.

"Hello?" Slightly-sour fumes of last-nights beer spills greet my nostrils.

Delilah's head pops up from behind the bar. "We're closed," she says, before recognition flashes on her face. "Oh, you. Parker's girl. He's in the back."

She has a cardboard box in her hands. She pulls a few beer cans out of it and sets them on top of the bar, then goes about breaking down the box.

She's acting like I should just let myself in through the swinging double doors I saw her and Parker go through last night, but I hesitate by the flap in the bar anyway. "Okay if I…"

"Come on back. Make yourself at home."

I lift the section of polished wood. "Hey, question for you, if you have a sec." The thick, rubber mat under my sneakers is slightly sticky. It smells like Pine-Sol back here, and soap.

Delilah arches a brow. "Yeah?"

"I thought Parker was just helping out around here. So, why is it that he was the one to go get the cash last night? And why is he in the back right now, anyway? And why does he know all about the next beer delivery?"

"That's three questions."

"I know, but… please?"

She grabs another cardboard box, peels back the top, and starts unpacking more beer cans. "He handles the cash because it's his cash. He's in the back making next week's schedule. He knows about beer deliveries because he sets them up. He owns this place. He's the boss."

My jaw drops.

I'm entirely too caffeine deprived to bother lifting it back up.

She shakes her head. "You really didn't know that?"

I can't answer her. I want to, but my type-A self is too busy getting hot and bothered about the fact that Parker's currently writing a schedule.

I love schedules.

"Ah… great," I manage at last. "Okay. Thanks for filling me in. Anything else I should know? Does he have an ex-wife and kids I don't know about, or a prison record?"

She snorts. "Man, you're hard on him."

"I'm best friends with his little sister. Thanks to sibling rivalry, I get heavily biased reports on what he's up to, here in Pines Peaks."

"I have an older brother, so I get it," she says with a grin. "You're in luck, though. I've known Parker for years. No ex-wife, no kids, no jail record. You know about the animal shelter, right?"

I narrow my eyes into little slits. "What, now?"

"He started one. It's over on second street. I volunteer there once a week. You should check the place out. Plus, he's got two apartment buildings on the east end of town. Low income housing, for the working class. There was a real housing crisis before he came to town, but he basically fixed it. I rent from him, too."

Holy cow.

If Carly only knew.

The Black Sheep of the Manning family isn't hiding out here in Pines Peak, getting into trouble and making mistakes like they all think.

He's here starting animal shelters and fixing housing crises.

Now I really am speechless. I hobble toward the doors, attempting to fit Animal Saver and Good Samaritan into my working description of who Parker Manning is.

It's a little tough, thanks to all the suspicions I've harbored over the years. It's a big jump, from Man Child Mega Flirt to Landlord-slash-Saint.

Delilah's voice flits toward me. "Hey, did you get in a fight or something?"

"Nope." I push through the swinging doors.

"Okay, well, tell him to remember I need next Friday off!" she calls.

In a daze, I walk down the tight hallway, toward the only door in sight. It's open and the scent of coffee wafts out.

Parker's seated in a leather chair, facing a computer.

An actual computer.

I didn't even know he was capable of using one. His big, strong hands rest on the keyboard, and he types like he knows how to type. Not finger-pecking. He's fast.

Why does the fact that he knows how to type make my stomach feel like it's a jar filled with fireflies?

I stand in the door quietly for a second or two, just watching him go. Plenty of girls have drooled over Parker's agility on the tennis court. I might be the only one to get this swoony over his typing speed.

When he swivels to face me, I give him a tentative smile. "Morning."

"Afternoon, actually, sleepy head." His brow pinches when he spots the hole in my legging, then my pink, scraped hands. He stands up and walks over to me.

I can't even stress about how to handle this first, post-kiss interaction, because the next thing I know, he's wrapping his arms around me. "Gem, what happened?" he asks, mid-bear-hug.

"*Mrrm im wvva mog*," I say into his sweatshirt.

"What?"

I pull my lips away from his chest. "Run in with a dog. Mopsey. Up at your trailer. Well, running *from* her is more like it."

Then I bury my face back into his sweatshirt. He smells good. Clean and manly and faintly of the coffee I so badly crave. His arms are strong, holding me.

"You were up at my trailer?" His fingertips glide over my hair as he smooths down stray strands. I feel the softest, sweetest pressure on the top of my head when he lowers his lips to my hair for a quick kiss.

"I wanted to see for myself if you had a rat problem," I admit.

"Take your pants off."

"Excuse me?" I yank away from him, and heat rushes up into my cheeks. Even though I haven't yet consumed a drop of the coffee in the pot on one side of his desk, I feel jitters jolt through me.

I give his chest a little push. "*What* did you just say? *No!*?"

He laughs. "Relax. Not like that." Then he turns and crouches over a duffel bag near the wall. When he hands a pile of silky maroon fabric up to me, I get it.

Shorts. He's handing me shorts.

Right.

No reason to have a heart attack. I've had a rough enough day as it is.

"You can't just tell a girl to strip like that, out of the blue," I quip, as I hold the shorts up, judging the size. "A little context would help."

When I glance over at him, I find that he's looking down at me like I'm the most delightful interruption he could ever ask for.

Like I'm beautiful.

"Would you turn around, at least?" I ask, pretending to be annoyed by his stare.

But I'm not.

At all.

I love when he looks at me like this.

His eyes hang on mine for another long minute, but then he swivels around and starts working over by the coffee pot, readying a mug and filling it. "Did you meet Randy?"

"Yeah, but I met Mopsey first. I thought, for a minute, that she was going to snarf my face. As in, with her teeth. I tripped and ate dirt. But then she just gave me a bath with that huge tongue of hers. I'm now covered in sweat and drool."

"Wow, sweat *and* drool. That's so attractive, Gem. Lucky me."

"Tough cookies. You get what you get. Unless you have a shower in this magical office of yours, too?"

"No shower. But I do have a first aid kit."

"You could've given me better hints about what was going on up at your place—which is beautiful, by the way." I have my leggings peeled down, now. The silky fabric of his athletic shorts feels like liquid against my skin.

I pull the drawstring tight and loop it into a double bow.

When I look up, he's facing me.

"I didn't say you could turn back around," I tell him, with a fake scowl.

"My office. My rules." He hands me the mug of coffee. "Figure you might need this, since you left this morning without breakfast. I made you a burrito and everything. Egg whites, spinach, all the healthy, girl stuff."

"Oh, sure, girls are the only ones concerned about nutrition. Says the man with an eight-pack." I slurp down a sip of rich coffee, and silently decide to put off my experiments in caffeine-weaning for another year. Or two. Or five.

Parker sets a white lunch box on the desk. He opens the plastic container's lid and I see rows of Bandaids and ointments. Ah, yes. It's that first aid kit he mentioned.

"For a sec I thought you packed that burrito for me," I say, before taking another long sip.

"It's back home, in the fridge. You could've asked me for a ride to your car, you know." He sets a few Bandaids and a tube on the side of the desk, and then douses a wad of paper towel with sterile saline from a bottle. "Sit."

I lower myself down into the chair, doing my best to ignore the way my dirt-packed skin protests against the movement.

"I know, but I was sort of—" I watch warily as he presses the wet towels to my scrapes. Instead of hurting, the cool dampness eases some of the pain. "Thanks. I was sort of… nervous about seeing you, I guess."

"Why?" He looks up at me with his gorgeous chestnut-brown eyes. There's no playful sparkle dancing in his irises. The pools of brown are dark and sincere. "This isn't our first rodeo, Gem. We've done this before."

"Not for a long time. We're both different people, now. Grown up. And I don't—" I bite my lip and suck in a breath.

I don't know how to say this, for one thing.

I also don't know why I'm talking this much.

We kissed a couple times.

It's not a big deal until I make it a big deal.

My mouth keeps moving, though, and words spill out in a rush. "And I don't usually do things like this, Parker. Hooking up, for me, isn't ever just for fun. It always *means* something, and I'm afraid that maybe it doesn't mean the same thing to you that it means to me."

He presses dry towels over my scraped knee. Peels back the papers on a bandaid. Carefully squeezes ointment onto the little pad of gauze on the backside of the bandage, and then smooths it over my wound.

Why is he being so quiet?

What is he thinking?

I said too much.

Way too much.

He's probably regretting what we did last night. Right now, he's wondering how he can get his needy, overbearing ex out of his office. He's wondering how he can let me down softly, because I'm Carly's friend and he doesn't want her to slap him in a few months, when the Manning's all get together for Christmas.

Way to go, Gemma.

Way to freaking pull him to you after a fun, carefree night, and then make it into something as wide and tall as the mountain towering at the edge of town.

It was just a couple kisses.

But, at least I voiced my truth, as ugly and dorky as it may sound. I really don't hook up just for fun. I don't even know what that would feel like.

Parker seems to be some sort of expert, though. I need him to know that I'm not up for some meaningless fling. That's not how I roll. It's not how I'm wired, as Carly so directly pointed out to me on the phone a few hours ago.

He runs his thumb over the bandage, working it so it's securely sealed to my skin.

"Say something," I whisper.

"Gemma…" He stops working the Bandaid and looks up at me again. "I would never have kissed you unless it meant something to me, too."

My breath hitches.

He rocks back on his heels. "We both fell in love, back when we were younger. We both know how intense it was. You think I'd just mess around with you, knowing how deep this connection is?"

"If it's—" Shoot, why is it this hard to speak?

I gulp, trying to swallow the lump in my throat. My vocal cords are tight. My lips twist into a frown, and my chin starts to quiver. "If our connection was that deep, why did you break it off?"

Hot, wet tears glisten in my eyes.

Now I understand the frown that's taken my lips hostage. I lift the back of my hand and press it to my nose. Great, now I'm covered in sweat and drool, and I'm turning into a crying, runny-nose mess.

I can't help it, though.

All the vulnerability and rawness I've let myself share with Parker for the past twelve hours worked away layers of defenses. All that's left right now is hurt.

"I l-loved you, and you loved me, and you left." My voice shakes, and tears spill over my lower lids and snake down my cheek.

He gently parts my knees and fits himself inside. He reaches up to swipe his finger along my cheek, drying a tear. "I left because I had to. You were so smart. So driven. So *young*. You had everything in front of you. The college scholarships. The potential. The big plans. And I had big plans, too. I wanted to go big with my tennis playing. I couldn't see how we'd make it all work. I wanted you to have everything you dreamed of."

"But I didn't have *you*. And you were what I wanted." More tears stream down my cheeks. His fingers can't move fast enough to clear them away, but he tries. Soon he's cupping my wet face with his palm.

"Gem, I swear, I didn't want to hurt you. I wanted you to be happy."

"It did. It hurt."

"I'm sorry."

He's sorry.

That's what I needed to hear. I didn't know how badly I needed to hear it, until right this instant.

"You are? Really?"

"Really. What can I do?"

I sniff, and press the back of my hand to my nose again. "A… a tissue would be good, I think."

He leans forward, reaching past me to his desk. It's sort of a Twister-type reach, seeing as he's sitting in front of me. The contact of his chest bumping against me helps, somehow, like maybe our hearts are lining up. And when he returns to his haunches with a roll of paper towel in his hands and a devastated look on his face, a smile breaks through my tears.

"This is all I got," he says like he's completely disappointed in himself. "At least they're not the cheap paper towels. They're soft. But if you want, I'll go out right now and buy twenty boxes of tissues."

I take the roll from him and pull a few free. "This is fine." I dab my cheeks, and more lightness creeps into my chest, totally unexpectedly; sun peeking out through clouds after a burst of rain.

"You sure?"

I sniff and pat under my eyes. "Yeah. I'm sure. Maybe I just had to get that off my chest."

I lay a hand over my heart to emphasize the point, and something about the gesture feels off.

With a start, I realize what it is. My fingers crawl along my collarbones and behind my neck, but I don't feel the chain of the necklace I always wear.

I swear under my breath. "My ring. The one my great-gran gave me…"

"What's up?"

"I wear this ring on a chain…"

"Yeah, the silver one, on the silver chain. I've seen it. Family heirloom, right?"

"From my great-grandmother." My fingertips scramble down along my tank top neckline, feeling for any hint of the jewelry. "Shoot, it must have come off when I was up at your place running from Mopsey. My shirt snagged on the gate. I love that ring…"

Parker, still crouched between my legs, pulls out his phone. "If you love it, we'll find it. Even if it means getting a search party going up there." He rests an elbow on my leg, holds his phone to his ear and listens as it rings.

His arm on my leg feels heavy and warm. He's so close I can smell mint on his breath.

"Hey Randy," he says into his cell, a minute later. "Got a favor to ask you. Can you go out to the gate and take a look around? My friend… yeah, her, she's missing a necklace that means a lot to her. It's a chain with a ring on it."

As he talks, I'm busy forming a strategy for finding my precious jewelry.

It's soothing to dwell on the logistics of getting my ring back. I'm good at making plans, and switching over to problem-solving mode feels familiar and comforting.

Re-igniting my relationship with Parker: not so comforting.

Exhilarating, yes.

In the way that bungee jumping or paragliding are probably exhilarating.

Like, 'I might crash and burn soon, isn't this fun!'.

With his body fit snugly next to mine and his arm resting heavy and warm on my leg, I feel like we've stumbled back into couples territory, somewhere between my crying and his apology. Could it have happened, that fast?

What does it mean, us sitting like this—*this* close? This intertwined?

When Parker gets off the line, I bounce up out of my seat.

I'm patched up, and I should probably leave his office.

I don't know what will happen for me and Parker—which is beyond scary, to my control-freak of an ego. But I know how to retrace my steps to his trailer and scour the ground next to that gate.

"I'm going to go do a little searching for myself," I say, before drawing in a big dose of coffee.

"If you give me a couple minutes to finish up this spreadsheet, I'll drive us," Parker says. "I think staff will kill me if I don't send this schedule out this afternoon, but it won't take me long to wrap it up."

"Hey, that reminds me. Delilah said she needs next Friday off. Oh, and Randy said he's all set and doesn't need help unloading his truck later." I hesitate as I slip into an internal debate.

The scared part of me wins, so I gather my purse. "Thanks for offering to drive, but I'm fine going up there on my own. A little solo windshield time will be good for me. I need to process."

As usual, he sees right through me. "Hey, don't overthink this, Gem. Let's just see where it goes."

That might be his style, but it's not mine.

"It's strange," I say, as I lift my crumpled leggings off the floor and deposit them in the trash. "I've been a licensed therapist for years. I'm used to helping people expose stuff so it can heal. But I guess I never bothered to do that for myself. It feels good, letting some old wounds breathe a little. See the fresh air. Get some first aid."

I walk up to him and give him a peck on the cheek. "Thanks for letting me come clean. Thanks for listening, and for apologizing. That meant a lot to me."

"Anytime, Gem."

"I really do feel better."

"I'm glad. Hey, I'll be done here in a couple hours. I'm taking tonight off. What do you say we head back to the tennis courts for another round?"

"Another round of me kicking your butt?"

He laughs. "You wish."

I smile at him from the doorway. "I'd like that. I'll meet you at the high school."

"Cool. Let's say four. I'll bring that racket for you… and you're already looking pretty sporty."

"Yeah, sporty, but maybe not season-appropriate."

"Here." He rummages through the duffel again, then walks up to me and presses a giant sweatshirt into my hands. Then he lowers his lips to mine and gives me a kiss much sweeter and longer than the quick peck I gave to him. "Good luck finding that ring," he whispers.

It's difficult to walk away from him, but I force myself to do it.

After pulling the sweatshirt over my head, I look back. Down the hall, he's in his office doorway, leaning against the frame and watching me.

I raise my arms to show off how the huge garment hangs off me like I'm a human tent. "It fits!" I call.

He laughs. Even from here, I can see his look is dark and smokey.

I turn and push through the swinging double doors, aware his eyes are still on me.

Out in the bar, Delilah's standing on a bench, dusting picture frames. She looks over her shoulder at me. "How'd it go? Get what you needed?"

Let's see…

Bandaids on both knees: check.

Caffeine in my bloodstream: check.

The feel of Parker's warm lips still lingering on mine: *check.*

"Yeah, I think I did."

I got something else, back in that office, too. He said he was sorry for ditching me like he did. It's wild what a difference it makes, hearing that a person is genuinely sorry for an action. Forgiveness is a powerful thing.

All this time I thought he left me because he didn't care about me. Now I know that I was wrong about that.

He ended it because he wanted us both to be happy. He couldn't think of any other way for us both to go after our dreams. I didn't know I needed Parker to apologize, but I did.

Now that he has, what's going to happen between us?

Chapter 20

Parker

There are certain things I know about Gemma.

I know she's crazy smart..

I know she takes time to process things.

I know that with her, I have to move slowly.

I've known all these things for ten years. I learned them when we were young, first dipping our toes into a relationship.

And now, I'm learning new things about her, too. I'm learning she's a wiz of a therapist. A talented and thoughtful CEO of her company. A super hard worker.

She likes maple syrup. A lot. Like, she'll drench her blueberry pancakes, or yogurt, or even strawberries in the stuff. The woman has a sweet tooth.

Also, she doesn't like to take no for an answer.

And, thanks to the fact we've been living together for a week now and playing tennis together every afternoon, I also know how she can improve her forehand.

"It's your grip," I tell her, after she hits yet another ball way over the chain link fence. "You're over gripping. Relax it. Loosen it up."

"Do you know how hard it is to relax?" Gemma says, as she jogs over to pick up another ball. "You can't just tell a person who has been in chronic stress-mode for years to relax. That's like telling a person with focus problems to 'pay attention'. It doesn't work like that." She bounces the ball down onto the pavement like she's preparing to hit it.

"Hang on," I say, as I jog her way.

It's a beautiful fall day. It rained earlier, but now the sky's mostly blue with a few gray clouds still lingering to the west. The court's dusted in a layer of wet leaves around the edges, in little piles where we raked them yesterday. Our bags are propped on the metal bench, and there are two water bottles over there, too, ready for when we want a break.

Gemma's cheeks are rosy, and she's wearing one of my baggy sweatshirts rolled up to her elbows. The thing goes down to her knees, like some sort of dress.

She smells sweet, like the vanilla latte she had earlier at the Steaming Mug, where we sat for hours, watching the rainstorm pass through.

"What are you doing?" she asks with a giggle, as I come up behind her. I wrap my arms around her body and grip the racket over her hand. "Showing you."

"Oh…" She wriggles a little, and I kiss her ear.

My hand cradles hers and the racket. "Pretend you're picking the racket up off the ground. That's how you hold it, all the time. Like you're carrying it around, easy, light."

I feel her hand relax, under mine.

"Better," I whisper. I kiss her neck, just below her ear, and then release her and jog back over to my side of the court.

I hit a ball at the backboard. It bounces her way, and

when she smacks it with her new grip, the shot's solid and strong.

She whoops with pleasure.

We keep playing, and not one single other ball goes over the net.

Soon we're both worked. Her, more than me, but I won't let her know that, because that's another thing I know about Gemma: she's competitive. We head to the bench and sit side by side and slurp down ice cold water, like we've done after sessions like this all week.

It's been so easy, getting into a routine with Gemma. I don't know what I'll do when she leaves.

It's Friday, seven days since she arrived in town.

We've talked about a lot of things this week.

We've laughed over shared memories, parsed apart family dramas, traded opinions about Wayland, Cambridge, and Pines Peak.

But we haven't ventured into 'future' territory. Gemma's always been focused on the future. I know that one day soon, it's going to come up.

This vacation of hers won't last forever.

But I wish it would.

"Parker?" She has her knees tucked up, and she looks at me from over the bare bumps.

"Yeah?"

"I really needed this. I want you to know that. I was on a one-way train to burn-out city. I can see that now. This week with you is saving me."

'This week.' That sounds temporary.

Is it only this week? When is she planning on leaving? What will happen when she does?

"I'm happy." She leans her head on my shoulder.

I wrap my arm around her, and rub her upper arm. "Good."

"Also, I asked Carly not to tell your dad that you're at the cabin, but she wants you to call her. Since you're an expert with that phone of yours now, you should. She says she's been trying to get in touch with you, but you're not answering."

I chuckle. "That's 'cause I'm expert enough to know how to master it, not let it master me."

"She wants to know what's going on with us."

"What'd you tell her?"

"I said we're having a really good time. She keeps threatening to drive up and talk some sense into me."

"Do you think you need some sense talked into you?"

She falls silent.

I know Gemma, how those gears in her overactive mind are turning double-time right about now. Making connections and leaps that a guy like me can't fathom, and could never replicate.

She swivels so she's facing me. "I think.... I think I never found my ring."

"Ha. Okay, help me get there with you. I'm not catching how that relates."

She reaches out to play with the zipper on the hip pocket of my sweatpants. As her fingertips worry the slider, she frowns. "I can talk to you about a lot of things, but I can't talk to you about that ring. Not right now."

Man, I really wish she found her ring. It's still missing, and that bums me out.

Randy looked for it. Gemma did, too. I went up there on my own a couple times, plus with Gemma a couple days ago. Even though we all searched carefully, none of us spotted the silver chain or silver ring.

I guess the thing has sentimental value to her. I don't really get why, or what kind of meaning she's attached to it, exactly. But I do know that when she talks about it, she gets a worried, sad look, like she has now.

I want to understand.

Not just about the ring. I want to understand how Gemma's mind's working, when it comes to *us*.

I want to understand, because maybe if I do, I'll be able to fight for her in a way that will actually work.

With a woman as complicated and deep as Gemma, there will be a fight.

It'll be a fight against the part of her that wants to pull away from me.

I'm sure she's torn about what's going on between us. I've caught glimpses of it a few times this past week. Sometimes she's all sunshine, keeping up with me on a mountain bike, or sneaking chunks of sugar-coated apple from the mixing bowl while I try to bake a pie.

But sometimes, like in this moment as she worries about her ring, she turns stormy. There's trouble brewing in her soul, and if I don't understand it I won't be able to fight for her in the way I know I have to, when the storm breaks.

"We could swing up there again, now, and take a look around again," I suggest. "Maybe someone picked it up."

"Like who?"

"The neighbors down the road."

She bites her lip. A crease forms between her brows. "That house with the horses? That was a mile away, at least."

I trace my thumb over the back of her hand. "We'll find it. I promise."

Her eyes connect with mine. There's a message in them, but I can't decode it.

She swallows and looks away. "Maybe…" She sighs.

"Hey, what was going on, out in front of the library? Those tents we passed?"

"Fall Festival. Happens every year. You want to hit it?"

"Um... do you really need to ask that to the city girl basking in the best Vermont vacation of her life?" She bounces up and grabs her duffel. "Yes, Parker. The answer's definitely yes."

I laugh, even though some part of me knows this is a distraction.

There's something going on with Gemma.

If I don't find out what it is, it won't matter how good my tennis shots are. This is a game that I'm going to lose.

Chapter 21

Gemma

How is it that I'm at a fall festival straight off of a postcard, sinking my teeth into a caramel covered apple, and I feel *worried*?

There's something wrong with me.

Really wrong.

Because I should be enjoying the smell of wet leaves, and savoring the feeling of the warm sunshine that's so busy drying them.

The sweet, buttery caramel under my teeth gives way to juicy McIntosh apple. The mix of flavors is sugary and tangy all at once.

Inside Parker's sweatshirt, I feel cozy and comfy. And he's at my side, talking to Delilah, who's running the animal shelter booth at this adorable little festival.

I should be enjoying all of this.

But a number keeps surfacing, in my mind.

93 percent.

My compatibility score with Mortimer.

The number first popped up in my head again on Wednesday evening, while I watched Parker coach Ransom. I had my cell phone in my pocket and it rang. Because I was expecting—and nervous about—a call from Jocelyn Radner, I checked the incoming call right away.

If it was Jocelyn, I wanted to pick up, to hopefully finally figure out what she was so eager to get in touch with me about.

But it wasn't Jocelyn.

It was Mortimer.

I didn't pick up, but I did listen to the voicemail message he left me. *"Hey, hon. It's me. Sorry again about that little mix up we had on Monday. I still feel like a goof for that. Give me a call back."*

Hon. He called me 'hon', like he used to. He sounded easy-breezy, which made me doubt everything I saw on Monday afternoon. How could he call and leave a message like that, given what unfolded in that hotel lobby?

He made plans to have coffee with me, forgot said plans, and then practically threw his current relationship with his raven-haired lover in my face.

None of that was hinted at in his message though. He spoke into my voicemail as though nothing at all had happened. So, did it? Or did I read into the whole thing, painting it the way I wanted to see it?

I was already into Parker when I made that drive to Broad Hollow. I get that now. My old feelings for Parker came to life the minute I walked out of the guest bedroom in that seaweed mask and saw him standing in the entryway.

So, did I mis-interpret my interaction with Mortimer, because I *wanted* to?

Doubt's a tricky thing.

It sneaks in, burrows down, and then refuses to leave.

Ever since Mortimer left me that voicemail, I've been wrestling with doubt. And with that number. 93%

I love numbers.

I *trust* numbers.

I know how fickle and unpredictable human behavior is, while math equations and statistical models remain constant, no matter what.

Once you solve a formula, it's always solved.

Forever.

Plenty of journalists have written about my Right Match formula, and all those articles say pretty much the same thing: that I 'cracked the code' for finding love. The articles applaud my company for our rigorous, scientific approach to romance. Thousands upon thousands of data points went into the making of the software we use for matchmaking.

The system has worked for hundreds of clients.

So… it should work for me, too.

In all my years of setting up matches for other people, I've *never* seen 93 percent compatibility.

86 percent, sure. Even 87.

On a rare occasion, 88 or 89.

But that's it. Never anything higher.

The fact that Mortimer's questionnaire and interviews, which were carefully processed by my staff, led to a compatibility of 93 percent is nothing short of a miracle.

Maybe we didn't give it enough time, a little voice in my head whispers. *Maybe me and Mortimer are a slow-burn kind of couple. One that takes years to actually shift from mutual respect and civility to something closer to love.*

What would that kind of love look like?

What would it feel like?

What I have with Parker feels like a free fall. I'm tumbling head over heels through space, and I don't even know what direction the ground is in. Maybe that's the point. Maybe that's why it's called falling in love.

Or… maybe the ground is closer than I expect, and I'm about to know what doing a cannonball onto rocks feels like.

The sight of the cutest kitten ever pulls me back to the festival—thank God.

It's much more pleasant to be here on this still-damp, sun dappled grass than in the shadowy, doubt-riddled corridors of my mind.

"Oh my gosh, she's adorable!" I say, as Delilah deposits the squirming ball of fur in my arms.

My new bartender friend looks wholesome today. The long sleeves of the waffle shirt she's wearing under her Shelter Volunteer t-shirt cover up her tattoos, and she has her hair in a long braid.

"*He*, actually. Max. He's looking for his forever home."

"Aw, I wish I could help, but I'm heading home to Mass soon and I can't take a kitten with me." The statement slips through my lips before I have a chance to filter it.

If I'd been a little more on it, I wouldn't say anything about adopting or not adopting the cat, personally. Because all that involves a future. A future where I'm not in Pines Peak. A future where I'm in Cambridge, steering a company toward international success—with or without funding from Mitch Manning. I'm seriously screwing up the assignment he gave me.

Not only that, but the assignment he gave me is screwing with me. I'm starting to doubt my own match-making process.

"You sure about that? I bet he'd love to see what city living is all about," Delilah suggests.

I know she's trying to be helpful and friendly. But right now, me going back to the city is a sore subject that I'd rather not talk about.

Parker joins us and scratches the kitten's head.

"My apartment lease allows for one pet only," I say. The little kitten seals his eyes closed and dissolves into mini-purrs. The sound is so faint, compared to the lawn-mower type noises my grown cat makes. I run the tip of my finger over the downy soft fur between Max's ears.

"Any luck finding your ring?" Delilah asks.

I swallow. The ring is another subject that nags me, painfully, like a blister getting bigger with each passing day. Every time I think about it, I think about my great-grand-mother and her long marriage with my great-grandfather.

Seventy years.

To me, that's what love's *really* about. Not flashy romance, hot dates and wobbly knees; grand gestures, roses, or diamonds.

Real love is functional. Mundane. It's about finding a life partner who will weather storms with you. Make you tea if you're sick. Drive you to the dentist. Not get bored, when they wake up next to you for the ten-thousandth time.

My great-grandmother wore that bent spoon around her finger for seventy years as a symbol of her love for the husband she accepted and treasured. She and my great grandfather grew old together, and that's what I want, too.

Someone to grow old with.

A couple times this week I've come *this close* to talking to Parker about what the ring really means to me.

But this thing between us just started up again. I can't dump all this stuff about marriage on him *now*. We're only getting to know each other again. I'd be crazy to talk to him about whether or not we could grow old together.

And besides, I ran our numbers.

I know Parker's Right Match profile isn't perfect, because I filled it out myself, and it's incomplete. But the fact that we only scored 81% together worries me.

According to my own Right Match system, that's not a green light for marriage.

I know I'm nuts to be thinking about this stuff—but that's me.

Nutty, control-freak Gemma.

I pass the sleepy, tiny kitten back to Delilah carefully, aware that Parker's studying my expression.

"Everything okay?" he asks, as we walk, hand in hand away from the booth.

"Fine."

"Nah. I don't believe that. What's eating you? You've been quiet since we left the school."

In my purse, my phone rings. *Whew.*

I pull it out and see that it's Claire Holt. This is the third time she's called this hour, so it must be urgent.

"I should take this," I tell Parker, as I swipe the screen and lift it to my ear.

He gestures toward a booth not far away. "I'm gonna get a couple pies," he says, as he backward-walks away from me.

I answer the call and greet Claire.

Her usually business-like voice screeches in my ear. "Eeeek! First of all, I am so totally excited and happy for you. Congratulations!"

Is it my imagination, or does she sound *not* happy for me at all? And frantic?

Her tone's testy, like she's upset with me. Also edgy, as though she's on the brink of a panic attack.

"Um… thanks? What's this about?"

"Your big news, obviously! Although—and I don't mean to sound harsh, or like a downer—you *know* it's sort of crazy to spring this on us while you're out of town, right? I mean, this is *insane*, Gemma. Now I'm scrambling to lay the groundwork that should've been laid months ago."

"Hey, could you maybe back up and start with some actual facts? Because zero of what you're saying makes sense to me right now."

"Mortimer's post…? It started a major buzz in the media. We're all super pumped for you, of course, but the phones are ringing like crazy and I have journalists emailing me, trying to get statements, and—"

"What post?"

She hesitates. "You're kidding me."

"Not even a little."

Silence.

"Gemma, his *post.* The one he shared this morning on all his social media pages."

"I haven't checked my accounts in days. Can you fill me in?"

"Oh my gosh. This is crazy. Okay, let me pull it up…."

Now she has me really worried. I pace over to a tree on the edge of the festival. With my back to the skinny maple, I slide down so I'm sitting on a carpet of damp grass and leaves.

"Okay, got it here," she says. "He wrote: *'Can't wait to speak at the hash-tag Economics Forum Pinnacle Series on Saturday with my number one fan in her front row seat.'* Then, in parentheses: *'Hope she says yes'*. Exclamation point."

My heartbeat skips in a way that can't be healthy. The happy sounds of the festival around me fade into a singular *womp-womp-womp*, like a helicopter's descending.

It's not.

This is my own anxiety lowering down over me, all-consuming.

"Wait—what? That can't be right."

She ignores my statement. "And the photo to accompany the text is of you and him. Looks like you're on vacation or something? You're on a balcony and there's the ocean in the background. The two of you are smiling and holding champagne glasses, and you're in a black, sparkly dress. This post is getting mega-attention. Hundreds of comments, people saying how happy they are for you two."

Why would Mortimer share something like this?

He's always been big on social media. It helps him sell his books, and more than that, I think he likes the attention. I remember when we were together, he loved mentioning me in posts. He knew that his audience loved seeing photos of us together.

Maybe seeing me in that hotel lobby reminded him of our relationship—and how much the public adored us, as a couple.

I CAN'T GET a clear grasp on what's going on, besides the fact that now the public thinks that Mortimer's about to propose to me.

Which is impossible.

He's with another woman.

I work on steadying my breathing. It won't do me or my Head of Marketing any good, if we both have panic attacks. While I draw in slow breaths, I search the crowd for Parker and spot him across the way, paying for two pies.

How am I supposed to handle this?

Mortimer and I broke up. Now I'm tumbling head over

heels for Parker, and Mortimer goes and pulls a move like this…?

What a freaking mess.

I could instruct Claire to pump out some press of our own to stop the rumors. That would involve coming clean to the public about the fact that me and Mortimer are no longer an item. Since we're sort of the golden example of my company's work, I have to make sure we handle this situation carefully.

Claire busily compliments the photograph of me and Mortimer, and gushes about how happy we both look. I know the photo she's talking about. It was taken while we were on vacation to Hawaii. I remember forcing a smile for that picture, because I was so annoyed at Mortimer for working all day, during our vacation.

While I fight off a wave of nausea, Claire goes on. "...and it's fabulous that you two are finally getting hitched. Really. But—couldn't you have at least given me some time to write a press release? Or make a plan for how we can publicize this?"

"I had no idea—"

"Oh, puh-lease. This can't be catching you off guard. You and Mortimer wanted this to come as a surprise to everyone, right? That's cute—gives it a spontaneous flavor that the press will love. But I'm *sure* you guys have already hashed out the details of the proposal. So at the least, you could fill me in now so I can line up interviews and all. We need to be proactive, when it comes to what kind of media reach we'll get out of this. He's going to pop the question in Broad Hollow, after he speaks at this conference, I'm guessing…?"

"Maybe." *How should I know?* This is all news to me.

She huffs with frustration. "Gemma, you're my boss, and I'm sorry if I'm getting worked up. Really. But this is big, and I'm freaking out. I mean, I hate to sound cynical, but you marrying him is a big-time advertising opportunity. Do you realize I already have messages from dozens of journalists from papers across the US and Europe?"

"Claire, slow down."

She sounds distracted as she goes on. "Okay, as an example. Just now—seconds ago—a new email came in. Saul Croft from the *New York Times* wants to talk to you so he can get a quote for the article he'll publish, once you say yes."

Once I say yes?

Whoa.

This is out of control.

I hate when things are out of control.

But how can I fix this? How can I make it right?

Claire's talking at a fast clip. "He already has the headline and everything. *'Gemma Lafferty, Leading Expert on Love, Says Yes.*'"

Now I feel legitimately sick.

But I can't stop Claire from going on. "And here's the tagline…now I'm reading right from his email. Get this: "*Gemma Lafferty, statistics genius and founder and CEO of Right Match, gifted the world with a numerical system for finding perfect love. Now she's about to marry her very own right match.*" I mean, that is good press. Great advertising. That's going to get us thousands of new clients. But now I'm totally crunched on time and—"

"Wait, wait."

I wish this helicopter feeling would stop, in my head.

I wish Parker wasn't walking toward me, two boxes of pie in his arms.

I wish I couldn't see the Animal Shelter booth, behind him, complete with cute kittens in a basket on the booth's table.

I know I have to deal with this issue Claire's brought to my attention. It's a fire I have to put out—in person, with care. But how do you leave a postcard-worthy town, Parker Manning, apple pie, and kittens?

Not easily.

Not happily.

I know I sound grumpy as I cut Claire off. "This is catching me off guard and I need a minute to figure out my next move. I'm thinking I need to go to Broad Hollow to talk to Mortimer about this face-to-face. Clearly, there's been some sort of miscommunication. We're not on the same page."

She doesn't get what I'm talking about, and I don't blame her. In Claire's mind, me and Mortimer are the smiling power couple pictured in his totally out-of-line social media post.

She tries to cut in, but I bulldoze over her. I am the boss, after all. "I do have some thoughts about some quick damage control. Can you get in touch with Nikko?"

My interview on *The Nikko Show*, scheduled for tomorrow afternoon, has been on my mind for days.

"Already handled that," she says, sounding pleased with herself. "I told him that Motimer's going to propose tomorrow, and he immediately changed his travel plans and booked a room at the Broad Hollow hotel. So he'll be there when all this goes down, and he can catch that interview with you right after. He's thrilled that he's going to be the first to interview the future Mrs. Laughlin."

I groan and rub my temples. "No, no… that's not good. Reach out to him again, please. Cancel the interview."

"What? Gemma, as your Head of Marketing, can I tell you that'd be a huge mistake? You remember he gets an average of a million views per video?"

"Get in touch with him. Cancel it."

I scowl as I hang up the phone, and then immediately regret my grumpy attitude. It's not Claire's fault that Mortimer's pulling this crap. It's *his.*

And… and mine, I realize, as I lean back against rough tree bark and look up at the sky.

This is my fault, too.

I was the one constantly acting like my split with Mortimer was temporary. I sent all sorts of mixed signals —most recently by calling him up and suggesting a get together… and driving halfway across a state to make it happen.

That made an impression, apparently.

Actions always speak louder than words, and my actions said 'I want you. I want us.'

I was in such deep denial.

But now I've pulled out of it. And I know for sure that don't want to be Mrs. Laughlin. Ever.

I'm not ready to figure out what, exactly, I want.

I worked hard for the Right Match system. I trust it. I know it says me and Mortimer are beyond perfect for each other. But this week, Parker's taught me that sometimes, I have to *feel* things without analyzing them. And deep down, I don't feel that me and Mortimer are Right, with a capital "R."

Does that mean my system's broken?

Does that mean I have to stop doing the work I love, and abandon Right Match as a company?

I bow down and burrow my head in my hands. As I rake my fingers through my hair, I think about the countless all-nighters I pulled in grad school. Notebooks, filled with formulas. Text books, stacked all over my various apartments.

I think about the night when me and Mark and Teagan

stayed in the office until four am, eating Thai take out, watching our brand new software churn through the first Right Match profiles. I remember how all three of us were invited to the wedding, when the first match we set up walked down the aisle.

My team and I worked so hard, for so many years.

I gave *everything* to my company.

Now it's like the very foundations of Right Match are quaking and shaking, about to crumble to dust.

And inside, I'm quaking, too.

Is this what it feels like, right before your whole life falls apart?

Parker lowers down onto the grass beside me. He takes one look at me and then reaches for my hands. "Hey—what's wrong?"

But the feel of his hands covering mine doesn't help. It makes me feel worse. My chin quivers, but I refuse to cry. This is my mess, and I have to clean it up. Dissolving into Damsel in Distress mode might be the easy route to take, but not the right one.

So instead of letting myself cry, I do my best to take a deep breath.

It's shaky, but at least it helps me get oxygen into my lungs so I can speak. "I have to travel to Broad Hollow to clear up a huge mess. It has to do with my company, and a weird, complicated mix of my personal life and my professional life." I flip my palm and squeeze his hand. "It's sort of difficult to explain it all."

He nods, like he was expecting this.

Which makes me want to stay here with him, not drive away.

He's wise, calm, and patient.

He uses his thumb to stroke my hand. "I know you have stuff going on, Gem. You're not a simple, surface-level kinda girl. I get that. It's one of the things I love about you."

Love?

Did he just say the 'L' word?

The confusion already swirling in me turns into a tornado.

He studies me. "Sorry. We're not saying stuff like that."

I get to my feet. "Let me figure out this Broad Hollow thing." I try to make it sound casual, but really my 'Broad Hollow thing' feels *huge*. Potentially life-shattering.

"Think you could give me a ride back to the cabin, so I can grab my car?"

"You bet," he says, his tone somber.

After he delivers one pie to the volunteers, and we both put up a good front, wishing them luck for the rest of the day, we walk to the truck in silence.

When we get there, he opens the door for me. "One thing I gotta say, and then I'll back off."

I stick my hand in my pocket, because he looks perfect right now in this golden lighting, strong arm propped against the door he's holding for me, and I'm tempted—so tempted—to reach for him. "Okay…"

"I don't want you to get back together with that guy."

"That's not my plan—"

"Not right now, maybe, but you're going there to see him. I know some part of you needs closure with him. I can't control how that's going to go. I don't want to see you get with him. I want *me and you*, Gem. I want us to be together. And I know you're not sold on that idea."

"It's complicated…" I say miserably. I wish it wasn't complicated.

"I know, baby. It's over my head. If I knew how to fight for you, I would. But I can't figure out what I can do, and all I can think is that I have to let you go sort through this on your own. Is that what you think, too?"

"I put a lot of myself into my work. I believe in it. Or, I did—and now everything's on the line. I've made mistakes. I want to set things right… and to do that, I have to go to Broad Hollow."

He nods. "I know you, and how you work, Gem. Go, if that's what you gotta do. I'll be here when you come back."

Chapter 22

Gemma

How do you drive away from a guy you feel out-of-control, terrifying feelings for? A guy you loved with all your heart, once, who you're starting to love all over again?

You keep your foot pressed to the gas, that's how.

Because if you don't, you might turn around.

I can't run from the problems in my life. I have to face them.

This tangled mess I'm in with my company has to be sorted through. I won't stick my head in the sand and hide out in Vacation Land, even if that place includes pie, warm kisses, and kittens named Max.

When I reach the Broad Hollow Conference Center, I have a headache. My neck and shoulders are stiff from clutching the wheel.

I spent half the drive talking with Carly, but even our long conversation didn't help me get to the bottom of what I have to do next.

All I know is that I have to set Mortimer straight. We're over.

The fallout from that conversation might be the end of my company.

Even if the story of our breakup doesn't ruin my reputation, it will ruin my faith and trust in Right Match. How could I work for even one more day, without believing in the product I'm selling?

I clench my jaw as I head for the row of revolving doors. It's early evening, and the panels of glass reflect the dark blue and indigo of the evening sky and a peachy glow from nearby lights.

I'm in the middle of pulling out my phone so I can call Mortimer and request a meet-up when the sound of my name stops me.

I release my purse and swivel my head toward the sound.

Jocelyn Radner's walking toward me.

Each step seems to take huge effort, because her belly is swollen with pregnancy. Her back is arched and she has both hands propped on the protruding mound under her blouse like if she holds it, she might not give birth right here on the paved walkway.

"Thank goodness," she says, as she nears, slightly out of breath. "Oooh, baby. Oh, mamma. Oh, Lordy." Then she moans and looks up to the sky.

My personal crisis can wait. Pregnant ladies demand full attention. "You okay?" I ask, as I take her elbow and guide her toward a bench near the walkway.

The wooden bench feels hard and cool under me when I sit next to her. A tall planter of brown and faded mums nearby smells earthy and rotten. "What are you doing here?"

"Whew. Got excited there, for a sec. I think I nearly popped."

"Don't pop. Please. Gosh, I haven't seen you in months. You've been trying to get in touch with me, right?"

It's a surprise, seeing her here in central Vermont. We're a long way from the South Shore, and I didn't know she had any interest in economics.

"You are a hard person to get in touch with," she grumbles, as she runs her hands over her belly, maybe soothing a kicking baby inside.

"Wait—you didn't drive here from Mass just to see me, did you?"

"Yeah, I did. I was trying to get up the nerve to call you, but…Well, you know how that goes. Sometimes I'm a big chicken. Mark gave me your cell number."

"I know… I've been waiting for you to call. He said you wanted to talk to me directly."

"Exactly. And that's why I'm here, really. I thought about the phone, but I kept talking myself out of it. Like I said, *buk, buk, bu-gawk!* A big old chicken. That's me. Besides, some things shouldn't be said over the phone, you know? So when I saw Mortimer's post about how he was gonna pop the question, I got right in my car. I've been sitting here for —ooooh, mamma." She sucks air through her teeth.

"You okay?"

"I get this back pain, when I sit wrong." She shifts to the right and rests back against the bench. "Oof. That is so much better. What was I saying?"

"You heard he was going to propose so you got in your car…"

"Right. I feel *so* incredibly guilty, Gemmy. You were a great boss. Can I just say that, first?"

"Um…." I glance over at the revolving doors.

I called Claire, during my drive. She said she wasn't able to get in touch with Nikko. Which means he might already be here, in Broad Hollow. She also updated me about a dozen more interview requests, plus the growing online frenzy about me and Mortimer.

"I hate to be rude about this," I tell Jocelyn, while still watching the doors, "but I am sort of in the middle of a catastrophic evening. I need to get inside and take care of something pretty major."

"I know," she says, wincing as she sits forward. "Mortimer's going to propose. I know. And that's why I'm here, and that's why I feel guilty. I better say this. The more I stall, the more stress I feel, and right now I really shouldn't let myself get stressed."

"Goodness, no. Whatever it is, Jocelyn, you can tell me." *And please be quick about it.* "Okay." She sucks in a breath. "I did something terrible. I'm sorry. Really sorry. A couple years ago, I was going to this gym on the second floor of the Grafton Center. And Mortimer was a member, too, and we both used the rowing machines. One day we got to talking and he found out that I worked for you. He said how pretty and smart you were, and how he'd love to have a shot with you. I told him you only dated guys who were vetted by your own system. You know, guys with Right Match profiles, whose scores were compatible with yours."

"Of course." I swallow and fight off a wave of nervous nausea.

Out in the lot, a car pulls out. Near the doors, a couple of middle-aged men stroll out and laugh as they walk into fading light,

"Well, he wasn't sure he'd get good numbers, with his profile. He sort of—oh, yikes, this is tough to admit. I feel like the worst human being on the face of the planet right now. Seriously."

She closes her eyes and pinches the bridge of her nose. When she speaks, the words come out in one big rush. "He offered me thirty grand if I'd fill out his profile for him and make sure the numbers worked with yours."

She opens her eyes and releases her nose. "There! I said it. Finally! I can't believe I kept it in so long. It was awful, the guilt. See, I had all this student debt. I was neck deep. I needed the money."

I feel heat rushing into my cheeks. "So you… you *faked* his profile?"

"I needed the money. Desperately."

I clutch my purse so tight, my knuckles turn white. Anger flashes through me, but I have nowhere to put it.

I can't be angry at Jocelyn.

She drove all this way to come clean and in her condition, hours in the car are surely not enjoyable. I can't even imagine how many times she probably had to pull over to pee.

Suddenly, it dawns on me that, while Jocelyn is not a suitable target for this anger surging in me, Mortimer is.

He lied to me.

From the get-go.

He *falsified* the only reason I was with him to begin with. Our whole relationship was built on those compatibility scores.

When, out of the corner of my eye, I see another gaggle of men and women spill out through the revolving doors, I catch sight of a tall forehead, and wispy, thinning brown hair. Long nose. Sleek, expensive suit, and that stupidly big, flashy gold watch.

Jocelyn, beside me, gushes on. "...And I'd never forgive myself, if you said yes to his proposal based on those scores. It was bad enough that you guys dated for so long. I never imagined you'd stick with it like you did. I was so relieved when you guys split—thought I'd really gotten away with something, you know? But then all this stuff's coming out about how you guys are going to walk down the aisle together, and I knew I had to confess."

I'll thank her for coming clean.

Later.

Right now I have a lying sack of bird poop to set straight.

I jump up off the bench with my eyes pinned on my prey. As I march up to him, it's like I can't even see all the other professionally-attired men and women around him. They fade to the background as I zero in on the man who cheated on his Right Match profile.

"*You*," I say, pointing as I near him.

His smile's wobbly and fearful. As it should be. He glances left and right nervously, checking in with his peers. As always for Mortimer, public perception comes first. "Hey, hon. I didn't expect you until tomorrow. Looking beautiful, as usual."

He opens his arms, like I'm storming in on him to hug him. *As if.*

"You lied to me. You sneaky, conniving, scumbag!" I keep my purse pinned under my arm, even though what I want to do is wallop him with it.

I'm only vaguely aware that the others around us have paused to watch the scene unfolding.

Mortimer holds up his hands. "Ah… haha… that? That was nothing, sweetheart. A testament to how much I loved you, don't you think? I went to a lot of trouble to get a shot with you. Let's talk about this in private."

He swoops in on me, and hooks his arm over mine.

The smell of his aftershave makes me want to vomit

into a nearby planter. I duck out from under his arm. "I was with you because we were a 93 percent match! The system can't work when you totally falsify the data points. Everything we had was a lie, Mortimer. Every minute we spent together—I wish I could get all that time back. I *knew* there was something wrong, but because of that number, I didn't trust my own judgment. Now I understand, finally."

"Gemma, hon, you're getting all worked up over nothing." His gaze darts about frantically.

I spot a man holding a big, bulky camera, in the periphery of the crowd.

In front of me, Mortimer's sweating. He pulls at his tie and collar as if they're choking him. "I love you. Seeing you Monday reminded me how beautiful and successful you are. I was lucky to be with you, and I see that now. I know you want to get things back on track. Let's do that. Hm…? What do you say?"

"No. No, no, no. We're over. We have been for a long time. We will never, *ever* get back together, and we definitely won't ever get married."

As I say those words, it's like my heart's a cage and the door's suddenly been flung wide open, and doves are flying out.

I'm free.

Blustering and red-faced, Mortimer protests. He'll do anything at this point, I'm sure, to try to save face. But I don't have to sit here and watch him do it.

I spin on my toes and stride away.

At the bench, I pause to give Jocelyn a quick hug goodbye and thank her for her honesty. Then I head for my car, practically at a jog.

This light feeling in my chest makes me want to run.

I don't have a plan for what might come next in my

life. The only thing moving my feet forward is a joyful feeling of freedom that's surging through my body.

When the same camera-wielding man I noticed earlier catches up to me and steps into my path, I nearly crash right into him.

A second guy joins the camera man. Given his unique caramel complexion and distinctive, green-tipped mohawk, I know who he is right away.

And I don't want to talk to him.

I want to get to my car.

"Leave me alone, please," I say in a rush, as I step forward, hoping the two will part and make way for me.

But they stand there on the sidewalk, blocking my way, and now I see that the big, professional-looking camera has a glowing red light on it. I'm being recorded.

Nikko steps onto the path with me. He's holding a mic.

He turns to his cameraman, and with a huge smile says, "Wow, guys, we're live with Right Match founder Gemma Lafferty, moments after her public smack-down with bestselling author Mortimer Laughlin. Gemma, what an honor to be here with you... Can you tell us more about what we all witnessed back there, live on *The Nikko Show*? Because I know we all have tons of questions..."

Chapter 23

Parker

I dump Fruit Loops into a bowl and add milk while keeping tabs on Queenie out of the corner of my eye. She's prancing along the counter, tail high.

Wanting some of this milk, probably. It's quickly turning pink in the bowl, a color that can't be healthy for cats.

Maybe not for humans, either, but I'm feeling too bummed out to cook.

Before she can stick her nose in the bowl, I swipe the dish up and out of reach.

"I don't think so," I murmur gently. "You got fresh grub down there. That fancy fishy stuff she gets you. Way better for you."

I carry my bowl to the counter, lost in thought.

I need to be a better man.

If I want Gemma, that's what I have to do. The problem is, I don't know how. I slurp down a bite, racking my brain.

I got her to loosen her grip on her racket. I remember how it felt, to feel her hand relax, under mine.

That first time we played, with the floodlights on and the field around us so dark, she said something to me. It was cold out, and we could both see our breath. I tried to kiss her, but she had other plans.

What was it, that she said?

Queenie passes in front of my cereal bowl. I pat my lap, and she jumps down. As I stroke her back, I try to remember…

It was about how I should think ahead and take action, instead of sitting back and watching things unfold. She was in therapist-mode, trying to be helpful.

At the time, her advice didn't register.

But maybe she had a point.

I like to be surprised.I like to see how life's twists and turns unfold. I've always played my hardest, but I didn't care about the outcome.

This time, with Gemma, I care about what happens with us.

A lot.

I care about our future. It's frustrating to care this much.

Uncomfortable.

Scary, even.

I want this thing with her to go a certain way. I want to *win*, when it comes to her. She's worth fighting for, so I have to try.

This doesn't come naturally to me—making strategies. But, with Queenie on my lap and a bowl of cereal in front of me, and two hours before I have to leave the ski house to pick up Ransom from work, I try.

Gemma's worth it.

After racking my brain a little more and stewing in my frustration, I grab my phone and dial my little sister.

"Finally," she huffs, when she answers. "I have been waiting forever for you to call me back. What is so hard about picking up a phone, anyway? Oh my gosh, what is that slurping sound?"

I lower my spoon. "Sorry. Getting calories in before coaching. Hey—question."

"This better be about Gemma."

"Yeah."

"You are *such* an idiot, messing with her."

"I'm not messing with her, Carly. I'm into her."

"If you hurt her, I will punch you in the throat."

"Whoa. Dude. Aggressive much?"

She groans. "Sorry—just finished battling rush hour traffic. Terrible work day. And *you*! You are screwing with my best friend, and she's a wreck over it."

"How do you know she's a wreck?"

"Um, the Nikko Show? She's totally flustered, obviously still in crisis mode. Plus, we've been *best friends* since we were two…? That's how. We talk. Unlike you, Gemma calls me all the time. We were on the phone for an hour this afternoon. You understand she's currently turning her life upside down all because you've been putting on your Perfect Parker act for her, right?"

"I'm not putting on an act. I'm being real."

Half of what my sister just said made no sense to me.

The name Nikko's only vaguely familiar, and I can't place it.

"Hey, maybe I shouldn't have called."

"Wait. Wait…" Long pause. Hopefully, she's putting her claws away. "Sorry, again, It's just—you don't get it. The effect you have. You do your thing, and women fall all over themselves, and even when you don't mean to, you cause a lot of damage. You can't see it, but I've been watching it happen over and over and over. I don't want to see that happen again when it comes to you and her."

"I know, I know..." I rub the stubble coming in on my chin. *I don't want to hurt her again, either.*

"You said you had a question for me, right?"

"Yeah. What should I—" I rake my hand through my hair.

Man, this is tough.

Hard to form the thoughts. Hard to get the words out. *Hard.*

Maybe the reason I've made myself not care about winning is that deep down, I'm afraid of losing.

What if I fight for Gemma, and I lose?

I push my cereal bowl away and clear my throat. The pendant counter lights twinkle, and out through the picture window, night's falling fast. "Carly, look. I need your help. I need to make a plan. What should I do to get her back?"

It feels so strange to ask my little sister for help. My family doesn't get me, and I don't expect them to. I've used that as a reason to distance myself, but maybe that's not serving any of us.

It's like Gemma said, that first night she was here. Everyone needs a little help. I'm no exception.

People always call me stubborn, and maybe there's a reason for that. It's time for me to change some of my ways.

"Wow," Carly says, clearly stunned. "This is new. You, asking me for help? Who are you and what have you done with my brother?"

"Hey, if you could not gloat, that'd be awesome."

"Fine. I won't gloat too much right now, mostly because we don't have time. First of all, you didn't lose her. You just don't *have* her, yet."

"I did lose her, though. She drove out of here this afternoon… to deal with her past."

"Yeah, and she did deal with it. Tell me you're watching the Nikko show."

"Hunh?"

"The Nikko Show? He-llooo….? The show Gemma's being interviewed on, as we speak? Get a clue, Parker!"

"Right… Nikko." Now I know why that name is familiar. "She did say something about an interview with that guy. I thought it was tomorrow."

"*That guy?* He's the face of our generation, not *that guy*. And her interview with him got bumped up apparently because it's playing on my laptop right now. Look, love's important to Gemma. She takes relationships seriously, and they mean a lot to her. Her career's based on love—you know that, right? She's an expert. She cares so much about that matchmaking company of hers. She's lived and breathed it for years now, and it's her baby."

She goes on, but I stop listening. A plan—vague and cloudy—is starting to form in my mind.

Two seconds later, I hang up on my little sister, mid-sentence.

I fumble with pulling up the internet and finding *The Nikko Show*. All my time on tennis courts, on mountain trails, and behind the bar has not made me a tech wiz, that's for sure. When I manage to find the show's current live broadcast, my heart hammers.

There's Gemma.

She looks flustered. Annoyed. And gorgeous.

Her eyes burn bright, and she keeps looking toward the parking lot on her right, like she's anxious to get there.

Nikko's standing in her way, though, and sticking a microphone in her face. "Wow, Gemma, this is big news. Really big. Here we are, thinking you're about to say yes to the guy, and you dump him and tell us that you're moving on. Way to go, girl. Tell us, how does one of the globe's leading experts on dating and marriage actually move on?"

Gemma pushes back a flyaway strand of hair. "Um… I'm actually trying a new thing, where I keep my private life a little more private."

"Hey, good for you. But at least give us a little hint, hm? You're brilliant, and a lot of us out here are clueless when it comes to dating. So, come on, a hint. Will you use psych profiling and all that jazz, or are you gonna just get out there, hit some bars, and see who you bump into?"

That actually gets a laugh out of Gemma.

She's so pretty, when she laughs.

She shakes her head. "I'm definitely not going the 'throw spaghetti at the wall, see what sticks' method. People used to have to do that, but not any more."

"So, Right Match, then? You're gonna find yourself a match?"

"All I can say is that the process my team and I came up with is important and worthwhile. Right Match can save people a lot of heartache and trial and error. I believe that's very valuable to all of us, myself included." Her eyes dart toward the parking lot again.

Nikko finally steps aside, giving her some space. "I'm sure you have to get on with your night. Thanks for taking the time to let us know what's going on. Real quick: Besides finding yourself a hot match, what's next for the great Boss Lady and trail-blazer Gemma Lafferty?"

"I think—" she blushes, and tries to fix a bump in her hair but fails. "I don't know—I think a little bit of a slow-down is on the menu. There's a lot up in the air in my life right now, and I'd rather not talk about it yet. I really have to run."

"That's it, folks! You heard it here, on the Nikko Show.

Gemma's back on the dating scene, gonna use her own amazing love-finding system, and she's gonna take it easy for a while. I'm your host Nikko and I want to say a big, huge thank you to everyone out there listening for your likes, comments, and shares. Your support means—"

I close the tab before he can go on.

Because, suddenly, the vague plan that stirred in me turns totally clear.

I know *exactly* how to fight for Gemma.

She has trust and faith in her company. Of course she does. She's worked her butt off to come up with a genius system, and here I am, being a total, stubborn idiot about it. I never did fill out that questionnaire she kept bugging me about. I refused to sit for the interviews.

It takes me a minute to locate a number for her office in Cambridge.

I wait as the line rings twice.

Three times.

Four times.

My knee bounces up and down.

After the sixth ring, someone picks up. "Yo. Right Match, this is Mark." The dude sounds young, and also like he has a mouth full of food.

"Hey, man. I have a favor to ask you. My name's Parker Manning, and I think there's some kind of profile thing I was supposed to fill out—"

"Parker Manning, in the flesh! Ho ho. I can't believe this. Here I was, about to leave for the night. Now I got you on the line. Parker, I logged some serious hours sorting through your psyche profile earlier this week, lemme tell you."

"Yeah, about that. I know I didn't give Gemma everything she needed."

"She said you were stubborn, among other things. And

yes, we did factor that in, when it came to your personality assessment." He chuckles.

"I'm thinking I want to start over, from scratch, and take a shot at it myself. I'll pay whatever I have to, plus extra if you'd walk me through it. I'm not great with tech."

"Man, she's going to be so psyched. Your profile means a lot to her, because of the major investment your father might make. How about this: no charge. And I will sit right here and hold your hand through the whole thing. Then I'm gonna get your info straight into our data so our software can process it. You got some time?"

I nod, though I know he can't see me. It feels good to be taking action like this. Really good. "Yeah, I have a little under two hours before I have to head out. That enough time?"

"It is if we get cranking. Okay, bud, we got sixty-eight questions to get through, and then a video interview. We use facial-recognition software plus a super involved lie-detection system, so make sure to keep your answers as honest as possible. You ready?"

I shake out my hand, trying to shed some nervous energy. I feel like I used to, in the early days of my pro career; like I'm about to pick up my racket and walk out onto a clay court.

"I'm ready," I tell Mark.

Chapter 24

Gemma

Main Street is dark, except for that crooked neon beer mug above the Tipsy Tavern. The other stores and businesses have been closed for hours now.

I pull into the bar parking lot and crawl down one row, then another, looking for Parker's truck. Is he here?

I have to talk to him.

I have to apologize for leaving in such a rush.

I don't want to hurt Parker, and I don't want to make him feel sad. But I know I did. I could hear it in his voice before I left town in a hurry earlier today.

The parking lot is dark. Great for kissing in, not so great when you want to actually see the shape and size of the vehicles nestled closely together. I wind my way down the last row of parked vehicles without a glimpse of his big black truck.

I nose my Prius out toward Main again. Just before pulling out, my phone rings.

The instant I pick up, a chorus of voices trills through the speaker. *"You have a match!"*

Mark's boyish tone mingles with Teagan's excitable soprano. Claire's in there, too, sounding much happier than she was earlier today.

I laugh, but shake my head. "Okay, guys, what is this about?"

Now Mark's voice fills the line. "Gem, your boy called in this evening. I spent two hours drilling him, and—"

"Wait, my boy?"

"Your family friend. Parker Manning. I was trying to eat dinner earlier, and he called up. I was a couple minutes from leaving for the night. I have this new video game at home that has—"

There's a muffled rustling sound, then Teagan's voice is in my ear. "Gem, you there?"

"Yeah, what's going on?"

"What Mark is taking forever to say is that Parker filled in his own profile. Mark called us all in to code it. We ran it through the system as a priority, because of how you've been going on about the funding on the line."

I hear another rustle as Mark yanks the phone back. "Gemma, this family friend of yours... his profile's airtight now. Spot on. Totally accurate. He asked us to run his numbers with yours, and you guys are a 94% match. Do you realize that's the best compatibility score we have *ever* seen?"

My hand starts to tremble.

I suppress the urge to squeal like a six-year old on Christmas morning, when it's time to open presents.

Behind me, headlights approach and then glare in my rear-view mirror. The car behind me is too polite to honk, but I catch the driver's drift when the headlights inch closer to my rear bumper.

"Thank you guys for doing this," I say through my smile. "You all are amazing, and I truly appreciate you. I have to run, but I will give you an update soon, I promise."

"Love is in the air!" Mark says.

"And bonuses!" Teagan adds hopefully. "Big, fat, bonuses!"

I laugh as I hang up.

The car behind me loses patience and honks, so I pull out onto the street. When I check the clock on the dashboard and see that it's now 10:15, I consider heading up to the cabin. It's late, and if Parker's not here at the bar, maybe he's up at the ski house.

Then I remember: Ransom's private lessons. Parker probably picked the kid up from that grocery store and then settled in at the high school for the session.

I step on the gas and cruise that way.

The feeling of freedom that blossomed in my chest earlier tonight has given way to full-fledged happiness. I can't stop smiling, and I have so much energy that I keep tapping my hands against the wheel like it's a bongo drum. Me and Parker are a match!

I want to roll down the windows and shout it: *'Ninety-four percent! He's my Mr. Right!'*

That might get me arrested for disturbing the peace, though, and I won't be able to run into Parker's arms if I'm locked behind bars.

And I really want to run into his arms.

Please, please be here, I think, as I spot the faded Highshcool sign up ahead. There's some sort of muzzle-faced creature painted under the school's name. It looks like a cross between a fox, a dog, and an alligator. Must be the school mascot, but what is it?

I don't have time to decide, because now I see a gaggle of shadowy forms huddled on the sidewalk not far from the sign. The half-dozen figures stand in a knot, chins wagging. I wouldn't even take a second glance at them, except for the fact that now I see Parker's truck on the shoulder of the road, not far from where they're gathered.

The pale beams of my headlights glitter against fragments of glass that are scattered across the pavement.

No.

I brake and ease my car to the shoulder behind Parker's truck. Cold air nips at my cheeks as I jog up to the small crowd.

"Excuse me!" I'm breathless when I reach them. "Sorry to interrupt, but can you tell me what happened here?"

Please, no.

I know now that Parker's my perfect match.

My Mr. Right.

Now I'm standing next to his truck, and I can see that the windshield is smashed and there's an angry dent in the front fender. The hood's crumpled.

This world's not always filled with sunshine and roses. I know that. Bad things happen. But the universe can't be so cruel that it'd serve up my Mr. Right with a side of delicious fries, and then… take him away, before I have a chance to tell him I love him, can it?

That's what I want.

I want to look Parker in the eyes and tell him how I feel. How I've *always* felt.

It takes me a moment to realize I'm crying.

A weathered woman in her sixties grips my upper arm. "Ma'am, are you a friend of his?"

"Yes—yes, a friend." And more than that. Much more. I hope. I look over at the truck again.

This can't be happening.

She goes on. “Well, we’re not supposed to gab about our calls. There are all sorts of laws about that, these days. But you look like you’re about to pass out right here on the sidewalk. You know what we call that, in the first responder community? An incident within an incident. So you ask what you need to ask, and I’ll do my best to tell you what I can.”

For the first time, I realize that her fleece has a white letters stitched on the lapel: EMT. and she’s in uniform pants, too, and black work boots.

“Is he—Is he okay?” I stammer, while trying desperately to stop my hands from trembling so bad. I glance over at the truck again and spot a dark stain on the driver’s side window. Blood.

That doesn't help.

I look away. “What happened?”

“Accident, honey, can’t you see? A truck hauling logs fish-tailed, came right on over into his lane. Nothing he could do about it, except try to get out of the way, which he did. See how he’s on the shoulder?” She points toward the truck, and I try to look that way but the sight of the smashed windshield—and blood smear— catches my eye and more tears blur my vision.

I swipe my eyes clear. “Is he okay?” I ask again.

“Paramedics took him and the boy to the hospital. If you like, when we’re finished up here, we can give you a lift over. We’re waitin’ on the sheriff to get back. Shouldn’t be more ‘n ten minutes. I take it you’re gonna want to see him?”

I do. And not just want. I *need* to see Parker, and I don’t want to wait ten minutes.

I’ve seen the hospital. It’s on one of the side streets I’ve driven down, on my way up to Parker’s trailer.

I thank the EMT as I back track toward my Prius.

Inside, I crank the heat in an attempt to ward off the chill that's making my teeth rattle.

It doesn't work.

My tense jaw is sore and hands are ice cold as I approach the clinic's front doors.

I jam my hands into the pockets of my fleece and try not to start crying all over again as I near the front desk.

A young woman with a nose ring and long, wavy brown hair looks up from filing her cherry-red nails. She stops chewing her gum long enough to mutter, "What's up?"

"I need to see Parker Manning. Is he here?"

A vision of a careflight pops into my head. Then a different possible scenario: the back of some ambulance filled with paramedics, carting him to a nearby town. Somewhere bigger than this five-bed clinic. A place with actual surgeons on staff, and maybe a receptionist who isn't filing her nails and looking at me like she's bored out of her mind.

"Yeah, he's down there." She waves in the general direction of a hamper-lined hallway. "Past Mrs. Millhorn's room."

I am so mad at her for not even bothering to give me a room number. And for assuming I know who the heck Mrs. Millhorn is. *And* for still filing her nails, even though now I'm crying again and there's a box of tissues on her desk and she hasn't even offered me one.

But it's worse. I'm not just mad at her.

I'm mad at myself.

I hate that I wasn't here when Parker got into this accident. I hate that I wasn't right there to help him into the back of the ambulance with my own two hands, and then sit next to him on the way to this crappy clinic.

I should have been there.

"I'm not from around here," I choke out, as I paw at my cheek and try to look like an adult, even though I feel like a scared teenager. "Mrs. Millhorn?"

"You know, she used to be the principal, now she's got major dementia? You'll hear her shouting. Well, Parker's probably in the next room down."

Probably? Great. She doesn't even know.

At least her casual, not-helpful vibe has worked to my advantage in one way.

Seeing as she doesn't seem at all worried about patient confidentiality I get to pass her desk, and make my way down the crowded hallway.

Please, please be okay.

A stern, feeble voice behind a closed door is doling out "detention for a week" to some unidentified "young Missy."

The next door is ajar.

I push it open gently and step into the room.

Chapter 25

Gemma

The first bed in the small clinic treatment room is unoccupied. Beyond it, a curtain's drawn, slicing the room in two.

I hear sounds coming from over there.

Awful sounds.

A pained groan, and then rustling sheets and a faint cry.

That's followed by a nurse's soft murmurings. *"There, now, that's better, with that t-shirt off. All that blood! My goodness. Let me get you a gown and another couple blankets."*

I head toward the curtain.

She pops out from behind it before I can make my way through.

"Heavens! You about scared me to death. What can I do for you?"

"I'd like to see him."

She shakes her head of thick auburn hair. "Oh, no. Not in the state he's in. He's not decent. Not a stitch of clothes on him, waist up, and I'm sure you know the paramedics sliced his pants right off of him, on account of the leg injury, which—thank goodness—wasn't as bad as we first thought. It's his jaw that's the real trouble."

"I didn't know." Now I feel shaky and woozy all over again. *Poor Parker.*

"You just sit here and give him his privacy. I'll be back in two seconds with a gown."

"Wait—can you—" I stammer, "This is all news to me. I just got back to town and rushed here. Is he going to be okay?"

"He's banged up, that's for sure. I think besides the cuts and bruises, the real damage is those three teeth that came out. A good oral surgeon will fix that up and patch his jaw, too. We've got his lower mandible all bandaged up tight and pain meds on board while Doc Stacey heads in to take a look. She's on call tonight, but I'm sure you know she's a good ways away. That all goes to say, don't expect him to chat with you. He can take sips through a straw, though, which is good news."

She steps past me. "I'm sure he's not happy with me, stripping him down like that and leaving him to wait. I'll be back in a tick. Just hang tight." She pats my shoulder as she passes, and then I'm alone, staring at a curtain.

"Parker?"

I feel sort of dumb, talking to a curtain.

But I also don't want to intrude on him, so I keep my feet planted where they are.

The rustling sound on the other side and a muffled groan make me hopeful that he's listening.

"I feel awful for not being around when all this went down," I say, my voice wobbly. "I was worried sick, driving over here. I thought for sure you were being loaded into a helicopter or the back of another ambulance, heading for major brain surgery or something, and that maybe I'd never get to tell you—"

I take one step closer to the curtain. "I *have* to tell you this. I know this is a bad time, with your jaw all wrapped up, and I'm sure you're in a ton of pain—but I don't think I can wait. We're a match, Parker. You filled in those questions and did that interview with Mark, and they ran our numbers, and we're compatible. *Very* compatible."

Behind me, the opening door makes a hushed sweeping sound against the linoleum floor.

The red-haired nurse bustles past me, a stack of gown and blanket in her arms. " 'Scuse me. I don't mean to interrupt." She slips behind the curtain.

I haven't said everything I want to say yet.

I'm too eager to get it out to wait. So, I keep going. "I know it might sound stupid to you, me being so hung up on those scores. You're so tuned into life, in general, but I'm not always and I needed those numbers. I know it's probably way too early to talk about our future, but at least this lets me know that it's there, if we want it… You know, a future. Together."

My face is flushed, my voice is coming out tighter than I want it to. It's hard to bare your soul to a curtain.

This room is stuffy and warm, and the muffled grunts and groans coming from the other side of the curtain are slightly distracting.

Is he in pain?

Did he fall out of bed?

Did the nurse turn her back and he's choking on a sip of juice from some sweaty styrofoam cup?

This isn't ideal, but I'm finally saying how I feel. To him, and to myself. And to this random nurse, but that's okay. It's good to be honest outloud.

"I love you. I really do," I tell the curtain. "You said

the 'L' word earlier today at that totally perfect fall festival. I guess I sort of freaked out, but it's only because I thought our compatibility score was low. And yeah, I'm a dork and a statistics nerd, but that worried me. But now that I know our score is high, I feel good about using the 'L' word, because that's definitely how I feel. I love you. I want to be with you, if you want to be with me. I've been happier this week than I have been in years. We'll make the distance thing work. I'll come here whenever I can... it's not really that far, and I love it here. You make me laugh, and feel safe and loved and like every day is Christmas, basically."

The curtain ripples. Then the nurse pokes her head around it. She frowns at me. "Well, he's all dressed and ready to see you."

"Thanks."

She won't quit frowning at me.

"Sorry you had to hear me get all gushy," I tell her, as she starts to slide the curtain back. The hooks along the ceiling squeak in protest as they travel along the rusty track.

"No, that part's fine. There ain't nothin' wrong with telling a man you love him. A *man*. I don't mean to stick my nose where it doesn't belong, but this one here's a little young for you, don't you think?"

She drags the curtain another foot, and I get my first peek at the bed.

Ransom's propped up on a pile of snow-white pillows, his head wrapped in layers of gauze equally as pristine.

He's starry-eyed as he gazes across the room at me. Then he starts writing something on a whiteboard.

I just spilled my guts to a crooked-toothed *kid*.

He flips the board. His letters are blocky and big: *'I think I love you, too, Ms. Lafferty.'*

Behind me, I hear a deep chuckle. The laughter's warm, and the sound resonates through me.

I turn and a smile flickers on my lips.

A warm, fuzzy feeling stirs in my chest.

Parker.

He's not that beat-up looking. Besides a thick, puffy bandage across his temple and a bunch of white gauze wrapped around one wrist, he looks damage-free. He's smiling, and carrying a big cup with a straw in it. His playful eyes flit over to Ransom's sign. "Back down, my man. This girl's all mine."

Ransom utters a grunt.

Parker crosses the room and sets down the giant cup. "I got you a cranberry juice." He holds up his hand and Ransom gives him a high five.

When Parker turns to me, I feel sparklers light up in my heart.

He walks to me, and soon he's so close I can make out faint speckles of blood on his t-shirt.

"Did you hear me?" I ask quietly.

His voice is just as low as mine. Gentle and intimate. "Yeah, I heard."

"Did it sound stupid?"

He chuckles and reaches toward me. "How could a statistics nerd be stupid? You're the smartest person I know, Gem."

That makes me smile for real. "You said once I was too smart for my own good, though."

"I take that back. You're smart. You're good. Period."

"You really think so? I know I'm a lot to handle…"

"You're a lot, in the best way." His fingertips brush along my jawline. He rests his thumb under my chin. "I could've told you we were a match without all the numbers, you know." His deep whisper sweeps through me, leaving my knees jelly.

I want him to kiss me, and I know he will.

His brown eyes carry that promise, and more promises, too.

"Yeah, but you were too busy insisting you had life all figured out." I splay my fingers across his chest, over his dirty t-shirt.

"It's a good thing you showed up to rescue me."

"That was my plan, but I think maybe you rescued me, in the end."

"This isn't the end." He guides my chin up as he lowers his mouth mine. Everything else I wanted to say to him suddenly flies the coop of my brain as we kiss.

I think I wanted to hear him say it: that he loves me.

I don't need that anymore, though.

He's saying everything to me, in this instant. As we kiss, he wraps his arms around me and holds me tight.

Chapter 26

Gemma

I hold the green-and-red striped sweater up so that Carly can judge it.

She tilts her head to the side. "It's not *garish* enough."

She yanks at the hem of her own holiday-themed sweater, a baggy thing with a big reindeer knitted into the front. The reindeer even has a big, red, puff-ball nose that sticks out an inch. "*This* is an ugly sweater."

"I figured you might say that, so I packed option 'B'." I drag a second sweater, tags still on, from the depths of my suitcase.

Parker and I arrived at the Manning's ski house a couple hours ago, but I haven't had a chance to unpack.

Mostly because Carly's occupied my time. I can't complain about the fact that we took a long snowshoe hike, sipped a glass of wine by the fire, and now we're getting ready for some mysterious "ugly sweater" photo shoot that Mitch Manning apparently insists on, every Christmas Eve.

It's been fun, catching up with her.

Ever since she took over as CEO for Manning Light Fixtures she's been a peach to be around. Less irritable. More fun.

She approves of this second sweater option, a neon green thing that says 'let it snow' in big, hot pink letters across the front, so I pull it over my head. "Hey, were you able to get Thursday and Friday off, so we can ski?"

I peer into the guest room mirror and try to flatten my static-crazy, finger-in-a-socket hair.

On the bed, she flops down to her back, sticks her leg straight up, and grips her toes."Ugh, my hammies are so tight. Yeah, I did! Yet another perk of being my own boss."

"You really love your new gig, don't you?"

"*So* love it. I can't believe it took Dad so long to see I was a good fit." She switches legs and repeats the stretch on the other side. "He had tunnel vision about getting Parker behind that desk, I think. I'm way better at bossing people around though. Parker's too much of a 'good time' guy, and he can't lay down the law like I can."

I smile at her description. Parker *is* all about good times.

It's one of the things I love about him.

One of the *many* things.

It's been a year and a couple months since we got together, and I'm slowly, steadily learning just how fun life can be.

I've backed off of my intense work schedule. I still love my job, but I'm finding balance. It felt right to put the move to an online business model on hold. Down the road, maybe me and my team will tackle that. But right now, I have other priorities.

It doesn't matter to me that I didn't find a wife for Parker, and I never got that funding from Mitch. His assignment got me here, to Vermont, and that's what matters to me. And, who knows…? Maybe I'll marry Parker one day.

Spending so much time up here in Pines Peak really helps, with the work-life balance thing. It's almost impossible to obsess about work after a long mountain bike ride with him. Or, a session on the basketball court, smacking tennis balls at those plywood backboards.

And lately, I care more about my volunteer shifts at the Animal Shelter than I care about profit margins.

I think that's healthy for me.

Those volunteer shifts could be a little problematic, though, if I keep adopting animals at my current rate. So far, I've managed to sneak two kitty friends to Parker's home permanently, so Queenie has friends when we come up to stay in Vermont. Little Max grew like a ragweed, and he's twice Queenie's size now but he still lets her boss him around. And the latest addition, an orange tabby named Dusty, is my favorite cuddle buddy.

Well, except for Parker. He's the king, when it comes to snuggling.

Parker's just as bad as me, when it comes to falling for animals. He brought a puppy home out of the blue this fall, and I think he has his sights set on another.

It's a good thing he started construction on a new house, up on his land.

Carly's phone beeps, and she stops stretching to check out the text. "Hey, speaking of my wild-card brother, he says I can quit stalling you. They're ready for us, out in the sitting area."

She bounces off the bed and hooks her elbow through mine.

"What do you mean, stalling me?"

I don't know what she's talking about, or why she's

dragging me out through the guest room door and down the hall.

But a second later, I find out.

In the sitting room, Parker's on one knee.

A fire dances in the hearth behind him and the big, bristly, Christmas tree's off to his left, in front of the snowy landscape pictured through the huge window.

Patty and Mitch are standing off to the side, both holding up their phones, aimed out into the room—either poised to snap photos, or ready for video. My dad's near them, with his arm looped over my mom's shoulders. She's beaming at me with total pride, like I'm about to be crowned Queen of the Universe.

Veronica's perched on the green couch, and Ransom's there, too, with his big, goofy grin, which is a little straighter since he had all that oral surgery a year ago. He's been around a lot this month, since the college he got a full tennis scholarship from runs on a trimester schedule and has a long winter break. It's fun having him around. Parker loves playing tennis with him, and still thinks he'll go pro one day.

Ransom has his phone in his hands, too, and I can tell by the way he's watching the screen that he's recording this, too.

One day, I'll get to watch this happen all over again.

I feel heat from the fire dance over me as Carly drags me in closer to waiting Parker. She gives my hand a squeeze and then joins her parents by the hearth.

I'm left looking down at my boyfriend of a year and two months. Longer, if you could all those years that my love for him was buried so deep inside me.

I fell for Parker at age eighteen, and some part of me has loved him every day since then.

My eyes are locked on his, so I've barely looked at the

box he's holding. But when he flips it open, I flick my eyes to the ring nestled in satin and gasp.

My great-grandmother's ring.

"You—you found it?"

"Took some searching..." His mouth hitches up at the corner. "Maybe I should've given it back to you when I found it, last August. I was out mowing, and the thing shot out of the back and almost took my eye out."

That gets a laugh from our audience in the wings.

From most of them, anyway. Not his mother. "Parker, you have to be careful!" she quips.

Carly smushes her finger to her lips. "Shh! Mom, let him talk."

Parker plucks the silver ring from the fabric it's nestled in and pushes the box back into the pocket of his sweats.

That's right. His *sweatpants.*

My man is wearing sweatpants and a t-shirt—with an ugly plaid sweater-vest pulled over the top— to this surprise engagement party.

He still manages to look smoking hot, though.

I think he could dress in a trash bag and still look gorgeous.

He holds the ring toward me. Orange and golden light from the fire dances over his chiseled, tatt-covered biceps.

I'm about to say 'yes' to a man with tattoos.

A man who can't mix a cocktail, but owns a bar.

A man who doesn't use a planner. How can that be? I own six.

That's why we're such a good pair, a little voice inside me whispers.

I've haven't yet dug into our compatibility score, because I've been too busy *living.* But I know it's all there: the weaknesses in me that Parker's quirks make up for; the strengths I have that fill in his weak spots. The ways we support each other; the ways we can grow together.

There are probably data points about how we both like to drench our pancakes in maple syrup, or how we both go speechless when a sunset turns wispy clouds to pink.

And there's definitely something in both of our scores about respect.

I respect and admire him, and he feels the same about me, and that might just be the reason we're here right now, in this sitting room.

The ring's bumpy, antique, silver surface looks freshly polished.

It is *so* good to see it.

I thought it was gone forever. But Parker found it… for me.

"You've told me what this ring means to you," he says, in that husky, intimate way, like we're the only two in the room and his words are only for me. "I want us to have what your great-grandparents had, Gem. What we're doing now—it feels really, really good. I want it to keep going. I love you, baby. I want to spend the rest of my life with you."

I can *feel* his sincerity.

It's coming off of him in waves.

It's in his eyes, and the quick, shaky smile he gives me. Maybe he's actually a little nervous, after all.

I know I'm supposed to speak, but I can't. If I try, my voice will crack, and this is being filmed.

"Don't leave me hanging," he whispers.

I swallow, and then bite my lip and try my hardest to compose myself. "You know what I'm going to say," I finally manage to whisper back, before biting my lip again.

I will not cry.

I refuse to be in an ugly sweater *and* a crying mess in these videos.

Someday, I might watch this scene with my children. I want them to see a lovely, mature, composed woman, not a sobbing mess.

"I think I do," Parker says. "But you're full of surprises."

"Not this time." I hold my left hand out. "Yes… yes, of course, yes, Parker. *Yes.*" I draw in a shaky breath, and have to bite my lip even harder as he slides the cool ring over my finger.

When Parker stands and pulls me in for a kiss, I weave my fingers around his neck and kiss him back. Then I pull my hand away for a moment, to take a peek at how the ring looks on my finger.

I wore it around my neck for so long, it's strange to see it on my hand.

Strange, but good.

Great, actually.

I wrap my hand around his neck and smile as I kiss him again.

"I love you, baby," he whispers between kisses, "I want to be the man that sees life with you. Maybe I'll even learn how to mix you a Cosmo."

"And maybe I'll learn how to kick your butt on the court."

"Ha. We'll see about that."

"Hey! Lovebirds!" Carly shouts. "Break it up already, would you? Some of us want to get this ugly sweater photo in the can."

Parker laughs as he eyes my sweater. "Some get-up, Gem."

"Carly said I had to wear it. If I knew you were going to propose, I would've refused to comply."

"I wanted to surprise you."

"You did."

You've surprised me in so many ways, I think, as I tuck in next to his side and let him lead me toward the tree.

Epilogue

Parker

It's my wedding reception, so I shouldn't be behind the bar.

But I am.

It's actually a nice break, to stand here at the taps, pulling a beer nice and slow so it doesn't fizz up.

Delilah hip-checks me just as I get the glass full. "Get out of here, Groom! You're on the other side, tonight."

"My best man's glass was empty. Figured I'd help him out."

"How's he holding up tonight?"

I check down the bar, to where Randy's currently holding his phone out to one of Gemma's co-workers, Teagan. "About as good as you could expect, for a newly divorced guy at a wedding. He's been trying to get chicks by showing off pictures of Mopsey."

"Good for him." Delilah sets a bottle of whisky down on the table and surveys the crowd as she readies a few shot glasses. "Your sister sure seems to be warming to this place."

I follow her gaze and spot Carly over at a table near the dance floor. She's all smiles. I'd take a minute to appreciate the fact that she hasn't once referred to this place as a 'dive' today, except I get distracted.

My wife is next to her.

My *wife.*

Gemma's beyond beautiful today. White strapless gown, with her hair swept up. Long, sparkly earrings trail down toward her shoulders.

She's listening intently to something my father, across the table, is saying.

How did I get this lucky?

When I was a teenager, Gemma was over at our house a lot. On the days she didn't come by, I sometimes wanted to see her so badly that I'd make up an excuse to go over to her house. When her mom or dad opened the front door, I'd offer to mow their lawn, or I'd ask for a tool that my dad didn't have in the garage.

All I really wanted was to catch a glimpse of her.

Then I would—and my whole day would be better.

Now, I won't ever have to make up an excuse to see her. I'll get to wake up next to her every morning.

I try to keep my smile under wraps as I deliver the beer to Randy and clap him on the shoulder. The guy's getting over his break with Lydia, and I hate to rub my good fortune in his face.

But I let my grin free as I amble over to the table where Gemma and my family are seated.

I grip my dad's shoulder and give it a squeeze. "Hey. What's going on over here?"

"Your dad says he has a special card for us," Gemma says, before flashing a quizzical look my father's way.

"How about this," my dad proposes, as he pushes his chair back. "You two come with me. It's over in my coat pocket. I didn't want to put it in the pile with all the others..."

Gemma shoots me a puzzled look as we follow my dad toward the coat rack. It's a silent question: do I know what this is about?

I shrug. No clue.

When we reach the thick row of coats, Dad pulls his parka off the hook and rummages in an inner pocket. He hands the card to Gemma.

She checks in with me again with her eyes before tearing it open, but I have no insights to offer, so I shrug a second time.

Whatever my dad's up to, it's big.

He rocks back on his heels and hums along to the song playing. He's pleased with himself, that's for sure.

Gemma scans the interior of the card. "Mitch! You don't have to do this."

"I know I don't have to, but I want to. You fulfilled your part of the bargain, Gemma. You found my wayward son here a fine, stable wife. More than that. A brilliant and beautiful wife. Now, I know you're taking it easy, as far as work goes. But I watched you grow up and if I know you like I think I do, you'll be back to it with gusto, one of these days. So I want you to have this handy, when you're ready to take the company online like you talked about, whenever that may be."

"Mitch, this is.... I don't know what to say!" She raises her wide eyes to mine as she hands over the card.

On the front, there's a picture of two birds, sitting on a branch. Out of the corner of my eye, I see Dad flash a self-satisfied grin. "You're not the only one around here who can play matchmaker, you know."

I open the card. Inside, there's a check...

A big check.

Now I know why Gemma's eyes were so wide. Five-hundred-grand.

I'd protest, but this is between my wife and my dad. I hand the whole bundle back to Gemma.

She immediately tries to pass it to my dad. It's like we're three adults, standing around playing hot potato.

He holds his hands up in refusal and chuckles as he shakes his head. "No way. Yours now, and I'll look forward to seeing your success in the years to come."

She's too smart to fight him. She gives a resigned nod and hesitates for only a moment before reaching out to hug him.

As the two embrace, I hear her ask, "What do you mean, about playing matchmaker?"

Dad releases her. She settles in at my side, her arm wrapped around my waist.

He slips his hands in his pockets and rocks back on his heels again. "I'm glad you asked. I really am. See, I pay a guy to check on the log cabin. He does a walk-through once a month or so. Well, one day he called me up and mentioned pizza boxes in the trash bin, so I figured I knew what was going on, there. Doesn't take a rocket scientist to figure that one out. Gemma, you came along asking for an investment, and I figured all I had to do was get you to the cabin and you two would take it from there."

"You set us up?" Gemma squeals.

I laugh as I pull her to my side. "How's it feel to be outsmarted, smarty-pants?" I ask, before kissing her temple.

She leans against me. "Pretty good, actually. Pretty freaking good."

Also by Evie Sterling

Single Dad Billionaire Boss

Protective Billionaire Boss

Fake Dating My Billionaire Boss

Printed in Great Britain
by Amazon

38549533R00145